THE WAYWARD SPIDER

JOHN HAAS

Renaissance.
Diverse,Canadian Voices

Cover art, design, and typesetting by Nathan Fréchette. Edited by Meaghan Côté, L. P. Vallée, and Jack Cimesa.

Legal deposit, Library and Archives Canada, September 2019.

Paperback ISBN: 978-1-987963-71-7
Ebook ISBN: 978-1-987963-57-1

Renaissance Press
http://pressesrenaissancepress.ca
pressesrenaissancepress@gmail.com

To my big sister, Janet.
Thanks for always laughing at my crazy antics.

CHAPTER 1
DEEP THOUGHTS AND DESPERATE PLANS

Timurpajan, that bustling oceanside metropolis and home to thousands, was gloomy and overcast. The city's mood matched mine to a T, as if deciding that cheering me up was a hopeless cause and joined me for a good sulk instead.

The show of solidarity was appreciated.

My name is Spider, by the way, and this is my story.

Oh yeah. Nailed that opening. Ugh!

I mean, *obviously* this is my story since I'm the one telling it... Okay, maybe the "Spider" part wasn't so obvious, unless I call this "Spider's Quest" or something.

Hmm, Spider's Quest?

Nah!

Okay, okay, moving on.

I wandered the streets of Timurpajan, going where my feet took me, allowing five years of memories to breeze in one side of my mind and out the other. Five *years!* The longest we'd stayed in one place, only settling here once life on the road had become too much for Dad.

Dad.

He'd aged so fast. And now he was gone, leaving me alone in the world.

A sigh escaped me, coming from the depths of my soul.

Thinking in bad prose must be one of the stages of grief, but it refused to be shaken off, clinging like some nastiness stuck to the bottom of a shoe.

Look, usually I'm a much more happy-go-lucky kind of guy, but burying Dad had been the most crushing event of my life. That man had always been my anchor in life, my rudder, my compass.

Okay, stopping at the docks to think may have been a mistake.

This part of the city spoke of adventure and change though, and that's what was needed. Change. I itched to leave the city's claustrophobic walls and get back on the road, to travel, wander, explore. That was my true home, where I'd grown up.

Grown up?

A snort of cynical laughter escaped me.

For seven years now, I'd been an "adult," at least by human standards. I still didn't feel like one.

Well, at least I'd managed a laugh, cynical or not, and that was one step closer to the true me.

"Snap out of it, Spider," I said since no one was there to judge me for talking to myself. "Maudlin and gloomy is not the way Dad raised you."

A murmur of voices off to my left.

Four sailors loitered at the base of a ship's ramp, nudging each other and staring in my direction.

"Funny how talking to yourself doesn't seem crazy until you have an audience," I said to them.

One sailor nodded at this sage observation while the rest stood there looking dangerous. I moved on, leaving the smell of salt air, the creak of mooring lines, and the threat of untold violence.

Dad would have handled that situation some other way. Judging from past experiences, he would have charmed the sailors, challenged them to a game of dice, and left with all of their money.

Now *that* brought a smile to my face.

Didn't we have some adventures, Spider?

Dad's voice and words. He'd been lurking in my head the past couple of days, offering random bits of wisdom. If talking to myself was a tad crazy, then listening to my dead father speak inside my head was drooling-in-the-darkness bonkers. Still, I wasn't ready to let him go just yet.

Now, if this were a story—

All of life is a story, Spider, but I'm still only memories.

I sighed.

Weren't we thinking about the old days?

Yes. Right.

Dad had been my life's only constant, back to my first conscious thoughts. It had been just him and me most of that time, always on the move, living the lives of traders with some honest thievery thrown in.

By the age of ten, he'd taught me how to drive a wagon and how to read people, how to pick some of the most difficult locks and more guarded pockets. Together we'd seen most of this continent, from the Opal Sea in the west to the ogre communities south of there; from the Razor Mountains rimming the land in the north to the edge of that more segregated kingdom in the east.

It was a wild and beautiful world, full of adventure and excitement.

But, where to next? It was fine talking about change and getting back on the road, but that took money. My only valuable was the set of lockpicks inside my tunic. The thieving tools Dad had carried most of his life. Now they were bequeathed to me and had more value than a purse of gold. How best to put them to use?

Good question. Any thoughts, Dad?

No answer.

Guess even my subconscious had no ideas.

Wonderful.

A meandering path led me past the thieves' dens and their secretive shadows, around the mysterious Tower of Wizardry which loomed over the city, and through the bustling, noisy market where traders hawked their wares.

A booth at one end of the market proclaimed:

See the world! Make your fortune!!

Join the Adventurer's Guild and explore the unexplored!!!

Keep 10% of all treasure found!!!!

They sure did like exclamation points.

These booths were set up in every marketplace through the kingdom, recruiting desperate young people to risk their lives for gold and glory. The fine print, which desperate young people willing to risk their lives for gold and glory didn't bother reading, stated the Adventurer's Guild kept anything unique or rare, and all items with magical properties.

Quite the racket. Still, ten percent wasn't zero, and the guild *did* outfit its people.

Further up was where our shop had been. Gone now, sold, along with all its inventory, and anything else Dad owned. A shop selling aphrodisiacs with names like The Basilisk's Horn now occupied the spot.

Just outside the market's other end was the Inn of the Sainted Ogre, our home for the last five years. The inn's name was a joke between the owners, Garveston Winterfield, Gar to his friends, and his wife, Lees Bonebreaker. Lees was a half-ogre who could crush stone in one hand while making her delicious spiced potatoes with the other—not that she stood around doing this. That would have been odd behaviour, even for a half-ogre who didn't care what others thought.

Gar and Lees were Dad's best and oldest friends, more like family, and were the main reason he'd chosen Timurpajan to settle down in when the time came.

To the right of the bright-blue wooden door was a sign showing a gruesome ogre in beatific contemplation, a ring of glowing holiness around his head. That sign had always amused me whenever we'd passed through Timurpajan. I've seen many ogres on our trading excursions but never met a sainted one.

Today, that sign did its job of lessening the heavy burden on my soul.

Heavy burden on my soul? Ouch! Was I some teen hiding in my room, composing poetry even a tavern bard wouldn't sing?

Enough already.

The heavy door swung open with ease, smells of beer, bodies and spiced potatoes fighting for my nose's attention. The inn's ground floor was a wide-open tavern with sturdy tables, surrounded by equally sturdy chairs, the kind which could take the weight of a man in armour, or a half-ogre woman. A table next to the door waited for patrons to leave their weapons.

This was a place for friends to share a drink or a meal, to laugh and sing. Grudges remained outside or were met with the wrath of Lees Bonebreaker.

Too late in the day for lunch but not yet dinner, and still the place was half-filled, mostly with patrons who had no better place to go, like me. Tonight, it would come to life again, but the Sainted Ogre didn't close for more than a few hours per night, catering to a diverse clientele depending on the time of day.

"There's the lad," Gar called from his spot behind the counter.

He gestured to his personal booth, and I made my way across the room, greeting familiar faces along the way. Gar jumped down from his serving crate and came around with two mugs. Like the potatoes, Lees made the beer herself, and it drew people from all around.

Sliding into the seat, I hesitated, then pushed the hood back to reveal my elfin ears, noting Gar's one raised eyebrow of reaction. Dad had always insisted on keeping my hood up and ears hidden while in public. It was easier than explaining why a human male travelled with an elf child.

That wouldn't matter anymore, hadn't actually mattered in years, but was an ingrained habit. In truth, my hood down made me uncomfortable, but there was no way to pull it back up without appearing foolish.

Gar jumped onto a step, then to the seat, and finally onto a raised section there just for him. Average for his race at a few inches under four feet, the halfling lived in an oversized world, compensating where he could around the inn.

As a child, I'd delighted in the fact that we were close in height, something which Gar enjoyed just as much. Everyone loved the halfling and Gar loved everyone back, finding the joy in whatever others did. His ability to cut to the heart of any topic and see past the people's masks was impressive.

Today his face was tinged with the same sadness it had worn at Dad's funeral. "How are you, Spider?"

I shook my head. "No more tears for me, Gar. I'm fine."

He raised an eyebrow, the weight of that stare boring into my soul.

"Okay, okay," I said. "As fine as can be expected. Trying to adopt Dad's realistic view towards life."

"Oh, you mean: *It's a wild ride, except for the sudden stop at the end*," Gar quoted.

The familiar words made me laugh, a real one this time, untinged by cynicism. Gar joined in, though maybe more in relief at seeing the old me than anything else. Then again, Gar could probably use a laugh too. We'd both lost someone vital in our lives.

Gar grabbed the beer mug, as large as his head, and raised it in salute. "To Warrick."

I grabbed the other and clinked it against his. "To Dad."

We took a deep, delicious drink.

One of Gar's servers, a human girl I'd spoken to several times, brought a plate of potatoes and deposited them in front of me. Gar had somehow signalled for food without giving any sign, and I was grateful for it.

The girl's eyes lingered. It was the ears, ladies always loved the elf ears.

"Thank you, Thari," Gar said, rather pointedly.

She returned to her spot behind the bar, covering for Gar. My eyes followed her path as she went, though the aroma of garlic, rosemary and a few secret ingredients soon pulled my attention back. I breathed that perfume in deep.

The recipe was known only by Lees, Gar, and myself.

Years ago, when I was young, curious and stupid... Hmm, okay, so I'm not all that old, if anything I am more curious, and as far as stupid goes...well, that's better judged by others, or from a distance of years. Anyway, one day while Lees made her potatoes, I spied on her, or tried to. She caught me and, instead of throwing me out a window, put me to work making them, trusting me with the recipe. Over the years she'd let me work in the kitchen with her whenever we were in Timurpajan, helping make the food and beer. That gruff, dangerous woman had a tender side and became a surrogate mother figure to me.

Had I said I was alone in the world? No, not as long as Gar and Lees were around.

"So, all done then?" Gar waved one hand vaguely which still conveyed his meaning.

"Yep. Shop sold and debts paid. Dropped off what was left at the orphanage earlier today."

"No temptation to keep some of it?"

"No, not with this."

A person pays their debts and doesn't steal from those needing the money.

One of Dad's first and favourite lessons.

I traced the ruts of ancient knife gouges in the table top.

"Why in the world did Dad keep travelling, Gar? He did better here in the last five years while sick than he had all those years on the road."

When Gar didn't respond, I glanced up. He'd been staring at me but looked elsewhere quick.

"What is it?" I asked.

Gar let out a pent-up breath. "Your father was a man obsessed with money, never could have enough of it and spent every waking moment scheming on how to get more."

I shook my head. "No. That doesn't sound like him at all."

"It wouldn't to you, but that *was* Warrick until the day he came through that door carrying a silent, squirming bundle."

"Me?"

"Oh, that man knew nothing about babies," Gar chuckled. "Not then anyway. Lees showed him how to feed you, change you, and we tried convincing him to stay so we could help, but he had to hit the road again. At first, we assumed it was his obsession with money, but that wasn't it. His focus had changed. He wanted to show you the world, make sure you didn't miss any experience."

That sounded more like my dad.

"You're fortunate he adopted you, Spider."

"Whoa! Hold on a minute," I said, one hand toward Gar, palm out. "I'm adopted?"

We both smiled. Then I giggled. Gar joined in, and soon we'd dissolved into uncontrolled laughter. It was a well-worn joke, but those are sometimes best.

My purebred elf heritage isn't evident from the name, or from my appearance, as long as I keep the hood up. Elves are reserved and lack that outward spark, that love of life.

As the story goes, Dad found me along the road leading to Derabi when I was a baby, lying in the shade of the giant elms which line either side of that road. He'd named me after the only other living creature in sight, a black spider crawling across my blanket.

"Warrick always said you were the one treasure he'd gotten for free," Gar continued, repeating words heard countless times but which had extra weight today. "Everything else he had to buy, trade, or steal. No one needed a baby less than that man, but he kept you anyway, raised you as his own."

"Taught me everything he knew."

By day it was trading, and how to deal with customers, and at night it was the art of thievery, emphasizing who to steal from and why: Only those that could afford it and never from friends.

Best of all, he taught me to enjoy life.

"I haven't met many other elves," I said. "Mostly adventurers who left the forests. They were all so sombre and reserved. Boring."

Another reason to keep my hood up. If people knew I was an elf, they would treat me like one.

"Elves don't laugh," Gar said. An old quote.

"This one does."

In all our years of travelling, we'd stayed clear of the elf communities in the eastern forests. Not difficult since they'd distanced themselves from other races, not encouraging visitors into their lands.

We sipped our beers in silence, me dreading what came next. Gar would resist it the whole way. But Dad had insisted.

I reached into my tunic and pulled out a money pouch, dropping it in front of Gar with a clink.

"What's this?" Gar asked.

"From Dad."

Gar shook his head, taking a drink from his mug. "We don't need charity, Spider."

"Not charity, Gar," I said. "Payment on the room you gave us these past five years."

Gar raised one eyebrow. "No tab was kept. That was me and Lees giving hospitality to family."

The sack remained on the table, and I had no idea what to do if Gar refused the money.

Gar took another drink. I did too.

"I told Dad you wouldn't take it, but he'd insisted. Said if you couldn't help those you loved then he'd misunderstood what life was about."

Gar rolled his eyes and grabbed the pouch, making it disappear without so much as jingling the coins.

"That's dirty fighting, Spider."

"Yeah, but I'm trying to fulfil a dead man's final wishes."

"Oh, enough already. I've taken the coins."

We both took another drink from nearly empty mugs. The potatoes were gone and this felt like the perfect place to remain for the day.

"Have you decided to keep the room?" Gar interrupted my thoughts.

"Yeah, for a couple more nights anyway."

"Stay as long as you want," Gar said.

I looked over at the serving girl, Thari, who had been glancing in our direction whenever she could.

"Hands off the staff though," Gar added. "It's hard enough finding ones that are trainable."

"Aw, Gar. No fair..." I laughed. "Yeah, okay. Understood."

Gar turned toward Thari who scrambled to appear busy.

"So, what's the plan, Spider?"

"The plan?" I asked. "Same one Dad had always intended for me. Get out there and find my own success. It's my—I don't know—quest?"

And the bad-poetry teen returns!

Gar nodded. "How do you plan to start this quest?"

A fair question, and one I'd been asking myself all day. "Well, thieving and trading are all I know, and I don't have enough to start a trading business."

"You can have the coins you just gave me."

"I appreciate that Gar, I really do, but the idea was that I make my own way, to build myself up from nothing."

"Hmm, a wise man once said: *If you can't help the ones you care about...*"

I grinned. "Okay, nicely played, Gar, but in this case, I need to prove to myself that I can take Dad's teachings and accomplish something with them, in honour of his memory."

"To honour Warrick, huh?"

I nodded.

"*And* you're looking forward to it."

"Of course. This will be a fantastic adventure."

"Just like your father."

"Am I?" I asked, hoping that was true.

"So, if you can't start trading, where will you go thieving?"

Another good question. My mind returned to the booth in the market. "I could join the Adventurer's Guild. See the world, make my fortune, help explore the unexplored. Lots of abandoned dungeons and keeps around."

I was only half joking.

"They always need a good thief," I added.

"A little desperate, don't you think?" Gar asked.

"Yeah, but maybe I could see a dragon."

Ooh, a dragon! Okay, closer to one-quarter joking now.

Gar signalled for fresh beers. "You know, most folk who go off with those groups come back dead, insane or possessed. The recruiters don't bother telling that part."

Yeah, dead, insane or possessed people did *not* enjoy life much.

"You know," Gar said, scratching at the smooth skin along his neck. "You could have kept that money you used to pay off Warrick's debts."

I opened my mouth, ready to repeat the part about making my own way. Gar was already waving the objection aside.

"No, I suppose not. Oh!" Gar slapped the table, the flat noise carrying across the tavern. "I've got it. You come back to our rooms tonight and steal *this* sack of coins. I'll let Lees know so she doesn't accidentally kill you."

I snorted at the idea of anyone stupid enough to steal from Lees.

"No. Thanks, Gar. That's not how Dad raised me. I won't steal from friends, even ones asking me to."

We stared into the fresh beers Thari had brought.

"Okay," I agreed, "so you're right about the Adventurer's Guild. Not much future in being possessed."

"Don't forget dead or insane. Those are pretty limiting too."

"Some thieving closer to home then. Merchants, royalty, politicians. Someone like that."

"Now you're talking."

There were plenty of patrons in the tavern for inspiration, and my gaze fell onto an expressionless wizard in rich purple robes only one table from us. He appeared to be in his late teens, though looks mattered little with that sort. A glass of wine, which he appeared barely old enough to drink, sat in front of him.

"The Tower of Wizardry has untold treasures," I said.

Gar coughed a spray of beer. "Are you mad? Better to go adventuring. At least you know what death you'll get there," he leaned closer to me. "And keep your voice down."

The seated wizard gave no sign of having heard, maintaining the vacant expression as if no emotion ever reached his face.

It seemed attentions other than just ours were on the wizard. A squat man with flushed face approached his table. Even to an inexperienced observer, it was obvious a scam was in motion. The man in front spoke in low, conspiratorial tones, holding the wizard's attention while an accomplice approached from behind. Each wore an aura of overconfidence assuming that, because the mark was young, he was also stupid.

That wasn't all they wore. Each had a single red sash dangling from their waist, identifying them as part of one group.

"River Rats, Gar? Why do you let them in here?"

The River Rats were Timurpajan's most pathetic, desperate band of thieves and beggars. Some possessed rudimentary thieving skills that could be refined with patience and practice, but in general, they were ones with no hope of joining the more distinguished Thieves Guild.

"If they have coins and don't cause trouble they can drink here," Gar said.

I turned toward him. "No trouble?"

"Oh, this isn't trouble. This is a life lesson. Watch."

Unsure who this life lesson was aimed at, I leaned back in the booth, watching the scene play out.

The thief in front moved his hands back and forth, distracting the wizard while his partner, a skinny man with slender fingers, searched the seated man's pockets. A bold move targeting an obvious magic-user.

Boldness and stupidity are separated by a thin line of common sense.

River Rats were not known for common sense.

The wizard himself was tall and slim, with wisps of half-formed beard starting on his chin. He wore the floor-length robes usual to his order and had one ring on each hand. Worthless baubles but flashy enough to draw attention.

The wizard's demeanour told me he maybe wasn't so unaware of what

13

was happening. He was a bit *too* focused on the thief in front of him, watching the man with great interest and allowing the other maximum opportunity.

For one brief instant, I wanted to warn the Rats but discarded that idea. Having the game turned around on you was part of thieving, part of learning to become a better one. As Gar had said, this was a life lesson.

The rummaging thief, presumably the one with more skill at pick-pocketing, pulled a palm-sized glass pyramid from the wizard's pocket. After a cursory glance, he placed it in the satchel over his shoulder. Next came a tiny sack, tied at the top. The River Rat struggled to untie it, and I groaned. Gar turned toward me.

"Never count the gains until you're safely away," I said in a low voice.

"Uh-oh," the wizard said, interrupting the thief in front. "Do you smell bacon?"

"Um," the squat thief said. "I suppose..."

The wizard's eyes glowed a soft amber.

"Magic," Gar said, making it sound like profanity.

"You expected something else?"

"No. Just that much power in one person makes me uneasy."

"No dull moments with a magic-user around."

"Greedy pig," the wizard said.

Sensing the mood had shifted, the slender thief jumped to his feet, trying to stuff the unopened sack into his satchel but unable to manage. He raised one hand showing a black hoof where fingers used to be. His mouth opened in surprise, a shout on his lips that came as a terrified squeal.

The transforming thief fell onto his hooves and raced past the wizard. The squat thief grabbed for the now-pig, missing completely.

Glow fading from his eyes, the wizard glanced around, as if seeing the scenario for the first time. Amusement creased his dour face while he watched the still-human thief chase his partner around the tavern.

The frightened pig-thief rebounded off one table in an effort to escape from reality. The other finally caught him and turned to glare at the wizard with fright and anger, holding his bucking partner tight.

"You should have been happy with the pyramid," the wizard said. "Take comfort that the spell isn't permanent and that it stopped with your friend."

With that, the wizard's eyes glowed amber again. The thief looked at his hand, face as pale as snow, backing toward the door. The wizard, still seated, raised one hand. This was enough for both thief and pig who turned and barely found enough presence of mind to open the door before fleeing.

The door slammed behind them, and the glow faded from the wizard's eyes.

"Life lesson," Gar repeated.

The wizard's demeanour softened for a short time, then his almost-smile disappeared in the space between heartbeats, like blowing out a candle. His face returned to its previous dourness as if all that was enjoyable in the world had died in an instant.

This man was out of his mind.

It was a relief when he stood and flicked a coin onto the table before leaving the inn as if nothing had happened.

"Now," Gar said after the door had closed. "Is that the kind of person you want to try stealing from?"

"No," I shook my head. "Of course not."

It would be a challenge though, *wouldn't* it? And wasn't that the best part of thieving? In earlier days, while still learning the art, I would break into rich merchants' homes and creep close enough to touch their sleeping forms. All this without them knowing, sometimes not even taking any reward, doing it for the thrill, the challenge.

"I know that look," Gar said.

"Look? What look?" I asked.

The halfling leaned in close. "The one that says you'll be visiting the Tower of Wizardry tonight, no matter what sense I try to talk into you."

"I have no idea what you mean."

"*Just* like your father."

CHAPTER 2
THE TOWER OF WIZARDRY

Five storeys of gleaming white marble loomed above the one and two level buildings surrounding it. The Tower of Wizardry was the most remarkable, most mysterious place in Timurpajan. No one had been inside that wasn't a part of the Wizard's Guild, and none of *them* were telling stories of what it was like inside.

A visit to this city had always seen me here at the tower, wondering what was inside, knowing my skills weren't yet ready for the challenge. Then, once we settled here when Dad was so sick, I didn't have the right to place myself in danger.

Now there were no more excuses, and my palms itched with the idea of exploring that tower. It wasn't *just* the curiosity, though that was a great chunk of it. No, it was also a test. Any thief who could break into the tower without their knowledge was a sneak worthy of the name. One that could make it to the top floor and out again, with some valuable treasure to sell, would be one of the best.

Throughout each year several would-be thieves would be found at the tower's front door, not even making it past the entry. Others would be found dead and broken in the nearby street, any discoveries dying with them.

The tower's pristine walls taunted me, daring me to come see for myself what was hidden within, if I had what it took.

Still, I wasn't about to rush inside.

For the remainder of the afternoon, I circled in a slow, discreet route, looking for information that wasn't already apparent. The tower refused to give up any secrets but did present one interesting question. How did a building only a few hundred feet around house all the magic-users seen around Timurpajan, plus their equipment and living quarters?

More mystery.

The setting sun lit the tower with a glowing halo for fifteen minutes before disappearing behind the horizon and surrendering to the night. Still, the marble gleamed.

Learning nothing from my tours around the tower, I settled into some shadows across from the front door and waited, watching. At a quarter to midnight, I pulled a sandwich from my satchel and ate, contemplating. In all that time watching, no one had entered or exited the tower, not through any normal means at least. It was as if all the wizards inside had gone to other realms.

Hmm, is that a possibility?

Guesses are dangerous. Work with the facts you know from observation and experience.

Midnight arrived, the moon high in the sky. The time of thieves.

Time to get to work.

The magical residents inside should have had plenty of time to settle down for the night—or perhaps, plenty of time to wake and start doing whatever they did when not turning regular citizens into pigs.

Detaching from the shadows I made my way across the street and to the front door without any notice.

The lock had seven tumblers with two poison dart traps.

Do they even want to keep me out?

Confidence is fine. Cockiness leads to mistakes.

When the memories living inside my head were right, they were right.

I pulled the lockpicks from my tunic's inside pocket, examining the lock for any surprises. You would think the wizards would choose a Zadi lock to secure this door. Then again those *were* in short supply and wide demand since the master locksmith's disappearance two years ago.

In any case, this lock was intimidating enough to make many thieves think twice, but not one who had spent his childhood in the back of caravans, practicing on every possible lock he could get his hands on, including one older model Zadi.

My fingers itched to challenge a more recent version of that master's work.

The picks made short work of the door lock, easing tumblers into place, avoiding the traps. Soon the door swung inward without a hint of sound. The Tower of Wizardry lay open, ready for exploration.

Rubbing hands together, I stepped inside.

On the other side was a wide, square lobby decorated with marble columns sculpted into dragons, wyverns, and other magnificent creatures. Oak chairs and tables lined either side of the room while gleaming porcelain tiles covered a floor. On the far side was a winding staircase, leading upward and down.

Astounding.

Outside, the tower was round and marble, inside it was square and the walls were made of plaster and wood. It was larger, too. How this was possible was one of magic's mysteries and beyond a humble thief's understanding, even if a wizard *did* deign to explain it.

It was unnerving.

You can't always understand what you're looking at, but that doesn't mean you can't appreciate, or profit from, it.

I don't remember my father ever saying those words. Was it my own inner voice I was hearing, now? The things he could have said?

A consideration for later. Now was the time for focus.

Except for my controlled breathing the lobby was quiet as a cleric's bedroom.

Torches and candles lit the area, floating in mid-air at regular intervals, making it easier to pick which tiles held pressure plates. Tracing a path from these triggers led to no evident danger, which was troubling. There should have been some sort of trap, a deadfall, an alarm.

Magical defences were tricky, the possibilities endless, the punishments for error fatal.

The pressure plates were easy to avoid once their pattern was determined. They'd been arranged so those that lived in the tower didn't set them off by accident.

I made my way to the stairs.

These were more worrying in that no trap could be seen at all. I searched again and again for several minutes.

If a good thief can't see a trap, then there's no trap to find.

And I was indeed a good thief.

Very well.

I took the first tentative movement up the spiralling stairs toward the next floor, moving with caution. One step. Two. Three. Four. Every step was an inspection, sure that the wizards arranging security wouldn't stop at what was on the ground floor. In short time the lobby was left behind, but still no traps presented themselves.

The remaining steps passed without incident or change until nearing the next floor. There a jagged hole had been punched into the plaster of the wall, at roughly the height and size of my head. A full minute passed while examining that hole, unable to gain further information except that it hadn't been put there by design.

At the final riser, I paused, scanning the second floor for traps before taking the step forward. A soft gong chimed somewhere in the tower, reminiscent of the ones hill-monks used as a call to meditation.

I froze, neither increasing nor decreasing the pressure placed on the last step taken. Had I set off some alarm? But no, no pressure plate underfoot. No trap.

A magical alarm then? Or was it all coincidence?

Thieves die embracing a belief in coincidence.

Damn it!

Okay, so until another cause presented itself that gong was all about me. The real question now was, stay or go? If that chime *was* about me, would it be possible to leave at all?

Silence and a faint, cool breeze wafting from the upper floors were my only answer.

No! Believing in coincidence was a luxury, but so was abandoning a job at the first hint of trouble.

Forward.

This second floor occupied even more space than the previous, giving the impression of an inverted pyramid. And why not? The tower had already broken a law of nature by being bigger inside than out. Nothing should be surprising at this point.

Passages branched off in the four main compass directions, each much like the others. Wooden doors lined each hallway, five to a side. Any untold treasure could be behind those doors, any mystery.

Oh, ho?

Each hallway was the same? No, not quite.

Halfway down the western passage, the wall held a long, jagged furrow, the kind caused by a sharp weapon. Someone had swung a sword or axe here, and the wall had suffered for it. Nearby was a deep scorch mark on the floor.

Something interesting had happened here.

Stories are everywhere. You don't have time to stop and listen to all of them.

Good point.

As much as knowing the story behind this battle would be fascinating, I am here to finance a trading business. There's no money in furrows and scorch marks.

Now, what about all those closed doors?

No, that's curiosity talking.

Looking behind each of them wasn't practical. The night would run out before the doors would, but a better reason to move on was that this floor wouldn't hold the tower's most valuable treasures.

That would be at the top.

The steps leading to the third floor were similar to the last. Nothing hidden. No traps. Easy going.

I froze.

A soft scrape of padded foot against floor from somewhere in a lower level.

Someone was awake and on the move. A wizard up for a snack? Or someone searching for an intruder? If not for the midnight silence and my keen elven hearing I might have missed it.

Two steps from the next floor I paused, listening to the silence of the tower. No other noise came, and I let my breath escape, reminding myself this wasn't the first time I'd snuck through a place with people awake... Just the first time with people who could turn me into a farm animal.

Adjusting the satchel across my shoulder, I gritted my teeth and took the last steps to the next floor. Lots of shadows here, plenty of places to hide.

Huh! It appeared each floor was constructed of varying materials as if they were different buildings instead of different levels. Bizarre.

On this floor, wide corridors of well-worn stone extended in every direction, like the spokes of a wagon wheel with the staircase acting as the hub. Magnificent, ogre-sized statues rested at the mid-point of every passage while heavy oak doors lined either side, the sort of door that would need several annoyed trolls trying their best to knock them down.

Like on the previous floor, these doors could hold anything...or nothing. Two floors remained to be explored and were bound to have greater treasures.

Yes. Onward and upward.

I took the first step back toward the stairs, congratulating myself on the ability to resist temptation and curiosity. Really, my strength of will was legendary, and deserved every accolade for—

What in the hells is that?

There came an audible *poof* sound inside my head, the sound of my legendary resistance turning tail and heading for parts unknown.

Each corridor ran up to a stone wall, except one which ended in a blood-red door. Over the door hung a sign saying *Enter Spider*.

Okay, so there wasn't any sign, but there might as well have been with something that out of place.

Not investigating would have been irresponsible. That is the sort of door which would hold great treasures.

More noise, this time from the floor below.

Furtive steps mixed with muffled whispering, someone trying to be quiet and not quite getting there. Much too noisy for such a silent tower. Whoever the noise belonged to, they didn't have a right to be in here any more than me.

That gong *hadn't* been for me.

Get out of here, Spider. Curb that curiosity.

Except, these other intruders were still on the second floor, and that gave me plenty of time to get through that door.

With all the swiftness and silence possible, which was considerable if I do say so myself, I rushed for the door, passing a gorgeous mermaid statue halfway.

This red door was spaced an equal distance from the others but very much apart from them. On top of the blood-red colour, the door also had a professional, prison quality lock securing it.

This would be no real deterrent, but it would take some time.

My hands twitched. This was it. Valuables had to be hidden behind the door.

With the speed of thought, the lockpicks were in my hand, flashing back and forth as I worked. This was somewhat more difficult than the one securing the front door, though there were no poison darts this time.

Yes!

The door swung inwards, hovering candles flickering in the red door's breeze.

What was it with wizards and candles?

Inside was a laboratory of sorts. Mixing stations, much like a kitchen's preparation area, were sectioned off on a workbench occupying most of the room. High shelves lined the walls, filled with ingredients. Most jars held unidentifiable powders or liquids. Some held skeletal bodies of creatures or eyeballs floating in fluid. The bench's cabinet doors revealed more of the same.

Nothing here! Nothing sellable, anyway.

One fence in the thieves' quarter bought magical items, but he wouldn't be interested in ingredients, not unless they were rare ones. Without knowing more, who could judge which ones were remarkable and which were the day to day stuff.

Valuables had to be hidden behind a door like this?

I ignored the sound of my father's voice, knowing that if he were here, he would have been just as attracted to that door.

That did explain the lock though. The front door was to keep intruders out while this one was for other wizards.

Still, a waste of time. No sense prolonging it.

I closed the door behind me as I left.

Always leave the area how you found it. Make them question that you were ever there.

My father's words registered through my disappointment. I turned and relocked the door.

Not even a magic wand in there. Were the stairs down back at the lobby the way to go?

No, surely the valuable objects would be at the top.

The area around the stairs was empty. The intruders still blundered through the second floor, not difficult to hear. They opened and closed doors, begging for attention from the residents.

Damn it!

Their noise and lack of skills could ruin the whole night, set the tower on alert.

In fact—why hadn't that happened already?

As if in response, a muffled scream came from the floor below, followed by the sharp sound of snapping bone. A moment later, a second scream, less muffled, echoing.

Footsteps, fleeing.

They'd entered the tower without permission and were now paying the price for it. Tomorrow, bodies would be found in the street outside, a warning to others. I had no intention of being with them, judged as just another common failure.

Heart pounding inside my chest, I rubbed sweaty palms against my leggings.

Real danger lurked here, the sort where death was a reward for mistakes.

It was so invigorating.

Whoever these blunderers were, they'd made returning to the floor below impossible.

Good thing I'd come with a backup plan.

But first, at least one of the intruders was still alive. Sprinting footsteps on the stairs headed this way.

No, thanks.

I retreated back down the hallway and into the shadows of the mermaid statue.

A man arrived at the stairway, panting and swaying, trying to see every direction at once. He was in full panic mode and if he didn't calm himself and focus, he would be finished. Turning, he looked back at the stairs, up and down, then at each of the hallways.

"No, no, no," I whispered to myself, seeing what would come next. "Remember, red means danger."

His gaze landed on the door behind me and, without hesitation, he headed straight for it and my hiding spot.

Wonderful. So, if he was being chased, that would lead them straight to me. Serendipity for some tower monster.

This intruder was about my height but scrawny thin and moving with slight grace. The red sash on his waist said he was a River Rat, but I'd last seen him in the market, begging. When had he joined the Rats?

It's this new leader of theirs, Grey Badger. He was uniting all the beggars, urchins and thieves unwelcome in more professional groups. He'd risen to the top of the River Rats and aimed to bring them professionalism and credibility. A long and difficult road.

This beggar rushed past my hiding spot without so much as a glance, headed for the red door. He saw the lock and stopped, shoulders slumping.

"There's nothing in there anyway," I said, pulling my hood into place.

He whirled at the sound of my voice, one hand in a warding off gesture as if expecting to be attacked. The other arm hung limp, drops of blood collecting on the floor at his feet.

"Spider! You!"

The relief in his voice was thick. I nodded, struggling to remember his name. Something buggy.

"You're...um, Tick, aren't you?" I guessed.

"Flea!" he spat, then calmed himself. "My name is Flea."

"Right. Of course." It still didn't sound familiar.

"And I'm not looking for something to steal, not anymore. I want a window to escape."

"You have rope?"

Flea shook his head.

"You know we're three floors up, right?"

Flea sagged, glancing back at the stairs. He leaned his uninjured hand against the wall for balance, leaving a smear of blood. He'd been raked along his left side and arm. A semi-serious wound but plenty of time to get out of the tower and find a healer.

"What happened?" I asked.

"Some...*thing* attacked us, on the second floor."

"What was it?"

Flea shook his head. "How should I know? It was like the shadows came to life."

The shadows? Interesting.

"I came in with three other Rats," Flea said, "including my trainer."

"Trainer?"

Flea turned a smug expression on me. "The Rats are training me to be a thief."

And who had trained his trainer? I bit back the comment. "Go on."

Flea glanced back at the stairs, his smugness slipping. "The shadow thing detached from one corner and hovered there, watching us. When it moved, it was like water flowing. It grabbed Rock first, then Tarnol, both died screaming without any marks on them. Brion, my trainer, turned and fled for the stairs. I followed."

At this he stopped, exploring his wound with the opposite hand.

"That was when you got hurt?"

He winced. "As we passed, the shadow swiped at us." His hand came away with blood on it, but less than before. "Brion headed down the stairs, but I went up."

He stopped and looked at me, as if for confirmation. Wish I could ask this Brion about leaving a green recruit behind, but he was probably as inexperienced as Flea.

"See," Flea continued, "I knew we'd be expected to go down."

"Sure. Good thinking."

He smiled—an expression that said he was well aware of how clever he was and didn't need my confirmation after all.

"Brion screamed as I climbed the stairs. I kept going."

"What else could you do?"

"Yeah, right. Right!"

"Is it following you?"

Flea glanced back at the stairs again, watching then shaking his head. "Nah, I don't think so. I waited on the stairs a while, listening. I think it was happy getting Brion."

That or it was patient, playing with the intruder. With luck, the creature was restricted to the second floor, but that was doubtful. My mind kept turning to those pressure plates in the lobby, and the gong which sounded through the tower. The wizards wouldn't set a trap for intruders restricted to the second floor, would they?

"What are you doing here anyway?" I asked.

Flea shrugged. "Following you."

"Me? Why?"

"No idea."

I levelled my best glare on him, crossing my arms.

"Okay, okay," Flea said, throwing up one hand. "We saw you at the tower door and figured you had a line on something worthwhile."

"Uh-huh."

The part Flea didn't mention was robbing me afterwards.

Curse my inattentiveness anyway! I'd been so focused on the front door, so excited about getting in, that I'd let myself be seen...and by River Rats no less!

"So, what *are* you here for?" Flea demanded.

"No idea," I said, throwing his own words back at him.

"Come on."

"No, really. Just looking for anything of value."

"You broke into the Tower of Wizardry, to look around?"

"Essentially."

Flea rolled his eyes, though whether that was because of them following me for no reason, or flat out not believing me was unclear. It didn't matter either way.

"Okay, Weevil, listen—"

"The name, is Flea."

"Oh, right. Anyway, I can get you out of here if you listen to me."

He glanced at the stairs, then at the red door, then me. He nodded once.

"You have to follow my instructions though," I said.

"I already agreed, didn't I?"

"You did, yes. Okay, follow me Beetle."

"Flea!"

For someone with a name like Spider, I probably shouldn't be making fun, but Flea's personality was too arrogant for my tastes. This annoyed him, and I wasn't about to give it up so soon.

We approached the stairs again, Flea moving with some degree of stealth. Perhaps he *did* have potential. There was the occasional shuffle of foot against stone, but that was as much his trainer's fault as his own, and not so difficult to fix. When we got out of here, I could show him a few tips.

What? No, no. What was I thinking? Last thing my life needed was some kind of apprentice. Adding Flea to my life would *not* bring me closer to my goal of that trading business, therefore it would take me further away. I travelled alone and liked it. Of course, I would help Flea escape the tower, if he would listen, but that's as far as this went.

So, this trip had gone from one of cat burglary to a rescue mission. Well, no reason some valuables couldn't be nabbed on the way out.

Nothing waited at the stairs. No living shadows. No wizards looking to nab intruders.

We started toward the next floor.

"Up?" Flea said, much too loud, voice carrying. "Why are we going up?"

"Shh!"

He rolled his eyes once again, making me wonder if it was possible to smack him in the head and still maintain I was trying to save him. Flea lapsed into a sullen silence and followed.

Good enough.

The next floor was one long hallway of smooth marble, like the tower's outside, ending in one single massive door. I slid forward, heading for the only possible destination other than further up. The annoyance coming off Flea was almost tangible. I gave him another fifteen seconds to stew before turning, making a show of looking around before speaking in a low voice.

"We headed up because your shadow monster will still be searching for intruders."

Flea glanced at the stairs. "You don't know that."

"True. Why don't you go scout the lower floors then come tell me I'm wrong."

"Um..."

"Up here we can hopefully find a window to escape from."

"I have no rope, remember?"

"Yes, Slug. I remember."

Flea didn't bother to correct me this time, which said this particular joke had run its course. Too bad, there were at least a dozen creepy-crawly names left.

"Luckily I come better prepared than your trainer," I said. "There's rope in my satchel."

There was no point mentioning that we had no guarantee the windows would even lead back to Timurpajan. In fact, if the tower could be larger than the outside, then it could also have more than just the five floors. The place could be infinite.

What a fascinating concept.

Greater signs of struggle marked the walls here. I slid a finger along one deep scorched wall groove, wondering how hot it had to be for marble to burn.

What had happened here? Some unexpected battle for sure.

"Wouldn't you love to know the story behind this?" I said, turning toward Flea.

He rolled his eyes. My hand twitched in response.

"Never mind," I sighed. "Come on."

We came to another statue, like the mermaid on the previous floor. This one was a wizard which had been smashed near the top, removing its head and entire left arm. Flea glanced at the sculpture and dismissed it with a shrug. I stopped to examine it, knowing that would annoy him.

Lucky thing.

I pulled Flea into the shadows on the statue's far side, my hand clasped around the beggar-turned-thief's mouth. A flicker of movement back at the stairs had propelled me forward on instinct.

"Shh," I warned.

Flea nodded under my hand. He may be untrained, but he was no fool... Well, not in this case at least.

A thicker shadow detached from the natural ones near the stairs, drifting toward us with slow breezy movements, red eyes boring into the gloom. An actual, living shadow. I'd never even heard of such a creature before tonight, and *living* probably wasn't the best word, but...well, whatever. This was fascinating.

Utterly terrifying too, of course.

Our only possible escape from it and the tower was the door behind us, which, now that we were closer, didn't seem like such a great idea either.

From top to bottom, four deep claw marks had been gouged into the wood. No apparent lock sealed the room but surrounding the frame were runes of greenish silver that kept forcing my eyes to focus elsewhere.

"Mmmph," Flea said, eyes wide.

One hand still covered Flea's mouth, grip tightening with each moment until his teeth were pressing into the flesh of my fingers. I released him.

The shadow had closed the distance by half, and we had no doubt on it discovering us. It was either horrible death or the unknown of that room, which could amount to more of the same.

"Okay, Flea—"

The runes glowed with sudden pale green light. Stabbing pain reached into my head like a knife twist. I gasped, one hand reaching for the statue to remain upright.

"What is it?" Flea asked.

Another bright spike drove me to one knee. The door runes glowed like green moonlight, brightening this entire end of the hallway. At the edge of light, the shadow wavered, as uncertain as any being composed of blackness could be. With the next surge of light and pain, it disappeared.

"Yes!" Flea leapt forward, bravery returning now that the danger was gone. "Hah! Take that!"

I groaned, forcing my feet back under me. The rune lights had dimmed but not disappeared and looking in their direction was pure suffering.

"What's your problem?" Flea said.

Unable to articulate with my head pounding as it was, I pointed at the runes, then reached up, sliding hands inside my hood to massage my temples.

"You..." Flea gasped. "You're an elf?"

"Huh? Oh." I'd knocked my hood back. Well, no denying it, and why should I? "You didn't know?"

Clockworks turned inside of Flea's skull, his mouth open in a slack O. His eyes went from me to the door and back again, coming up with the obvious explanation.

"Yeah! I get it! That, um, writing stuff drives everything not-human away, like the shadow. And *you*."

I chose to ignore the emphasis and disdain. Right now, getting away from those runes was more important.

"Gotta be a window in there, right?" Flea turned toward the door. He brightened. "Hey! Maybe even some treasure."

On his first step, the runes flared, and my head screeched.

"Stop!" I gasped.

Flea gave a condescending snort and continued.

Those runes were a warning, to keep people out, but they also kept something in.

33

"Don't," I managed.

Another flare drove me back to my knees.

Flea stopped and returned, crouching next to me.

"I'm okay," I said, collapsing to one side. "Just—"

"Oh, what a relief."

Flea rolled his eyes again, and I wished I had taken the time to smack him earlier. He flipped open my satchel and grabbed the rope. With that, he headed for the door again.

I pushed myself away, from the runes and the pain, sliding along the smooth marble floor. "Don't."

Flea guffawed and grabbed the door handle, pulling it.

"Damn," I muttered.

Everyone follows their own path.

I would have gotten him out if he'd listened.

The marble slid under my tunic without friction, allowing me to pass out of the rune light. With the help of one wall, I stood up, swaying.

The hallway was filled with deep, heavy breathing. A blast of frigid air swept through the open door, filling the hallway as far back as the stairs. Frost crept along the walls in icy spider webs.

Flea's destiny now lay behind that door while mine was back toward the stairs. Still, one stray thought came, pulling me back around.

"Dragon?"

Whatever lived behind that door was much too huge to get out of the tower to sell. But, if it *was* a dragon, what was seeing one worth?

Flea sneered at me, dropping the rope at his feet while struggling with some flint and tinder.

An added strangeness about that room, it was dark, yes, but my elven vision should have been able to pick out the body warmth of whatever was inside. Unless the room *was* empty after all.

But, what was breathing?

A blur of blue-tinted flesh, then a monstrous meaty fist enveloped Flea from neck to waist. Then Flea was gone, pulled inside the room. The door slammed shut like a clap of thunder, clipping off Flea's frantic screams.

"Huh!" I said, pulling my hood back into place. "Not a dragon then."

The rope had dropped on this side of the door and huddled there. Better than even chance it would be needed on the next floor, though I still wasn't convinced the city would even be outside for me.

One problem at a time.

I inched forward, eyes on the rope and trying to ignore the runes. They pulsed brighter but not as much as earlier. Was it because I had no intention of entering that room and didn't need the warning?

My head ached, my brain inside pulsing, but the white-hot agony did not return. I retrieved my rope, slipping it back into my satchel.

What if I just reached out...?

The runes flared bright, drawing a gasp from me.

I retreated for the stairs and started for the next floor while it was still possible. At the top was a locked door, stopping my advance and whetting my curiosity. Dad's lockpicks flashed into my hands and I got to work. The lock was straightforward, though a less experienced thief might have missed that poison dart for punishing the unobservant.

They *do* like their poison dart traps.

With a click, the lock opened. I cringed at the noise, cursing myself as an amateur.

Inside was a room, much larger than it should have been and lit by hundreds of floating candles, neither of which surprised me. A subdued fire floated in the middle, keeping the room a comfortable temperature.

First time I'd ever seen a fire burn from all sides. It was beautiful but wrong.

Off to one side, a workbench with all the bizarre paraphernalia that went with the realm of magic waited for someone to return. Smoking vials of bubbling liquid, giving off fumes undoubtedly fatal to inhale. I wasn't about to test that theory. Ingredients in jars which followed my path with their eyes. Books with more slippery runes, these changing while I gazed at them. At least these didn't hurt my head.

Three chests sat in one corner, sealed with several locks each.

Locked chests in a sealed room? Now we're talking. They *must* hold the best treasures. Rings and wands would be perfect, even without knowing what they did.

Space needed to be made inside my satchel first.

The room held one window and it *did* look onto Timurpajan. I pulled out the rope and attached it to my collapsible grappling hook. This combination would take me back to ground level once the satchel was full.

My hook bit into the marble window sill while the rope disappeared into the night below.

"Huh!"

Seeing the city from this perspective was surreal. Below was the entirety of west side, lit by a bright moon. It was like a giant map of the city.

"Okay, back to work," I said, turning toward the chests.

"It took you longer than I expected."

I stopped in mid-step, sighed and turned toward the voice.

A paper-thin, ancient woman occupied a wooden chair which had been empty a moment ago. An easy confidence emanated from her. She certainly showed no fear of being alone in a room with a thief and no witnesses.

She chuckled. "I was aware when you entered the front door. As I was with the other four intruders."

"They were not with me."

"No. I didn't think so."

Even now it was important not to be judged as an amateur. I was a better thief than any River Rat could ever be.

"And yet." The woman got to her feet with a grace which belied her shrivelled body. "I knew you were there as easily as the others, so what is the difference?"

"I'm alive and they are not."

"True. For now."

Well, better a quick death than a slow one in prison. I opened my mouth to say as much but the sorceress held up one hand.

"No explanations, please. No insincere apologies."

I wasn't about to offer either but let her think what she wanted.

One possibility, one hope remained though a slim one. As she cast her spell, there might be time to dodge and rush for the window. Maybe I could get out of the tower before she prepared the next. A long-shot to be sure, but better than giving up.

"You are no doubt wondering why you're still alive," the aged woman said.

"Well, now that you mention it." I shuffled to the left, trying for a straight route without being obvious.

"You *are* a brash, confident young man, aren't you?"

She eased to her right, between myself and the window, hiding it from sight. I forced an air of nonchalance, keeping both eyes focused on her until she had moved out the other side of my path.

Now!

One full step forward followed by an abrupt halt.

Where the window had been was more marble wall. I spun around, knowing it hadn't simply relocated but hoping anyway.

The door was gone as well.

"Nice trick," I said.

A smile quirked the corners of her mouth, enjoying the game she played. Cat and mouse. No, more like sorceress and powerless mortal. Her gaze bored into my soul.

"I am impressed with your skills." She gestured to a chair near the floating fire, and I sat, empty satchel in my lap. The sorceress moved to an opposite chair, a scent of lavender and burnt ozone following in her wake. She picked up a gem-studded goblet that appeared, and sipped, watching me over the rim until I felt naked. "I am in need of someone with your skills, to retrieve an item."

She was offering me a job?

"The item is rightfully ours, though I presume a thief wouldn't care about such details."

My eyes narrowed, mouth tightening into a line.

"Ah, I've insulted you," she said. "Interesting."

It was a common misconception that all thieves were the same, stealing anything not nailed down, and even then. "I don't steal from friends or those that can't afford it."

The sorceress considered this, sipping from her goblet in silence.

"Churches, orphanages and the like are off limit," I explained. "The rich and royalty are fair game, as are the evil and anyone who could help others but don't."

"And which am I? Evil, or someone who doesn't help others?"

My eyes flicked to the gemmed goblet which could have fed all the orphans in Timurpajan for a year.

"This task will take great thievery skills," she continued, ignoring all I'd said. "It is imperative they do not realize the item has been taken for as long as possible. Most importantly, this cannot be connected with us."

"Got it. And if I don't like the job?"

She laughed. "Do you have a choice?"

"There's always a choice."

"True, but the other option is never leaving this tower again."

Yep. That window was still missing. "Well, I should at least hear what the job is. Wouldn't want to be rude."

CHAPTER 3
PAYING A DEBT

A ramshackle warehouse occupied an entire city block of the waterfront, one floor high, sparsely lit, and long abandoned for any legitimate business purposes. Once it had stored goods coming in from ships, now it only housed secrecy.

From the shadows of a nearby alley, I gathered information. Night still had several hours left, too many judging by the position of the moon. It should have been much later.

Did time pass at an unnatural pace inside the tower?

I gave my head a shake.

Nope. Forget it. There was no hope of ever understanding the true nature of that place without going utterly mad.

All that mattered was enough time remained to be in and out of that warehouse before dawn came.

Even so, the move would need to be made soon.

Guards patrolled the outside, each one wearing the familiar red sash. Someone wanted passers-by to think this was a River Rat hideout, but observation made that illusion fall apart. The Rats were far from stellar thieves, but they still moved with more grace and stealth than some of these people. Under their cloaks, the occasional flash of chain-mail could be seen, and no thief ever wore more than leathers. Who could sneak around sounding like a pot and pan salesman?

Still, no one ever took more than a glance at a person wearing those red sashes. Like any other beggar, they simply weren't seen.

These pseudo-Rats moved with the precision of soldiers. One point to another, each path overlapping with that of the next patrol then back again, no holes in their sweeps, guards at every critical point.

Trained. Organized. Unknown.

Who *are* these people?

If you don't have confidence in a job, walk away.

Given the choice, I would do just that, but the sorceress had been clear that option didn't exist. This bit of thievery would cancel my debt for trespassing, but bolting from here would mean a life on the run. There was nowhere that she wouldn't find me.

What a mess. This was *not* bringing me closer to setting up that trading business. But what other choice did I have?

Gather as much information as you can to make yourself successful.

Yes. Helpful.

According to the ancient sorceress, I just needed to break into this building, sneak my way through to the lower levels, and find the item she wanted. An item she wouldn't name, but insisted would be obvious when seen. After that it became easy. A return spell cast on me would bring me back to the Tower of Wizardry as soon as I touched this treasure.

Defensive spells surrounded the warehouse, cast by their own magic-users and preventing spells by wizards from the tower. The sorceress had maintained the return spell, being passive magic, should work fine.

Should work.

Wonderful.

Another fifteen minutes passed to confirm the guards had a definite pattern to their movements, watching for a weakness in their routine. One, in particular, was interesting. A guard on the roof moved from one corner to the diagonal opposite, then along the back edge to the next corner and another diagonal. In all the hourglass-shaped route he followed took a count of four hundred and sixty-eight seconds, two hundred and thirty-four of which didn't focus on the roof's access door. Plenty of time.

Well, time to get going or go home.

THE WAYWARD SPIDER

Under cover of the night, I made my move, crossing the street and through the ground patrol's sweeps with ease. Up the side of the warehouse, using a crumbling drainpipe, then pausing for the sound of metal boots on wood which said the roof guard was above me.

Waiting. Listening. Moments which felt like hours.

The guard turned, heading back across the roof, and I pulled myself up. Ten feet ahead he stomped his constant, unhurried route.

My internal count was up to twenty-two.

Without a sound, I snuck along the roof, following the guard until he passed the roof access door.

Fifty-seven.

Lockpicks ready, I examined the door. Sure enough, it was locked. Nothing too professional, but enough to slow me.

Eighty-five.

Tumblers turned and fell into place without a sound. At least no traps waited in this lock.

One hundred and fourteen.

Uh-oh. No traps, but the lock was higher quality than first glance told. The tumblers were sensitive, and one wrong move caused a restart, eating the seconds.

One hundred and forty-four.

No point looking for the guard's position. Either he was continuing his journey as he had every other time or he would turn toward me. If he saw me, there would be a warning, a gasp or change to his stride.

One hundred and fifty-six.

A calming breath then another assault on the lock. One tumbler. Two. Three.

One hundred and ninety.

Four tumblers. Five.

Two hundred and eleven. Thirteen seconds left.

Last tumbler. Not even a click to say it was done, just a door swinging inward. Time for self-congratulations later.

Two hundred and twenty-one.

Through the door and into the shadows.

Two hundred and twenty-nine.

The door pushed back into place without a sound.

Two hundred and thirty-two.

I released my pent-up breath. Two whole seconds to spare.

Close. Too close.

Time for recriminations later. For now, Ammara, goddess of thieves and rogues, was watching out for her favourite son. In the entry, a set of hooks held disguises like the guards outside wore. I grabbed a red sash and tied it in place. My own cloak would do fine with the hood pulled far enough forward.

One deep breath and dive in, like jumping into a cold lake.

Downstairs, a vast, well-lit room occupied half the warehouse. Lining the centre were five rectangular tables, each able to seat forty and currently holding a tenth of that.

All ate, silent as stones. Some wore the cloaks and sashes of River Rats, while others had armour, well maintained but also well used. A smaller group in unfamiliar reddish-brown cloaks ate with their hoods pulled up and faces hidden.

Good. I wouldn't be the only one with my features hidden.

On the far side was a door that, whenever opened, allowed the aromas of cooking meat to waft out and about. The kitchen. Opposite this were two other doors, the first of which saw tired men and women headed toward what must be general barracks. That left one door, and few people passed through it. This must be the way to the stairs the sorceress said would be here. At least I hoped so.

No way around it but to head for this door and look legitimate.

Each person focused on their food, paying no attention to another hooded figure passing through. Well, that was easy—

"Hey!"

The challenge came from behind as I reached for the closed door. In as casual manner as possible I turned, surveying the room and judging the quickest escape would be back to the roof, setting the odds at well below even of reaching there. Still, they wouldn't be expecting me to bolt, so the element of surprise could act as a wild card.

A rough, muscled woman stared at me, chain-mail to the waist and a sword on her belt.

Okay, that heavy armour would slow her reactions, allowing me—

"Don't forget this," she barked, throwing one of the reddish-brown robes at me.

With that, she turned back to the table and her plate of food, while I stood dumbstruck. Should I thank her? Would that be out of character?

When in doubt keep your mouth shut.

Following Dad's advice, I slipped this robe over my existing one, hoping no one found that strange, and passed through the door, sparing one quick glance back. No one paid the least bit of attention.

For one brief, lunatic instant, I wanted to step back out and scream that I was an intruder, come and get me. It's an ugly cousin to the sensation a person gets on a high ledge, finding themselves wondering what jumping would be like.

I closed the door.

On the other side was a corridor of heavy shadows which felt more like home. Stairs led down at the far end, and I headed for these with all my thiefly speed, scratching at this irritating robe where it contacted my skin.

What was it made of anyway, ox hair? It smelled of earth, with an underlying coppery scent which had to be blood.

This was *not* a place for me. Except, now that a mystery had presented itself, I wanted to know what was happening here.

Next floor I paused at the bottom, trying to appear as casual as possible to those moving about. All wore the same itchy, reddish-brown robes and moved with the purposeful speed of those assigned important tasks. They were out of sight in seconds.

Doors lined either side of an east-west corridor with a north-south one intersecting about halfway.

This wasn't a secret area. Not yet.

The first door had the deep bellows breathing of some massive animal, destined to end its life in the upstairs kitchen presumably. I kept moving, heading along the hall and through the intersection with a quick glance in both directions. To the left was more hallway and doors, much like this one. Storage? The right passage had no doors at all, ending with a set of stairs cut into dirt and rock. It was where I needed to go, but two thickly muscled men blocked the way. They became more alert as I passed through their vision, eyes following me. Each had the air of casual violence and easy murder about them.

The old sorceress had stressed this mission needed to be stealthy. Whoever these people might be, they couldn't know the item was missing. It *would* be discovered, in time, but when it was no suspicion could be falling on the tower.

I searched my pouches and pockets for ideas, already knowing the items inside. My father's lockpicks wouldn't be any help. Other than that, there was flint and tinder and another of Lees's sandwiches. At my back were two concealed daggers. Another knife, this one for throwing, was tucked inside my boot. Only one of those, and murder didn't sit right with me. Nothing stealthy in that, anyway.

So, how do I get past those bruisers?

Bluff my way through? Not without knowing more. Besides, those two were on guard to keep their fellows out.

Doing an about-face, I passed through the intersection again as if I had a mission, heading for the room with heavy breathing. I opened that door and rushed inside.

The beast inside the cage could stop anyone in their tracks and did with me. It was a pig of sorts, a monster boar as tall in the centre as a man's chest. Two tusks came to wicked points which gleamed like scimitars. A ridge of coarse hair ran along its back, sharp as a knife blade. The pig drew snorting breaths through its mouth and expelled them from a mashed-flat nose in low, squealing grunts. Both baleful, mismatched eyes stared at me, one a deep black, the other shining blood red.

It was magnificent, *and* it gave me an idea.

The door pushed in further and stayed open against the wall. Lucky for me since there was nothing to hold it with except the cage, and the boar inside weighed as much as two of me, plus the cage. No, that was staying right where it was.

I rushed across the room and leapt on top of the cage to a low, annoyed grunt from my new friend. It gave an ineffectual thrust of the tusks.

"Hey now, I thought we were friends," I said.

Another displeased grunt, but it gave up trying to spear me.

Now, as long as it wanted to get out of there as much as any trapped animal should...

With relief, I pulled the itchy brown robe off, resisting the urge to scratch all over. Plenty of time for that later. I squatted, laying the robe flat across my knees.

The cage lock was no more than a hinge, with one thick pin holding it closed. The easiest barrier I've come across tonight. With a grin, I grabbed the pin and pulled.

Squuuueeeeeeeeaaaaaaaaakkkkkkkkkkk.

The high-pitched noise filled the room and *had* to carry to the entire floor.

Overconfidence is—

"Nope, nope, nope. Don't want to hear it."

His voice went quiet, as did everything else. Brother boar cocked his head to one side, but that seemed to be all the attention I was getting for now. The pin was only halfway out though.

Below, the boar pressed its face against the bars, red eye staring up at me.

"How do you see out of that?" I asked.

It snorted.

"Okay, hold on."

Squuuueeeeeeeeaaaaaaaaakkkkkkkkkkk.

With the pin free, the monster pig was on the move with a dash, slamming the cage door open. As it passed beneath me, I flung the robe outward, over its face and snagging the two great tusks. The animal stopped, twisted in a circle, trying to remove the intruder from its face and getting more enraged with each second.

I leaped over the boar, landing near the doorway while it thrashed and bucked, twirling the robe tighter.

"Hey, piggy," I called.

It stopped. Listening. One hoof scuffed at the floor.

"Over here."

The boar turned toward my voice.

"Come and get me."

It charged. I jumped out of the room, dodging to the right and pressing

47

against the nearer wall. The boar bolted through a moment later, slamming the wall across from me. It shook off the impact and stood facing my general direction, the robe hiding both eyes. The next part of my plan waited. I stepped backward in silence, hoping to reach the intersection before—

The boar charged, squealing its fury.

I dodged to one side, flattening tight to the wall while muscular pig flesh passed within inches. As the boar shot past, I gave it a solid slap on the rump. An indignant squeal of surprise, a snort of pure rage and the pig careened down the hall, thrashing and bucking, colliding with walls.

It reached the intersection as both guards did the same, the three barrelling into each other. All went down in a pile of grunting, cursing flesh and tusks.

In the carnage, I dodged around the three and into the hallway opposite the stairs.

"Help, help. It's gone mad," I yelled.

The boar, recognizing my voice, struggled to rise, trampling the two guards in its effort.

Shouts of pain. More cursing.

"How did that get out?" guard one shouted.

"How should I know?" the second replied.

Other voices, shouting, approaching from several directions.

The boar slammed one hoof into a guard's crotch, trying to charge.

I dodged around the struggling pile and headed for the stairs, enjoying every grunt and squeal behind me. I neither paused nor looked back until down those stairs.

The next floor was a wide, natural cave, lit by torches. Stalactites hung from a rock ceiling thirty-feet above. The walls and floor were damp, water dripping in fat, lazy drops to the floor.

On the far side was something less natural, an altar carved from the solid rock into a smooth, flat surface that gave me an uneasy sensation. Even from here it was obvious the top and sides had been stained a reddish-brown, matching the colour of that scratchy robe.

It was a wide cave. I kept to the edges where shadows were thickest, skirting the outside until reaching the altar. This close, the scent of blood mingled with other waste, hanging thick in the air, confirming my fears.

Sacrifices.

Who in the hells were these people? Some cult for certain, and a well-organized one at that, but who did sacrifices these days? That went out with the ancient gods. At least this altar was too small for bipeds. The cult was only performing the odious act of sacrificing animals.

Right. Only animals...

...In the secret dinginess of a hidden cave.

...Two floors below Timurpajan.

Sure.

I shook my head.

Time to get what I came for and get out. None of this was about me, none of it helped me complete my quest to become a trader. No, in the morning I could report this to the city guard, but for now I had a job to do.

Here's hoping that boar managed to do considerable damage, to people *and* property before being subdued again.

And now I felt guilty about that slap on the rump.

Focus, Spider!

On the far side of the altar hung curtains of blood-red fabric which, unless the altar opened into a secret passage, hid the stairs down to the next level. I rushed toward them, wanting nothing more than to get away from this cave.

Then I saw something I wanted more than to get away from this cave.

Behind the altar gleamed a gem-encrusted goblet. In the flickering light of the torches, it appeared expensive, like the one the sorceress had been drinking from.

Yes, pop the gems and fence each one on their own. Melt the gold down. That would fetch enough to get a modest trading business started.

Unless this goblet was the item to retrieve. I reached for it.

"And I says we should check," a voice carried from the stairs.

"Paranoid, I says," answered a second voice, coming closer. "But if it makes ya's happy."

Damn it!

That could only be those two muscle-brained guards. The boar hadn't kept them occupied as long as hoped.

Two choices, curtains or goblet.

I dove for the treasure. If it *was* the item, then touching it would return me to the tower before the guards could finish their descent. My hands wrapped around the stem of the goblet and...

Nothing. No shimmering return spell.

Fine. Guess the goblet is mine then.

"What's ya think'll be down here," asked the second voice, nearing the bottom of the stairs. "Goblins?"

I rushed for the curtains, through them and—face first into a metal door.

"Oof," I said by way of observation.

Not only closed but locked too, and nowhere near enough time to open it.

"What I expects is nothin'," the first guard said. "But I likes to play it safe."

Almost here.

The cave held many dim shadowy spots, but nothing dark enough to stand up to scrutiny. I rushed for the altar and hunkered down behind it, trying not to breathe in the scent of blood and waste.

"There! You sees? Nothin'," said guard two.

"Yeah, yeah."

The voices echoed off the walls of the cave. They were standing at the bottom of the stairs now.

Go back upstairs, I willed them. Go! Nothing to see—

The weight of the goblet registered on me. Too light. Not gold at all, but some lighter, cheaper metal. Tin? The gems were also junk, sparkling and worthless.

Wonderful.

"Cans we get back upstairs?" guard two said.

"I s'pose."

Yes. Go.

"Lemme check b'hind the altar."

No!

The second guard snorted. "Jus' hurry up."

The slow sound of boots sliding against stone as the guard approached my hiding spot.

Dammit! This was exactly what the old sorceress told me to avoid. Not exactly my first choice either, but what other options?

None.

Guard two at the stairs was my first concern. He couldn't be allowed to rush off and sound the alarm.

I placed the goblet down, freeing both hands to draw out my throwing knife and one of the daggers, and readied myself to spring into action.

Boots against stone approached from my left and I went right, around the other side of the altar, keeping low. I would need to get closer to the stairs to use my throwing knife. Luckily surprise was on my side.

Now! Attack while—

"Any goblins backs there?"

The guard at the stairs stood flexing his arms, examining his shadow cast from the torchlight. One arm up and one arm down. Both up. Both down. He certainly did love those muscles.

"Nah. Nothin'," came the voice from behind the altar.

More boot scuffs as guard one came around the altar and I scrambled back in the opposite direction.

"You was right," the guard nearest me said, crossing the cave.

"Course I was," the one at the stairs answered. "But I guess it didn't hurt ta check."

The two scuffed their way back up the steps to their guard positions. I peeked over the altar, sure the two would be standing there looking in my direction, but that would have been more subtlety than they could manage. No, they were gone.

I collapsed with my back against the altar.

Gods! That was too close.

Time for relaxing when the job is done.

Yes. Back to work.

Exchanging knives for lockpicks, I approached the curtained door. In any other place the lock would have been a welcome challenge, but having that altar at my back and those guards not so far away was unsettling. Like listening to a minstrel with no idea how to play the violin, but not letting that stop him from playing.

Crouching, I inspected the lock. A thick, professional grade type built into the door. Not Zadi quality, but still a serious one that would take time.

Nothing to be done except get to work.

Behind me, drips of water hit the floor, each one becoming a fat drop of blood falling from the altar, or a fat-headed guard sneaking up on me.

Eyes closed and one deep inhalation. In through the nose and out through the mouth. The opposite of my pig friend upstairs.

Now, focus on the lock.

Minutes passed, tripping tumblers into the correct place one by one. Not a great challenge, but time-consuming.

Without fanfare the door swung inward, taking a slow, lazy arc.

Yes.

I started forward then turned back toward the goblet of tin and fake jewels.

With luck, it held great religious significance for the cult and would distress them if it disappeared.

I rushed over and grabbed it, slipping the cup into my satchel.

Serves them right for leaving it lying around.

I passed through the metal door, closing it behind me, though not locking it. Better to have it ready to open if a quick retreat was needed. Any cultist coming along would question who was careless enough to leave the door unlocked.

Inside, steep, narrow stairs looking old as time led down, curving before the shadows swallowed them. I started down, scanning each step for possible surprises.

All that earth between me and the city above weighed on me, reminding me just how far underground this was. Though, maybe it was more the altar and knowledge of what must happen there that truly weighed on me.

This was not a happy place to be.

Forget the guard, I would pass this information directly to the city commander, through Gar of course. As a well-respected merchant, he would be listened to.

The next level was even dimmer. A roughly burrowed passage with sturdy timbers every few feet to support the weight of rock and dirt. This level was not natural like the cave above and had been dug out with brute force over time.

This would take *years* of workers coming in and out, removing rock and earth. How had no one ever noticed all the activity?

"Magic. Had to be."

A magic-user could cast a spell for encouraging eyes to look elsewhere. I'd seen such a spell in the city of Targ many miles north. Still, these sorts of spells could only last days at best, needing recasting over and over. The spell should also lose its potency over multiple castings, as far as I understood spells anyway. One thing for sure, this meant a magic-user of some sort was close by, more likely several.

Every piece of information made me like this less and less.

Torches had been inserted into the dirt walls every thirty feet or so, insufficient for illuminating the passage, but working wonders at messing up my elvish vision. Normally I would be able to see the outline of the cavern ahead, but with torches, even meagre ones, the best I could hope for was seeing a living creature's body heat. That would give me advance warning at least, assuming any creatures here *had* body heat.

Work with what you have.

Thanks, Dad. Helpful.

No verbal platitude followed. Instead, I had an image of Dad shrugging, an expression of *you're on your own kid*, on his face.

This current passage led in a straight line, sloping downward with no other options until coming to the next set of stairs. These were also made of stone, cut to be flat and smooth, leading in a gentle curve.

The next floor sent a chill through me. On either side of the passage glared four heavy wooden doors, each with barred windows the size of my head at the top, and a sliding door for food at the bottom.

Cells.

Another cheerless turn in this adventure.

What if there were prisoners inside?

The answer was evident, not even needing a comment from my father's imagined voice. If someone was imprisoned by this cult, I *had* to free them.

But could I get them out of here?

With great care I crept to the first door, peering in through the opening. One lumpy cot with dirty bedding and little else.

Empty.

The breath I'd held was released in a slow, quiet sigh as I moved to the opposite cell. This was a mirror image of the first, and also empty. Moving in this way back and forth, I found four more empty cells, all made up the same.

Two remained. One on each side before reaching the next stairs.

The left-hand cell looked like the others, sparse and empty, and I allowed myself the happy conclusion that these cells were all unused for whatever reason.

Jinxed myself.

Inside the final cell, a man hunkered down with his back against the far wall, head resting against his knees. He wore the brownish robes of a cultist.

Was he one of them? No, if he was in a cell, he couldn't be. This was a punishment, a warning to others.

Maybe he could help me find the item. Would the teleport spell take another person if we were touching at the time?

"Hey, hold on in there," I whispered. "I'll have you out in a minute."

No reaction. No movement.

I started on the lock, a thick type built into the door and usually reserved for prisons. Not difficult and requiring more brute force than skill.

As I picked the lock, an idea hit me: What if the item was, in fact, a person? *This* person. The longer I worked, the more I liked the idea. It made sense.

The door swung open on creaky hinges.

"Okay, you're free."

The man still didn't move.

I hesitated to enter the cell. Any thief's worst nightmare was being trapped where the lock couldn't be reached. Glancing left and right I made sure we were still alone before rushing across the room.

"Come on," I said in a low voice, reaching for the man's shoulder. "Let's get out of here."

The man pitched forward at my touch and sprawled at my feet. No sign of life at his neck or wrist and only cold silence from his chest.

I'd rescued a corpse.

"Run for it," I told him. "The door is wide open."

With regret, I left, closing the door behind me with a creak, then a clank, and headed down the next set of stairs.

Another floor empty of rooms was next, just a short hallway followed by more stairs. As was the next, and the next. Deeper and deeper into the earth, as if this path would lead straight to the underworld.

My breath was coming in rapid bursts with the awareness of how deep into the ground I had come. Anything could happen down here. If I disappeared in these depths, I wouldn't be heard from again.

And how does that differ from any thieving job?

Well, Dad, sometimes they only call the guard.

So the guard makes you disappear instead.

I had no answer, so continued on, quieting my nerves.

Five more floors of rock, stone and dirt before I arrived on the bottom steps. The end. A short corridor with one windowless door on either side and a plain stone wall straight ahead. No exit other than the way I'd come.

The doors were thick metal, secured by... I gasped. Genuine Zadi locks, one built into each door.

They were beautiful.

My training kicked in before taking that first rushed step forward. The floor ahead was fine, no traps or alarms. Nothing on either door. I eased forward, inspecting the locks without touching, aware of the greatness I was approaching. Yes, they were definite Zadi locks, so much like the one I'd had as a child, practicing in the wagon between towns.

The lock design was unfamiliar, though that wasn't strange since the gnome locksmith made each lock unique, tailored to the intended task. The tumblers of every lock were sensitive, fitting with their respective keys, like a well-worn glove on a particular hand. If a lock were attempted to be picked and any tumbler tripped the wrong way, or in the wrong order, the entire lock could seize and become little more than a chunk of metal. Given that they were a mixture of ogre steel and sky-metal, they were virtually unbreakable and needed to be melted off at that point.

These people were not taking chances with what the rooms held. Whatever was inside, it must be my reason for being here. The item was behind one of these two doors.

I chose the left-hand room first, inserting my picks into the lock.

It swung open.

Unlocked. Unbelievable.

My spirits sank at the aborted challenge.

The room was spacious considering it was a cell and showed signs of recent occupation. A low table, acting as a workbench, filled the length of one wall, holding papers and sketches, tools and writing implements from one end to the other. A sense of orderly chaos that only the owner of this desk could hope to understand filled this space.

I stepped inside, taking time to scan each of the desk's items. The tools were what they appeared to be, but the sketches were incredible. Plans for Zadi locks unlike any ever seen before.

This! This was the item to retrieve. It must be.

On touching the drawings, I was shocked to find I wasn't transported back to the Tower of Wizardry. In any case, the sketches, rolled up with appropriate reverence, slid into my satchel.

"No," I whispered.

Underneath the sketches was a pristine, shiny padlock. Solid and serious, and of unfamiliar design, sketched with tight, equally unfamiliar runes on front and back. Heavy too. The key was in the lock, which was disappointing, like being told to take whatever I wanted. It slipped into my satchel, a puzzle to play with later.

With nothing left to investigate, I backed from the room and headed across the hall. This cell *was* locked, and I crouched, ready for the challenge.

It took fifteen slow-going minutes, tripping the tumblers in their correct order, ignoring the false one leading to a trap. That one almost got me. The lock was ingenious, far surpassing that earlier childhood model. This was pure pleasure to work with, and a real challenge, even for a thief who had spent thousands of hours practicing since childhood. Zadi had outdone himself.

This was no lock, but a work of art.

Click.

The rewarding sound of the lock releasing. The door swung inward.

A single bed was pushed into one corner of the tiny room. The linens were in need of changing but still smooth and meticulously arranged. A plain wooden stool with chipped water pitcher rested against the opposite wall. Cold stone floor matched the surrounding walls.

"Well, 'bout time," a scratchy voice said off to the right. "Was beginnin' to think that lock might be too much for you."

A wizened gnome rested cross-legged on the floor. So motionless was he my eyes had skimmed over him, his back against the bed's end and hands resting on his knees, as if in meditation.

"No," I answered, leaning in the door frame. "Just making sure I do it right."

The gnome snorted. "Fair enough, I guess. Now, what d'you want? You're not one of them maniacs."

"No, I'm not," I answered, coming to a realization and embarrassed that it had taken this long. "You...you're Zadi."

The gnome nodded again, making no move to rise.

Of *course* it was Zadi. Who else would it be with his sketches next door.

This was the reason I was sent here, to rescue Zadi. *The* Zadi. "The sorceress, from the Tower of Wizardry, she sent me."

"Armentia, the high sorceress?" the gnome harrumphed, leaning his head back against the bed. "Great. One cell to another."

Not the reaction I'd expected.

"Problem, kid?" Zadi asked.

A quick review of all I knew, or thought I knew, brought me to a disconcerting conclusion. "I'm not rescuing you at all, am I?"

The gnome harrumphed again and closed his eyes.

I leaned against the door frame, staring at the floor. "As soon as we touch, a spell will transport us back to the tower. They want to make sure you get there safe, I guess."

"I'm sure they do."

"Why do they all want you so badly?"

Zadi opened his eyes, watching me. "Let me tell you somethin', when you're the best you get two types comin' after you. First, there's the ones who want to prove they're better. Mostly blowhards and fakes lookin' to make a quick name. If yer the best, you don't need to shout it from a roof, yer work speaks for itself."

I digested this bit of wisdom.

"The second type are dangerous. They want to control you, use you. And what they can't control they destroy or hide away so no one else can have it. These are the selfish, evil people of the world. Locks are somethin' everyone needs. Wizards and kings, ogres and cultists. They all have somethin' precious to lock away. Thieves more than anyone understand the value of a quality lock. You know that sayin' about honour among thieves?"

"I do."

"It's a lie. There's no honour. A thief is waitin' for other thieves to turn their backs and leave valuable treasures unguarded."

I joined Zadi on the floor. My father had said much the same words to me while urging me to act with more honour. "Who are these people holding you?"

"What, you don't believe I'm here for a vacation, kid?"

I smiled.

"No idea," Zadi said. "Some cult. Whoever they are, they want me to make some kinda lock that could be imbued with magic."

"Magic?"

The gnome nodded. "An interestin' idea I'll admit."

"What good would that be?"

"Well, for lockin' up magical items that don't want to be locked up, or maybe magical creatures."

"Huh. And that's why the high sorceress wants you too?"

"Who knows?" he thought about it. "Yeah, prob'ly somethin' like that."

Zadi turned, staring at me. I was about to ask why when he spoke again.

"You owe Armentia a debt, kid?"

I nodded.

"Hmm, powerful person to owe," Zadi said. "Magic-users shouldn't be fooled with."

"Wish you'd told me that last night."

Zadi laughed. "Yeah, you don't seem like the type who listens well."

I laughed too, thinking of Gar's warnings. "No, I guess not."

How messed up was this? Sitting next to a hero of mine but unable to enjoy it because I had the task of making sure he stayed a prisoner.

"I, uh, have your sketches here," I said, patting the roll of papers sticking from my satchel.

Zadi nodded, making no move to take them.

"These cultists have dug pretty deep into the earth to keep their treasures safe," I said.

"Oh yeah, they're completely paranoid. They keep me away from all tools 'cept when under strict supervision, and they strip search me every night before returnin' me here. One lockpick could have spelled my freedom months ago."

"Huh! Thief or locksmith, I guess we both have the same fear of getting trapped somewhere without the proper tools."

The difference being that thieves expected it and kept extra picks hidden on them.

I got to my feet, heading for the door, sure that cultists would be creeping along the hall, but it was empty.

"Hold on a minute. You said months?" I asked. "You disappeared almost two years ago."

He stared at me, telling me I was missing something which should have been obvious.

A bolt of comprehension struck me, like studying a difficult lock and understanding it all at once. "You didn't disappear, you were in hiding."

"I tried to retire," the gnome said. "I'd hidden myself pretty well in a village called Blue Valley... Well, not good enough I guess. They found me a couple months back and I've been here ever since."

I glanced outside the door again, coming to a decision. "Okay, let's get out of here."

The gnome got to his feet, coming toward me. "Yeah, okay. Every cell's different. Could be the wizards'll be less vigilant with security."

"No. I meant out of this dungeon. I'm not bringing you to the tower."

Zadi raised one eyebrow.

"Whether magic-users are to be fooled with or not, I won't sell another into slavery to save myself."

The gnome considered me. "Ah, my boy. They will hunt you to the ends of the world."

I shrugged and looked toward the stairs. It was quite a few levels but shouldn't take too long to arrive back at the warehouse above. With Gar's help, we could get Zadi out of Timurpajan, to somewhere safe.

We would need an itchy robe again. Another distraction too, a bigger one.

"Just make sure you don't touch me," I said.

"Yeah, kid. I remember."

I felt Zadi's rough hand grab my lower arm.

"No!"

The dungeon disappeared, replaced with the high sorceress's opulent room. She stood before us, a surprised expression on her face.

"Back so soon? I am impressed."

I spun on Zadi, but the gnome only stared straight ahead. He gave one quick shake of his head, and my mouth snapped shut on the unspoken question of *why?*

Zadi knew what touching me would mean. I would have gotten him out of that warehouse and he could have been free.

But I would have been hunted. *Powerful person to owe,* Zadi had said.

The ancient woman stepped forward and bowed to the gnome. "Lockmaster Zadi."

"High Sorceress Armentia."

She clapped her hands and two acolytes appeared to escort the gnome away.

"Search him," she said, and they did, finding nothing. "Fine, take him away."

"Hold on," Zadi said. "The kid's got my sketches."

The acolytes stopped, looking to Armentia who waved her consent.

Zadi came to me and pulled the plans from my satchel then stopped, a strange smirk on his face. "Kid, I want ta say thanks for gettin' me outta there."

Then he hugged me, actually *hugged* me. Zadi! Even though I had only delivered him to a substitute dungeon. The hug was brief before he turned and pushed past the acolytes, smacking one on the back of the head with his rolled-up plans.

"I hope my room's better than the last one," he called over his shoulder. "I want ta take a bath."

"Provide our guest with what he needs," the high sorceress said, watching them leave.

Armentia spoke to me, though I heard none of it. Zadi. I had just met *Zadi.*

He'd *hugged* me!

Then I found myself outside, staring at the tower's front door.

It wouldn't be so easy to get in a second time, nor would it be forgiven, but I had to free him. I couldn't abandon the gnome to a life of servitude.

I glanced at the moon. Still a couple of hours before dawn, but not enough time to do the job now.

Tonight.

Absently, I patted the inner pocket which held Dad's lockpicks.

"Huh?"

I patted it again with more awareness but felt no bulge of something being there. I pulled my tunic open and glanced inside, confirming what I already knew: the lockpicks were gone.

Zadi had said all he needed was one.

When he hugged me, he'd been picking my pocket, the lightness of his touch impressive.

Still, it was sad to lose Dad's lockpicks, even for a good cause.

People over possessions.

"Quite right, Dad."

In the end, all I had to show for my night was a goblet of cheap metal and junk jewels, and the memory of having met greatness. Oh! And an incredible Zadi padlock to play with.

I turned and headed for the Sainted Ogre, whistling a tune.

CHAPTER 4
MORE TROUBLE

The sunlight came through my window, landing in a gentle golden blanket which brought me back to the waking world. For several minutes I lay with eyes closed, enjoying the comfort.

It had been a strenuous night and one which hadn't brought me any closer to my goal. I'd earned a sleep-in, but my bladder had other ideas. With a sigh and a stretch, I opened my eyes.

"Good morning," a scratchy feminine voice said.

"Gah!" I replied.

In my room's one chair leaned the High Sorceress, Armentia, staring at me, unmoving.

Was this a dream? I rubbed my eyes with the heels of both hands and looked again.

"Still here, Spider. Quite real."

"Right. Yes. Well, not that I don't appreciate the visit, but *why* are you here?"

Surely not for any happy reason.

My tendency to sleep naked jumped to mind and I pulled the top sheet higher, aware of my exposure.

"You're an elf," she said.

I reached a hand up, as if I sleeping with a hood was natural and it had somehow disappeared in the night. I keep forgetting to not care about exposing my ears. Old habits and all that.

"I am."

"Interesting. I knew there was something..." She waved the thought away, refocusing on me. "You were naughty."

"I..."

What was she talking about? It couldn't be last night's break-in, but what else? I shook my head.

"No?" She tossed an item into my lap without appearing to move.

"My lockpicks!"

Oops, that was a mistake. Shouldn't have admitted to recognizing them.

Too late.

"Yes," she said. "Zadi left them behind when he escaped."

"Zadi escaped?"

But why hadn't the gnome taken my picks with him? No, I saw how that would've played out. Without the lockpicks, Armentia would have accused me of breaking in and freeing Zadi myself. This way, well, this way it still wouldn't work in my favour, but at least he could return my property.

"I can explain," I said, "but that won't make any difference, will it?"

"Not really. You'll say Zadi picked your pocket, or some other equally probable action, but in the end, you gave him the means to escape, and that's what matters. I have to hold someone responsible."

"Why not yourself?"

"Oh, I prefer to blame others."

"Have you considered holding someone against their will is wrong? That they will always find a way to get free?"

Armentia gasped, one hand rising to cover her mouth. "Oh, Spider. I've never thought of it in quite that way. You've changed my entire world with those few words."

Well, that was some impressive sarcasm. "Excellent, glad I could be of help."

Her glare bored into me.

My complaining bladder was getting more uncomfortable, and if she didn't wrap this up soon, there would be no choice but to use the chamber pot. I'm not a shy person, but no way was I 'showing the merchandise' in front of this woman.

"You still owe me," she said.

A spark of anger flared in me.

"Oh, come on! I still owe you?" I said, voice rising. "I broke into that warehouse, snuck my way through and did everything you asked."

"Nevertheless—"

"Who were they anyway?"

She blinked twice before answering as if having some inner debate. "The Cult of the Sightless Eye."

That was almost enough to make me forget about holding my bladder.

The Cult of the Sightless Eye was the stuff of legends, and not the *hero rescues the girl and lives happily ever after* type of legend, more like *a thousand years of death and suffering*. They were bloody maniacs performing acts of murder and violence in worship of an ancient, banished god named Aniha-Morgo.

"But, they were destroyed a century ago," I said.

"And now they are back. You can see why we didn't want to be associated with retrieving Zadi. We have power and can hold our own, but this cult is an unknown and could be far-reaching. Until we know *how* far we would rather not upset the wrong people. If you take my meaning."

Yes, I understood, as I also understood what would have happened if I'd been caught last night. I would already be dead, or more likely wishing I was, living the rest of my life like that boar.

"You could have warned me."

"Would knowing who was in that warehouse have influenced your decision to go in?"

"Yes!"

"And that is why I didn't tell you. You owed me a debt and I needed you to perform a task."

"And I did!"

"Yes."

"But me breaking into the cult's murder house doesn't square us for me breaking into yours?"

"No."

"Oh. Well, when you put it that way."

The aged sorceress came close to smiling—at least I think she did. "Let us say that the job last night paid for your intrusion, but now you owe for Zadi's escape."

My bladder tugged at my attention with some urgency, making it difficult to focus. I wished she would get to the point and leave so I could obey nature's call.

"I have another task for you," she said.

I gritted my teeth. "Of course you do."

"You'll accompany one of our order."

"No, thank you," I said. "I work alone."

"I'm sure you do, but this will be necessary."

"You don't trust me?"

"Not in the least, but that has nothing to do with it."

"Uh-huh."

"What do you know about magic, young elf?"

I shook my head. "What everyone else knows. You point, crazy stuff happens."

"Crude, but not inaccurate from an outsider's perspective." She leaned back into the chair. "Magic is a force of nature, like water or fire. With proper control, all can be used to advantage."

"Okay, with you so far," I said, bladder momentarily forgotten with this interesting topic.

"And without control, they ravage and destroy."

"Sure. We need water to drink, but it can also flood a valley. Fire keeps us warm, but it could destroy entire cities."

"Very good," she said. "Now, most branches of magic involve a wizard in long hours of study, memorizing spells. Then, once used, the spell is gone and needs to be re-memorized."

"Sounds tedious."

"It can be. Magic takes dedication, focus, a willingness to put all else aside. With time and control, we are able to memorize more spells at once and take less time rememorizing old ones. But the novice wizard spends many hours learning to cast a spell so simple as lighting a candle before moving on to other more difficult, more dangerous ones."

"Are you sure you should be telling me all this?"

"I'm not giving any trade secrets away. This is the process for most magic-users."

"Most?" I latched onto the word. "Not all?"

"No."

Not all? Why would she be telling me...? "Then, this one you want to come with me is different?"

"Yes," she laughed, sending a chill through me. It contained no humour and was close to, what? Fear? "He is different. A novitiate with a natural talent for chaos magic."

"Isn't all magic chaos?"

"Only because you don't understand. To one who spends their life studying, magic is a tool to be used, with rules and processes to follow."

"But not chaos magic?"

"No, not chaos magic. The best that can be said is the magic-user gets an idea and points the magic in a specific direction and, how did you phrase it? Crazy stuff happens? There's no studying, no discipline. It just happens, and sometimes the magic does as asked, and sometimes it does not."

"It sounds...exciting to be around."

"Oh, it is! Exciting *and* fascinating. It's also destructive and unpredictable, making it impossible to keep the tower in any state of order."

"Is it?" I asked, willing to punish my bladder as long as she continued providing interesting information. "How so?"

She scrutinized me, making it clear I wasn't fooling her, and that she continued only talking because it suited her. "Did you notice signs of damage in the tower last night?"

Clawed scratches in a door. Scorch marks in marble. I nodded.

"That was caused by a frost giant summoned from nowhere. It took ten wizards every spell they'd memorized to trap it in that room."

A frost giant! Of course! I saw the giant fist grabbing Flea and was glad the door had slammed closed again...though seeing a frost giant close up would have been amazing. Not *dragon* amazing, but still a sight worth seeing.

"So, this isn't a task so much as me taking your destructive wizard away."

"While the tower is still standing and the order is in one piece. Yes."

"And what am I supposed to do with him? Lead him into the woods? Find him a new home?"

"He's not some inconvenient pet to be abandoned. Graves is a powerful magician, needing to learn better control. He simply needs to learn it *away* from the tower."

"How will he do that *away* from other wizards?"

Her eyes wavered from me for the first time. "We can't teach him any more than we have. It's as if he speaks another language."

"But how have you taught chaos magic in the past?"

"We haven't." Armentia shifted her weight. "Graves is the first user in this branch of magic. Ever."

"Wonderful." I considered the entire situation and shook my head. "I'm a trader, not an escort."

"What you are," the sorceress said, steel back in her voice, "is a thief looking to cancel his debt."

"And a difficult debt to shake, it seems."

We stared at each other, neither willing to drop our gaze first.

"Look," I said, "all I want is to start my own trading business, to find my own success, but everything seems determined to take me further from that goal."

She closed her eyes and took in a deep breath before reopening them to focus on me. "Very well. There is also a payment that comes with this task."

"Payment?"

Why would she pay me when I was at her disadvantage? A whole series of warning alarms jangled inside my head. Either she was desperate, or this was a suicide mission without the likelihood of me collecting. Maybe both.

I opened my mouth, some cocky comment ready to fly when Armentia pulled a palm-sized ruby from the folds of her cloak. She held it in the open for two heartbeats before making it disappear again.

My mouth snapped shut on the comment, my inner trader calculating the value on what I'd seen. That gem was enough to start a more than modest trading business. I could accomplish my goal with this one job. Wasn't that my reason for entering the tower in the first place? This was a more roundabout way but—

"Graves has been told he is going on an important quest. You will accompany him, guide him, keep him company."

I'm no guide, but for that gem, I would drag this Graves to the ogre kingdoms and demand audience with their chieftain. "What's this quest supposed to be?"

"I don't care. Create some story. Just make sure it's away from Timurpajan. Far away."

"Hmm, this is sounding like a long journey."

"Yes. Graves will need years to learn control."

"Years!?" That gem wasn't such an overpayment now. "This isn't a journey, it's a life. You expect me to babysit your magician for years?"

"What I expect is for you to do what is asked and be grateful for the opportunity."

I stared back helplessly, seeing my life dwindling to this one function, any dreams of a trading business gone.

"However," she continued, "I am only asking you to guide him for the next year, until he has better control, and disaster doesn't follow him everywhere."

A year of my life, in exchange for that ruby.

"And if I pass on this offer?" I asked.

"Don't."

A crackle of blue energy flashed in the aged woman's eyes. Yes, she had great power within her, that much was certain. As was the message of *guide this magician and his madness magic or be snuffed like a candle.*

"Well, this sounds delightful," I said, clapping my hands. "We'll need money of course, for travelling expenses."

A sack of coins jingled onto the bed in front of me, next to the lockpicks.

"That will get you started. I trust a thief of your calibre is able to supplement that by whatever means necessary."

I made no move to look inside. "As long as I am not expected to betray my personal code."

"Morals do tend to cost their owner in the end."

"As does a lack of them."

She laughed with genuine delight while waving the debate away. "How you make your living is your own business."

Why was I off balance every time I spoke with her?

Now that the terms of our contract were known, the urgency of my bladder had returned. "I'll come around the tower later after I've gotten dressed and had breakfast."

"No need," she said, then, "Graves."

That last word was spoken at the same conversational volume as the rest, but the door opened immediately. The wizard who entered was familiar, a young man of perhaps seventeen or eighteen, wearing purple robes, with the wisps of a half-formed beard on his chin. His face was dour as if no joy ever found its way into his life.

"The wizard from the tavern." I snapped my fingers. "You turned that Rat into a pig."

Graves stared a moment. "Oh, yes. I'd forgotten about that."

Forgotten he'd turned a man into a pig the previous day? Wonderful. Graves just might be a complete lunatic. I turned toward the sorceress to tell her exactly that but wasn't surprised to find her gone.

"Graves, was it?" I said, turning back.

He nodded, with no sign of emotion.

"Would you mind waiting in the hall while I get dressed and use the chamber pot?"

Graves turned and left without reaction or comment. I dropped my head into my hands.

"How did this happen to me?"

When things go wrong, be prepared to pay the price.

Yes, Dad. I remember that one. Helpful.

No other bits of fatherly wisdom were coming so I shoved the sheets aside and headed for my chamber pot. There were only so many things to be done before passing through the door and embracing the joy of joining that madman.

Unless...

The room's window opened toward the front of the inn. I could be down the side of it and gone in no time. Without a doubt, I wouldn't be able to return to Timurpajan until the old bird died, which may not even happen in my lifetime.

Armentia.

She scares me, and I don't mind admitting that. There's a power and a promise of unknown horrors behind that face. Graves had turned a man into a pig, temporarily he said, I could imagine her changing me into a dung beetle and leaving me that way.

Would there be anywhere to hide from her?

No, I don't think there would be.

Fully dressed, with no more excuses and an eagerness to remain in elf form, I got moving, grabbing the recovered lockpicks and sliding them inside my tunic. The satchel, leaning in one corner, had a surprising weight to it. Oh, yeah. The cheap tin goblet with its junk jewels. That could stay in Gar's storage until I returned.

Graves waited without expression outside the room, staring at the door as if it had closed only a moment ago. I pulled my hood up and stepped out next to the wizard.

"Ready?" I asked.

Graves shifted a backpack to show he had everything necessary. I would need something similar.

"You eat breakfast yet?" I asked.

"No."

"*Do* you eat?"

Graves cocked his head to one side as if he'd been asked if his parents were bog zombies. "Of course."

I shrugged an apology and headed for the stairs. "The food here is excellent and will set us up to begin our trip."

"I come here often. I find people fascinating to watch."

The words held no emotion at all as if Graves had no real interest in the topic.

CHAPTER 5
MY NEW PARTNER, TWO SANDWICHES SHORT OF A PICNIC

Downstairs we took a seat and Gar came over, smiling until he saw my companion.

"Two breakfasts, then?" he said without missing a beat.

I nodded, and Gar headed back to the kitchen.

Graves didn't peer around, staring into nothing. His fingers drummed a beat to some internal tune against the table top.

"So, your name is Graves. Named after your father?"

"No."

"No, your name isn't Graves, or no, you aren't named after your father?"

Graves brought his attention around as if seeing me for the first time. No, that wasn't quite it. This kid wasn't used to anyone wanting to hear him talk. I adopted an appearance of quiet interest, encouraging the wizard. If we were going to be travelling companions for the next year, we might as well start off on the right foot.

"My name is not truly Graves. That is just what the children at the wizardry school called me."

Wizardry school? I hadn't heard of such a thing and stored it away to bring up later. "Why 'Graves?'"

The wizard looked at the table, shrugging his right shoulder. "A bit of cleverness by one of my fellow students, Jorgen."

I leaned forward, hoping it conveyed interest. Graves stared at me before taking a breath and talking again. "I am a naturally quiet person."

No kidding.

"Jorgen said 'As quiet as the grave.' He called me Graves from my first week at school and encouraged everyone else to do the same."

"Jorgen sounds like a dick."

Graves's mouth twitched, like he wanted to smile but didn't quite know how. He gave a brief nod before resuming his silence. Gar came a moment later with two plates of eggs, bacon, toast and potatoes, depositing them in front of us.

"I'll be leaving after breakfast, Gar."

"Back tonight?"

"Afraid not. I have a job and won't be back for a while," I said. "You can rent my room."

Gar glanced at the wizard who had started to eat, then back at me. He shook his head. "I warned you."

What could I say? Gar had indeed tried to warn me. I kept a pleasant expression on my face to suggest this wasn't so bad, and thoughts of that gem parading through my mind made it easier.

"Oh!" I said, holding my satchel toward Gar. "Would you mind keeping this somewhere safe until I come back?"

Gar reached for it without hesitation or question and started back across the room. That goblet would keep until I returned, especially since I was just hoping to inconvenience that cult by taking it.

I slapped my forehead with one hand and jumped to my feet.

"Be right back," I told Graves.

I rushed after Gar and stopped the halfling before he reached the bar, leaning in close to whisper.

"That old warehouse by the docks, you know it?"

"Yeah. I hear the Rats hold it now."

"That's just appearance. It's actually a hideout for the Cult of the Sightless Eye."

Gar retreated a step before catching himself. "They were destroyed ages ago, Spider."

I shook my head and Gar clenched his teeth, looking at the ceiling as if an answer were written there.

"Damn it!" he said, then refocused on me. "Okay, I'll get word to the city commander, Norn."

"Thanks, Gar."

"What's all this about?" Gar whispered, gesturing toward Graves.

"What do you mean?"

"Thought you wanted to start a trading business, make your own way and all that."

"I do, Gar. Hanging out with Graves for the next year will get me there."

"A year?" Gar looked over at the wizard, then back at me. He shook his head. "If you say so."

"I do," I said, hoping it was true. "Don't worry about me."

"I'll always worry about you, Spider. Lees and I both."

"Thanks, Gar. Truly."

With a nod, the innkeeper made his way back behind the bar, the satchel disappearing as he did. His sad eyes remained on me and my new partner at our table.

"I *was* named after my father," Graves said around a mouthful of eggs as if there had been no interruption. "But he disowned me when the magic manifested, so I have no claim to the name anymore."

"That's horrible."

"Well, I was making quite a mess at Father's castle."

With all the signs of damage to the tower, I believed it. Wait a minute. Castle?

"At first he believed I was possessed," Graves continued. "That might be because of the imps flying out of my room one morning. I was exorcised, twice, before Armentia came to tell them it was my innate magic, not demons."

Exorcism was a brutal process, to both body and mind. Going through it twice—

"My father was just glad I was leaving, going to the wizard school. I was ten. I've been Graves ever since." He shrugged. "As good a name as any."

"Ten?" What parent would ship their ten-year-old child off to a bunch of strange wizards at such an early age?

"The other students had been together four years already. Friendships had been formed, alliances made. I spent the next five years being tormented."

That would make him, what? About fifteen? No, he *had* to be older than that.

"They hated me because I was new, because I was quiet, and because the magic came to me with ease. They were jealous. While they studied hours to memorize a spell for lighting candles, I levitated."

Once again Graves spoke in his flat, emotionless voice about memories which should have conjured anything but emotionlessness.

"I am not skilled at making friends," he said. "I spent my first decade with four older brothers who had no use for me. I never learned interaction."

Graves looked up, leaning back in his seat when he realized I still paid attention. He gave another one-shouldered shrug.

"In those days, still with my family, the chaos magic was sporadic, building over weeks or months until I couldn't hold it back. You see, that's the reason I was so quiet, I had to concentrate on keeping it in."

My own upbringing was normal compared to his.

"In the tower, after some time, I studied and practiced by myself." He cocked his head to one side. "Especially after what happened to Jorgen."

79

"Jorgen?"

"He didn't just name me, you see. No, Jorgen was always first in line to torment me, knock scrolls from my hands. One day at breakfast he put salt in my porridge, and that was enough."

"What happened?"

"Distracted by Jorgen's trick, the chaos magic coursed through me, seeking a purpose. I pointed at Jorgen and said *go away*. The magic flew from my fingertips, surrounding Jorgen in a jelly-like sphere."

I leaned further forward. "Then what?"

"I can still see Jorgen's face pressed against the inside, stretching it. It started to shrink, and when the sphere was reduced to nothingness, Jorgen went with it."

"Where did it go?"

"Not even Armentia could figure that out," he said, his voice dreamy and far away. "As far as anyone could tell he'd never existed. No parent came looking for him. Only those in the tower remembered him."

I made a mental note to not mess with Graves's food.

"The next three years were better. I ate alone, slept in my own room away from the main dormitory."

Three more years? Yes, that would put him around eighteen. That made more sense.

Graves shook off his dreamy state and refocused on me. "My magical control is much better. Bad things hardly ever happen now."

"No? What about the pig yesterday?"

"Oh, that wasn't a bad thing. They got greedy."

"So, you intended that?"

"Not exactly. I had an idea that they were greedy pigs and let the magic go."

I shivered at the idea of that power. "What about the frost giant in the tower?"

"You heard about that?" Graves asked, a gleam in his eye the only show of emotion. "Well, I did say *hardly* ever."

"So, how often *do* spells go awry now?"

"Awry," Graves repeated, rolling the word around. "Awry."

Graves's eyes were unfocused and a wan smile came to his lips. Magic appeared to be the one item that got some vague emotional reaction from him.

"Graves?"

The wizard shook his head, all emotion gone. "It depends. Some days a dozen spells cast will have no unintended effects or be close enough. Other days, even the most harmless spell goes...awry."

Well, he liked that word. "I see."

"Last week I tried to heat up my tea and turned all the tower's water into wine." He gave his half-shrug. "No one complained about that one."

"And you use magic every day?"

"Of course. I *am* a wizard."

"Hmm, have you ever considered not casting spells for a few days?"

Graves was on his feet, jostling the table. His eyes darted, breath coming in rapid gasps through clenched teeth.

"Okay, I see that was a bad suggestion," I said. "Just forget it. My apologies. I'm not a magic-user and don't understand."

Graves gawked at me, the horrified look working. I leaned back, draping one arm across the chair next to me, trying my best to appear casual, non-threatening. Reaching out, I grabbed my tea and drank it. That scene remained frozen a full minute before Graves retook his seat, the expressionless mask returning.

I filed that reaction away, comparing it to what I'd seen in the drug dens of Carn. Many thieves ended up there, or people who ended up there became thieves. It was difficult to tell cause from effect.

One bit of knowledge from the story Graves told was he could cast several spells a day.

"Did your high sorceress explain about our quest?"

"She said there was an important task only I could do. I would be paired with a guide, an able thief."

Able thief? High praise coming from someone in her position.

With effort, I pushed that thought aside and focused on Graves, mind scrambling for some believable plan. I could give it to him in instalments, tell him the high sorceress is giving it to me a bit at a time, telepathically. Was that believable? It would give me time to think.

"Okay," I began, leaning forward in a conspiratorial manner. "So, this quest of ours—"

"Is a concocted excuse to get me out of the tower."

"Ah... I..."

When all else fails, try honesty.

"Yeah, it is. You knew?"

"Most people don't want me around. I've picked up a sensitivity to it."

"I'm sorry," I said, finding I meant it.

I'd had my dad, plus Gar and Lees. What must it be like to be wanted by no one?

Another half-shrug, only the right shoulder. "Armentia wants me to learn better control but wants me to learn it away from the tower. Unlike my father's home, I understand I may return one day."

Assuming you *ever* learn that control, but that wasn't my concern.

"Are those the only two places you've ever known?" I asked. "Your father's home and the tower?"

"Well, recently I've started coming here."

"To the inn?"

"I find it interesting to watch people, seeing if I can guess what they'll do, what they'll say. It's pure chaos, like the magic."

"Okay, then," I said, clapping my hands together. "There's our quest. You need to see more of this world."

Graves leaned back, away from me and my idea. "Watching is one thing, but I'm not good at interacting. I seem to anger people."

Yeah, that was very believable.

He shook his head. "I'd rather find a quiet place where I could practice, near a city with an inn serving good wine."

"Yes, that *would* be ideal."

Graves relaxed.

"Unfortunately, the old sorceress—"

"Armentia."

"Armentia, yes. She didn't give me enough money to sustain us the full year. We'll need to find a way to supplement it."

Graves's hands clenched and unclenched.

"Besides," I tried, "if you understand the chaos of people better, maybe that will cross over into controlling your magic."

I was grasping and knew it, but Graves rolled his eyes then nodded once.

"I have one idea," I said. "Can you sit tight here for about fifteen minutes?"

"Sure."

"Without turning anyone into a pig?"

"Oh, the magic wouldn't do the same random effect twice."

I stared at the wizard until he half-shrugged.

"I'll try," he said, then signalled for more tea.

CHAPTER 6
A JOB

Seventeen minutes later I returned, having stopped to purchase a backpack with some of the money Armentia had given. I approached the Sainted Ogre in time to see a mass exodus of Gar's breakfast crowd. The innkeeper appeared last, pulling a stunned Graves behind him.

"Aw, crap," I muttered.

"Your pet wizard here," Gar sputtered as I raced over to the two, "he brought all the bacon back to life. Every slice became its own pig."

"I was trying to warm up my tea again. I don't know why that particular spell goes awry."

Gar let go of Graves's arm and turned to me. "You will always be welcome here, Spider, but please don't bring him with you."

"I have already apologized," Graves sniffed.

"Apologized?" Gar rounded on the wizard. "Apologized?"

"Gar," I said, pulling my friend's attention back to me. "Did you say *every* piece of bacon became its own pig?"

"Yes, right there on the plates. Even the ones in the kitchen."

"Hmm. Gar, it seems you will turn a hefty profit on this."

At the word 'profit' Gar stopped fuming and turned toward me. "Explain."

"Well, you'll have to slaughter them, or pay Digby the butcher to do it, but you have a lot of free pork here, and not just bacon."

"Yeah, well—" the halfling began.

"And if you keep some for breeding then you can cut out Farwell the merchant's fees."

Gar was silent, looking from me to the Sainted Ogre and back again.

The calculations worked behind his eyes.

"I've still lost all my breakfast clients."

"True, but you'll make it up at lunch with all the curiosity seekers who come. May I suggest a special on something other than bacon sandwiches?"

My friend half-laughed. A good sign.

"I could turn the pigs back," Graves said.

"No," I placed on hand on his shoulder. "No, no. Let's quit while we're ahead."

Gar took in a breath and let it escape as a slow controlled exhale. "Will you be here for lunch?"

"Afraid not. We have a spot on the caravan to Grand Gesture, as protection."

"Protection?" Gar said. "What do you know about protecting caravans?"

"Plenty," I said, half offended. "I worked enough of them with Dad to know a show of power discourages bandits. If it looks too difficult, they'll let the caravan go by."

"And a caravan with a wizard who turns bacon into pigs will be left alone?"

"That's my thought."

"Hmm," Gar said. "I thought that caravan was protected by Farrobane and his boys."

"It was. Until they got drunk and wrecked a brothel last night. This morning they're in jail awaiting the judge."

Gar chuckled. "Well, best of luck to you, Spider." Then added grudgingly, "To both of you."

Graves peered up the street as if he'd lost all interest in the conversation.

Gar gritted his teeth, shot me a farewell nod, and rushed back inside the Sainted Ogre to start herding his pigs. I turned and headed back the way

I'd come, Graves following.

"I don't know anything about protecting caravans," my companion said.

"You won't need to," I said, quickening my pace. "Oh, this all fits together perfectly."

"What does?"

"Well, you need time to practice, right?"

"Yes."

"And we need money, right?"

"I suppose."

"And this caravan needs protection on the road."

"Here I start to have concerns."

"Relax. The caravan moves slow, allowing you time to practice. Any bandits will see you practicing and not want to tangle with magic, so you will be protecting the caravan by doing exactly what you wanted."

Graves's mind worked behind those eyes, looking for a hole in my logic.

"And," I continued, "if there is any trouble, well, no one is going to mind a bunch of bandits turned into pigs."

He shook his head. "I told you, the magic wouldn't do the same random effect twice."

"Well, chickens then."

Graves looked away, mouth pressing into a tight line that almost disappeared.

"Look," I said, "this is your best chance at having time to practice without interruption."

"Okay, fine." He threw his hands up in surrender. "When do we leave?"

"Now. They're expecting us."

We marched like this for several minutes, following the road and turning at corners until coming to a clearing near the edge of town. Twelve wagons waited in a line, each hitched to a strong horse with one driver in control. The wagons were all covered except the lead one, loaded with kegs of beer, and the rear one, filled with sacks of coffee.

"Here we are," I said.

A man detached himself from a group surrounding the wagons, heading for us. He was dressed in much finer clothing than the others and looked like the dust of travel would offend his highly polished boots.

"Narvin," I greeted as he approached.

"Spider. So, this is your wizard friend?"

Graves stared at the caravan, dubious expression clear on his face.

"He's contemplating his magic," I explained.

"Uh-huh. That doesn't change the fact I am leery about sending this caravan out with only two protectors, and one of them a thief."

"Trader," I corrected.

"When you have your own caravan, you're a trader. Until then, you're a thief."

"Fair enough, and that day will come. In a year's time, we'll be standing here discussing my caravan."

Narvin huffed out a short laugh. "Yeah, well, we'll see on that point. You have your father's temperament at least."

"My thanks, Narvin."

"Now, back to me being leery. Don't think you distracted me with your patter."

"I wouldn't expect to."

"Uh-huh. In any case," Narvin turned his focus on Graves, "I would normally be sending a squad of eight to ten swordsmen to protect the caravan, but Spider tells me how powerful a wizard you are, despite your age. I'm hoping this will make up for the numbers."

Graves cast a sideways look at me and gave a nod, saying nothing.

"See," I said. "Always in silent contemplation of his magic. You know these people."

"I do not." The dapper man turned back to me. "Out of respect for your father's memory and all of our dealings together, I am willing to entertain the idea of you two taking this job, but if *anything* happens to this caravan—"

"Nothing will happen. The caravan will arrive in Grand Gesture just fine, you'll see."

Narvin contemplated the twelve wagons. The lead driver, a career man with thick arms, who had been bronzed by the sun of countless journeys, scowled back, making motions that he was ready to go. Eleven men and women rested in the driver's seats of the other wagons, watching for the signal to move.

"Of course, if you have no faith in us, you can wait for Farrobane and his boys to make bail," I said.

"Those idiots made a great mess last night, tore up Madame Leona's," Narvin spat. "They won't be out anytime today."

"Are there no others you could get on such short notice?"

"Enough. You've made your point, and I acknowledge my spectacular lack of alternatives. You have the job and my faith."

Narvin and I shook hands.

"Your pay is with the lead driver, Zachariah. You'll receive it when the caravan arrives at Gesture in one piece."

It was the usual arrangement.

"Come on Graves. Let's go find our horses," I said.

A couple of steps from Narvin, Graves leaned closer to me. "I am unable to ride a horse, *and* practice spells."

Without missing a stride, I changed course for the lead driver, Zachariah. "Morning. Is my wizard's spot in the rear caravan prepared?"

The man peered back at me, impatient. "What?"

"Well, a wizard can't concentrate on his spells while jostling about on a horse, now can he?

The driver considered this then sighed, jumping from his perch in the lead wagon. He strode the length of the caravan, muttering, us a pace behind, then gestured at the last wagon's driver. Together they re-arranged burlap sacks of coffee to create a comfortable space for Graves.

"Better?" Zachariah asked.

Graves looked like it was anything but.

"Perfect," I said. "Thank you."

"Never had magical protection before," Zachariah looked from us to Narvin who remained to one side, wringing his hands.

"No fears," I said, recycling the reasoning used with Graves. "With my wizard in the open wagon, practicing his spells, the bandits will be too intimidated to attack. If they decide to cause problems anyway, then Graves will have a clear line of sight to cast spells."

The lead driver shrugged and headed back to his own spot.

Each other driver cast quick glances at Graves before readying to leave.

"Your horse is there," Narvin said, pointing to a strong mare off to one side.

I mounted the horse with ease and took her reins, hoping to give everyone a sense of my competence, but no one seemed to notice. Graves pulled himself into the back of the caravan and rolled onto his crude but somewhat comfortable seat of coffee beans.

Father's caravans had been protected by all sorts of rough men and had given me enough of an idea of what was expected on my part. To start, I spurred my horse forward, taking the lead. During the ride, my job was to range back and forth along the line and make sure all was well. When we approached possible dangerous areas, the task would change to riding ahead and ensuring no ambush waited.

Finding problems before they happened was a great strategy, but Graves was the failsafe if it all went Cyclops-in-the-wine-cellar. Even a spell that didn't turn out as intended should be enough to scare bandits unused to dealing with magic.

The caravan passed from Timurpajan and onto the road.

#

A few minutes shy of the first hour, Graves cast a spell. We had no danger of attack and wouldn't until we got closer to the hills, but there could be eyes on us already.

Two hours, more or less, separated the spell Graves had cast at the Sainted Ogre and this one, giving me an idea on what dependency the wizard had on casting spells. Could he have gone longer? Was he casting a spell from boredom or for practice? Necessity?

The rear wagon's driver turned to glance on hearing the muffled *wumpf* of Graves's spell. At least he seemed more curious than concerned about the magic, watching the pale yellow globe soar over the caravan.

"What was that?" I asked.

"A light spell."

"Ah, okay. Um, why?"

"So I can see at night, maybe read."

"Oh, of course. Makes sense."

Only, caravans don't travel by night. The horses and drivers need that time to rest, and there's too much danger of a horse stepping in a gopher hole and breaking their leg. Then again, if we *could* travel at night, that would speed up the journey and make the caravan more profitable. If Graves had better control over his spells, it might be worth suggesting to Zachariah.

Graves's eyes had already de-focused. He leaned back into the coffee beans. The spell hadn't been all that remarkable, but it was enough to satisfy the wizard.

Again, useful to know.

For hours the caravan followed King's Road through the Desert of Nan, a route created generations ago, now maintained by people like Narvin, with financial aid from King Vernion. Crossing the desert took two days, with one chilly night spent at the centre point. That was why Zachariah and Narvin were so anxious to get the caravan moving. No one wanted a second night in the desert.

A couple of hours later, when my route brought me around to the rear wagon again, I pulled up beside Graves and kept pace. He looked at me from the corner of one eye and let out a grunt.

I'd discovered that the greater interval between spells, the more short-tempered Graves got.

"I've been thinking," I said, "for your next spell, could you cast something to protect the caravan?"

The wizard harrumphed. "Oh, yeah. Why not. I'll just cast some passive spell that will wait for us to get into trouble."

"Can you do that?"

Graves didn't respond but looked thoughtful. He concentrated on the desert retreating behind the wagon before closing his eyes and after a minute raised both hands, muttering. He made a complicated gesture, then lowered his hands to gaze out at the desert.

I turned in my saddle and did the same. "What is that?"

Graves squinted at the shape scuttling onto the road. "A scorpion."

"One scorpion? That's our protection?"

"No, there's more."

"Oh, so there are. Yes. Two. Four. Ten... By all the gods!"

"That *is* a lot of scorpions," Graves agreed.

Scorpions of all sizes and colours flowed from the desert, doubling in number with each passing second. The creatures reached the road, turned, and followed the caravan. The procession of scorpions soon became a swarm, then a plague, gaining on the wagons with each second.

I spurred my horse forward to Zachariah, and soon the caravan had doubled speed, outdistancing the scorpions. The rear driver gave no sign of having seen what followed, and it would have been difficult to ignore if he had.

"How exactly were *they* supposed to protect the caravan?" I asked, returning to Graves.

Graves gave his half-shrug, and I made a note not ask him for help in that way again. If he just kept casting his usual spells, that should be enough to dissuade any bandit attack.

Of course, if any bandits were watching, they should have second thoughts after seeing those scorpions.

Everything works out, except when it doesn't.

That's when you find a way to make it work, right Dad?

That was a lot of scorpions, more than should have been available. They must have been conjured from Graves's spell. I shivered at the thought. All those scuttling legs were unsettling.

The rest of the day passed with little fanfare, the caravan continued rolling forward, and Graves cast his spells every so often, with the scorpions being the most spectacular and horrific. I shuttled back and forth, alert for trouble at one end or the other, finding more to consider on this job than I'd ever suspected.

As the sun started its journey toward setting, Zachariah held up one hand, slowing his wagon. The others came to a halt behind him, the drivers dismounting and massaging aching backs. Horses were unharnessed and allowed food and water while tents were erected for sleeping.

I took a breath through my nostrils and let it escape through my mouth. One day done out of the next year. One less day until I held that ruby.

A sentry schedule had been created for the night, with Graves and I scheduled first. Normally protectors would take turns through the night, allowing drivers to sleep, but with there being only two of us, and needing us to be awake and aware the next day, Zachariah had made adjustments.

After a quick dinner around the fire, each driver retired to a two-person tent, except for Graves and me on first watch. For a job where all we did was sit all day it was quite exhausting.

Our watch passed without incident, though I wished I had brought that Zadi lock to play with. Graves cast one of his spells toward the end without any real effect, unless that slight increase in wind was his doing. Once relieved of watch we crawled inside the tent, sliding into our bedrolls. The wizard was snoring in minutes, and I followed soon after.

An unknown, disorienting amount of time later, I was pulled from my sound sleep to full alert. No noise, no apparent danger, but I knew better than to question my instincts. Freeing myself from the bedroll, I got into a crouch, reaching to wake Graves.

He was gone.

I scrambled from the tent, looking around. Off to my right, Graves shuffled away from the camp into the desert. I pulled my hood forward and followed, keeping a distance.

Over the nearest dune Graves disappeared, without so much as a glance behind him. I crawled to the top of the same dune and gazed over at the wizard in his familiar gestures of casting a spell. Whatever Graves cast satisfied him enough that he turned back toward the tents. Halfway up the dune, he saw me.

"Oh. Hello, Spider."

The contrasting facets of Graves's personality were getting clearer. For a few minutes after casting a spell, he was pleasant and amiable, just before he was openly hostile. The rest of the time he was a typical eighteen-year-old moody pain in the ass.

"Nice night for a walk," I said.

Half-shrug.

"Why are you casting spells at this time of night?"

He peered up at the moon as if needing confirmation that it was indeed still night.

"I often get up at night to cast. The night is long...and nightmares wake me."

I should have seen this coming really. During the day Graves needed to cast every couple of hours, so getting through an entire night would be a challenge. Nightmares was another level to his addiction though.

We started back toward the tent.

"What are you two doing?"

Graves stopped, and I walked into his back. Ahead was this hour's sentry, the driver of our rear wagon, with sword drawn and aimed toward us. The man's sword arm twitched, as if unsure whether we were a threat or not.

I stepped from behind Graves and gave my best amiable face. "Just obeying the call of nature."

The sentry looked from me to Graves then back again, one eyebrow raised. He had some misconception here but— Oh! I realized what it was. "No, no. Nothing like that. I was... You know what, never mind. Think what you want."

I nudged Graves forward, back toward our tent. The sentry raised his sword, resting it against one shoulder. As we passed, the man brought it whipping back, pommel first to crack against the back of Graves's skull. He went down like a sack of coffee beans.

"What did you do that for?" I demanded, drawing my knives.

The driver held the sword, aimed toward me now. "Because he's the more dangerous of you two."

That was indeed true but didn't answer my real question. I started for the man, ready to go in low, under the sword. Movement to either side caught my attention as body heat registered in my vision. Men, unfamiliar ones, stepped from the shadows to join the sentry.

"Bandits?" I said.

I opened my mouth to shout a warning to the rest of camp when a blow to the back of my own head took consciousness away.

CHAPTER 7
WHAT HIT ME?

My eyes fluttered open. I was inside one of the covered wagons, hands bound behind me in what felt like the metal of city guard restraints. Don't ask why city guard restraints are so familiar.

The others were there. Ten drivers, Zachariah, and Graves who was still out cold.

"Fat lot of good you were when it counted," the head driver spat before both my eyes were open.

I rolled those eyes and groaned at the throb in my head.

Of course, my daggers and lockpicks were missing.

"This was the exact situation you were supposed to prevent."

What could I say, the man was correct. How would Farrobane and his boys have handled the ambush? Better probably. He would have had at least one of his men on sentry at all times, wouldn't have been caught unawares by—

"Hold on! It was one of your drivers that ambushed us."

"One of...?" Zachariah looked around. "Arn is missing."

"Yes, Arn," I confirmed.

"Well, I—"

"Good," a voice said from the wagon's rear, behind us. "I'm glad to see you are alive."

We twisted toward the voice's owner. In the covered wagon's flap was a robed man. Two others behind him were less distinct.

"You don't look like a bandit," I said.

"I am not, though some of my people used to be." The man shook his head. "No, we are the Cult of the Sightless Eye."

A chill shot through me. The drivers all gasped. One of the men started to weep.

I glanced at Graves.

"No, he isn't dead either. Just drugged. We can't have him casting any spells, now can we?"

"No, I suppose not," I said, trying to sound relaxed.

"He's the one," the cultist said over his shoulder, then looked back at me. "Our head priest will be most interested in you."

How had they found me?

"I don't have your goblet."

The man cocked his head to one side, shrugged then spoke to the rest of the prisoners. "You will be brought to our temple for the honour of sacrifice to great Aniha-Morgo. Do expect to suffer."

At the mention of that malevolent, sightless god each driver deflated, more than one sobbing now.

The cultist let the flap of our ersatz tent fall closed.

As soon as we were alone, I pulled my hands from behind my back, dropping the shackles onto a sack.

"How did you—?" one driver began.

"Please. I've been getting out of these without picks since childhood."

I started on Zachariah's bindings next. Each of the driver's restraints took less than a minute to unlock, the metal binding being intended for short-term incapacitation, and that only while being watched.

"Most of them are around the fire," Zachariah whispered, one eye to a tear in the wagon's covering. "Two guard this wagon, one at the back and a second which circles."

"How many?" I asked.

"Twenty that I can see."

"What are they waiting for?" one driver said, voice high and panicked.

Outside a guard chuckled. "We wait for morning."

"They need daylight to see the trail," Zachariah said, then in a lower voice, "And to remove evidence that they were here."

The reality of the situation hit several of the drivers. We were about to disappear, and no one would ever know what had happened, though bandits would be blamed.

"What do we do?" Zachariah asked me.

Well, the lead driver didn't think me worthless after all. Placing one eye to the same hole, I scouted the camp. The cultists *were* all gathered around the fire. Made sense in the desert's night air.

To the right, our horses were all tethered.

"If we can get to them," I said, "we could ride back toward Timurpajan."

"These are caravan horses, bred for endurance, not speed," Zachariah said. "The fastest they go is a quick trot, except yours. We would do better to run."

"Okay, that's what we do then. Up the road, hide when they come after us."

"And your wizard?"

"My responsibility," I said.

The lead driver cursed. "If they catch you, they catch us. No, between the twelve of us we will carry him."

Good! I didn't really want to carry Graves's unconscious body across the desert all by myself.

"Two at a time, out the front flap and into the desert," I said. "After the circling guard passes."

Zachariah pointed at two of the least panicked drivers, one man and one woman, who got ready. They would show the others how it was done, and that it was possible.

I watched at the slit, one hand raised to signal when they could go.

"What in the hells is that?" one voice outside said.

The guard circling came to a stop, right where we needed to exit. I turned to the drivers and waved my hands in a motion to stop.

"Hey, Farnde," the guard at wagon's back end said. "Come see this."

"I'm warm and got no interest in moving," someone, Farnde I guessed, said from near the fire.

A shuffling, scuttling noise.

"Somethin's movin' on the road," the guard said. "Farnde, you have to... No. No!"

The noise of many small scuttling creatures.

"Scorpions!" screamed one guard.

Once again I pressed my eye to the canvas, other drivers finding similar holes, and watched as thousands upon thousands of scorpions flowed in off the road. They swarmed across camp and over the cultists who struck out with whatever was at hand. Sword. Boot. Blanket. In one case a frying pan, which was more effective than any other weapon. In the end, it didn't matter. There was no escape. Too many scorpions covered the cultists in a sea of eight-legged, stinging horror.

"We need to run for it," one driver said.

"Are you mad?" another responded. "We'll be dead the moment our boots touch the sand."

Instinct told me that wasn't true. The scorpions were ignoring our horses, only going after the cultists.

"Be ready," Zachariah said. "I don't know what brought this abomination but we won't die without a fight."

Fight? That would be futile. The cultists were better armed and had the freedom to move, but most were dead or dying.

"I might know what brought this," I said

Quickly I told the story of the spell Graves had cast. The drivers looked both impressed and horrified, topping off the emotions with something that hadn't been there a minute ago, hopeful.

The last cultist, their robed leader, which was somehow proper, swung a flaming stick back and forth. The scorpions surrounded him as if the man were a preacher spouting the most fantastic rhetoric from some scorpion god. All attention was on him and him alone.

Flames inched their way along the stick, closing in on the cultist's hands. Soon he would drop the stick, and it would all be over.

It happened sooner than expected. As the first scorpion climbed the man's body, his expression changed, from wild-eyed fear to blank-eyed death. The man was dead before he hit the ground.

"We're next," Zachariah said, eye to another slit.

"I don't think so," I said. "Look."

Outside the scorpions stopped, turning around as if asking themselves how in the hells they'd gotten here, and just where *here* was. Then, like a receding flood, they all headed back into the desert, moving off in every direction.

We huddled inside the wagon for several minutes, waiting for someone brave enough to head outside first. Zachariah was already staring at me, as were several of the other drivers.

"Ah. Right. I'll go take a look then."

I pushed the wagon flaps aside and stepped onto the sand, looking all around for any scorpions that may have been slow to leave the party. I'd seen them leaving, knew it had been Graves's magic that brought them, but I was sure one would be leftover for me.

Death everywhere. Dead, squashed scorpions mixed in among the bodies of poison-swollen cultists. I felt sorry for the scorpions.

"It's safe," I called.

The other drivers, Zachariah in the lead, exited the wagon in a cluster, staring at the carnage. Once one moved away from the perceived safety of the group, they all went about the business of packing up camp. There would be no more sleep tonight, and none were willing to linger the couple of hours until daylight.

Our horses were indignant at having their rest interrupted, oblivious to all else that had occurred.

"I just wanted to point out that if it weren't for us, you would all have been sacrificed to Aniha-Morgo."

Zachariah stopped and turned toward me, his mouth working. He looked around at the death and destruction before speaking. "I cannot deny that you have made up for allowing us to be ambushed."

"We were taken by surprise, I must admit, but that was by a cultist in your group."

"This is also true," Zachariah sighed. "It reminds me we are down one driver as well. You'll need to drive the rear wagon."

"That will make scouting ahead difficult."

"Once your wizard is awake he can take the reins, and you can return to scouting."

Knowing what lay ahead was invaluable and I didn't like the idea of giving that up. Still, we should be okay until Graves awoke, though whether he would be able to drive a wagon was a mystery.

"We'll receive the driver's wages as well, of course," I said.

"You know, if we have to leave a wagon behind you don't get paid, right?" The lead driver crossed muscled arms over his chest. "According to contract, the wagons need to arrive intact."

"Ah, right." I thought about the wording of that contract and would have to speak with Narvin next time I saw him. No, forget that. It's a fair expectation, as long as it isn't taken too far. A broken wagon wheel could be interpreted as breach of contract. "Well, if there's a danger of us not being paid we could leave now."

Zachariah threw up his hands. "Fine. You get Arn's wages for driving the wagon to Gesture. You get the protector's wages for the wagons arriving intact. Agreeable?"

We shook on it before Zachariah stalked away, performing several tasks at once while keeping an eye on the whole production. I was seeing why these caravans were protected by more sizeable groups. There were so many possible jobs to do. Still, if Farrobane and his boys had been here, they might have been just as surprised and would have needed to fight their way out of it *if* they'd been able to free themselves.

Graves had been placed in the back of our rear wagon again, in a bed of coffee beans where he could sleep off whatever the cultists had given him.

The cultists. They'd known me, recognized me. Were they tracking me because of the goblet, or because I'd freed Zadi?

Great. Like I needed more complications to keep me from my goal.

After retrieving my lockpicks and other belongings I climbed into the driver's position and grabbed the reins. The caravan moved out, Zachariah following the road by moonlight at a snail's pace.

Sunrise was shy by an hour when Graves gave his first groan of displeasure. Five minutes later he crawled over coffee beans and leaned into the front seat, glaring at me.

"Before meeting you, I'd never been struck unconscious."

"This is quite the adventure so far."

"So far?" Graves's surly voice was back, though that could have been from being knocked out and drugged as much as needing to cast a spell. "What happened?"

I filled him in.

"Huh, well, you asked for protection."

"Yeah, the scorpions did the trick."

Graves crawled into the front seat and started the gestures of casting a spell. Before I could ask what he was planning, a glowing orb shot from his hands and hovered over the lead wagon. It would have been more useful an hour ago, but the lead wagon did pick up speed.

"I didn't think you would need all that waving," I said.

Graves looked at his hands. "I don't really. The teachers used them, so I guess I acquired the habit. They help me focus."

So, Graves could still cast a spell if his hands were tied. Another piece of useful information.

Minutes after sunrise Zachariah called a halt and we ate a quick breakfast. The caravan was making better time but would pay for it later in the day as horses and drivers got tired. Sleep would be much needed tonight.

Stops that day saw Zachariah much more vigilant with sentries, having three on the lookout at any time. Their gaze alternated between the horizon, for following cultists, and the ground, for scorpions.

Graves had taken the task of driving the wagon with a combination of annoyance and short-tempered snappishness. At least he'd proven adequate at the job. Driving had taken away from his ability to cast spells until he'd hit on the idea of casting one on the reins, giving them a certain limited-intelligence. He still rode up front, but the reins did the job of keeping the wagon on the road while he cast spells whenever he wished.

After lunch, the caravan passed out of the desert and onto a grassy plain which began inclining toward distant hills.

We drove in this way for several more hours until sundown approached. Going further would bring us into the bandit's hills which would be treacherous to navigate at night, even with a glowing light spell over our heads.

This night passed without incident. Zachariah set two-hour sentry shifts, three people per shift except for mine which had the extra person, Graves. The wizard woke in a foul mood for our midnight shift, spoke to no one and headed off from our watch to cast a spell.

I hesitated, wanting to follow and ensure we weren't surprised by another swarm or worse. In the end, I stayed with the other drivers on watch, staring at the spot of blackness where Graves had disappeared.

Deep breath in and slow release.

What's the worst that could happen?

Do I really want to ask that question?

There came a muffled rush of air and flash of light. Then he did return, a smear of black soot on both cheeks, his hair singed on one side.

I didn't ask.

CHAPTER 8
BANDITS

Next morning, the sun barely up enough to say it had risen, we ate breakfast while Zachariah spoke to the group.

"We're heading into bandit territory," he said. "When we encounter them, let me negotiate. Don't do anything foolish."

All agreed though this entire warning seemed aimed at myself and Graves. I nodded, knowing our part.

Zachariah would offer the bandits some bags of consumables as a toll for passage through the hills. The more impressive the caravan protectors, the more reasonable the bandits were in accepting the toll.

Caravans had three options for getting to Grand Gesture. The first being what Zachariah was doing, have some caravan protectors and pay some toll. The second was to have enough protectors that bandits let the caravan pass, but the cost of these extra warriors ate into profit and was reserved for shipments of gold or gems. The final possibility was taking a circuitous route around the hills and coming into Gesture from the east, doubling the length of each journey. Dad always took this last option, refusing to pay bandits to rob him.

"I'm thinking about transforming my horse," Graves said, climbing into his wagon. "Making it younger, stronger."

"You can do that?"

"Never tried it before."

I looked at the horse, then toward the lead wagon. "Better not. If that horse explodes, you and I will end up pulling this wagon."

"Cheerful thought."

I gave him my best what-can-you-do shrug.

"Tell me, are we ever going to stay in one place so I can practice?"

"What do you mean? You're practicing now."

Graves was silent, staring ahead at the wagons moving onto the road.

I nodded. "After this, we can find a place for maybe two weeks. Longer if we aren't too extravagant with our money."

"Extravagant." Graves was able to pack a lot of disdain into that one word.

"Well, if you're okay sleeping outside like this, catching our own food we can stretch that to a month."

"Pass. I miss a real bed."

"Agreed. Then we'll have about two weeks."

Graves wasn't excited by that time frame but said nothing, leaning back in the seat. He waved his hands and recast the spell on the reins, which snapped to attention. He exhaled in a slow way, eyes closed.

"Ready to go?"

"Yes."

It was interesting that the degree of difficulty on the spell, or the magnificence of it, didn't affect his satisfaction from it. Any spell would do to fill Graves's need to cast. If he kept them simple, circumstances shouldn't go too awry.

Right. Simple. Like heating a cup of tea?

I spurred my horse forward to lead the caravan.

An hour later we passed into Bandit Hills. If the hills had an official name, it had been abandoned long ago. The pass we followed was wide enough for my horse to get between wagons and rock walls to check on the rear wagon from time to time.

Another hour and we reached a wide opening. Zachariah halted his wagon on the far side, raising one hand to warn the wagons behind. Each came to a stop in turn, Graves negating the spell on his reins without a problem. This one spell, and negating it, had become a specialty for him, not backfiring once.

Ten minutes passed.

I was about to go forward and talk with Zachariah when the bandits arrived. They thundered into the clearing on horses, two dozen in all, surrounding the caravan with drawn swords and crossbows at the ready. A true show of force.

Several of these bandits seemed only days into adulthood, punk kids with fearlessness to prove, or indignity to avenge. These were the dangerous types, the unpredictable ones.

Zachariah descended from his wagon as the lead bandit dismounted and came forward. They shook hands, speaking in the low tones of people doing business. Not friends but people used to dealing with each other.

They were haggling on price. I recognized the signs and was curious to see how well Zachariah handled himself, how much he could talk the other man down. If these bandits had been paying attention, then the unknown factor of having a magic-user as protection should influence negotiations.

"Wizard!" one bandit blurted, an unseasoned man with a crossbow. One of the unpredictable ones.

He urged his horse forward, crossbow raised in Graves's general direction. Two other crossbow-wielding nervous types joined the first, all attention on the young wizard.

It was an obvious attempt to show that the thought of magic didn't intimidate them in the least. They had to have known Graves was here, seen him from a distance. Was their reaction all part of the act? If so these boys should be on the stage instead of doing banditry.

"At ease, boys," the head bandit said without looking around. If he had, he might have seen that his words had no real effect.

No, these kids weren't acting. They were nervous.

For his part, Graves did his best to ignore the extra attention, but his eyes kept wandering back to the crossbows. Fingers twitched against his legs, and his lips muttered words only he could hear.

"Look out. He's casting," the first nervous bandit said, jostling the one next to him.

The jostled bandit jerked his crossbow arm, hitting the trigger and sending a bolt hurtling.

"Graves!" I shouted.

The projectile passed through one sack behind the wizard, coffee beans spilling onto the ground. The wizard's eyes grew huge and panicked as he spun in the seat, like a trapped animal. His fingers twitched, already casting, his gaze glowing amber.

A second nervous bandit started raising his crossbow, and I urged my horse forward, slamming against his. The crossbow, still on an upward angle, went off and sent its bolt over the wagons in a high arc.

"Protect us," Graves shouted.

We were too far from the desert for scorpions. What could—

A deep growl of surprised anger, followed by a second. The bandits looked away from Graves and down at their horses.

"Bear!" the first nervous bandit screamed. "Bear!"

Nope, more like *bears*.

The spell had transformed each bandit's horse into a bear, not only in shape but in nature as well, each one furious at being saddled and ridden. The bears reared, dislodging riders not quick enough to dismount on their own.

Then the bears were on them in a blur of claw and tooth.

Our caravan horses remained just that, thankfully. I urged my wild-eyed mount forward, anxious to get away from the carnage and around the other side of our wagons. Zachariah and the bandit leader spun around to an unbelievable scene, the lead driver rushing for his wagon while the bandit made the unfortunate instinctive decision of heading toward his own horse. That horse, now a bear, was already heading for him, perhaps remembering every time a spur had been put to him.

The bandit went down, screaming, under a thousand pounds of bear.

The caravan horses had the wide panicked eyes of animals surrounded by predators. Each of them reared in their harnesses before trying to bolt in every direction, drivers doing their best to control them.

Two wagons collided, wheels locking together, sacks hurtling from the back of each and splitting open like fruit as they hit the ground. I pulled my horse a hard right to avoid Graves's rushing wagon. Zachariah had just gotten feet onto his own wagon when it bolted out of control. To his credit, he gripped on with feverish strength, trying to get into the driver's seat and grab the reins. At least his wagon was headed away from the carnage.

The bears, finished with their offending riders, turned toward the caravan and fresh horse meat. If they'd been black bears, we might have frightened them off, but Graves had changed them into grizzlies, and those don't spook.

"Graves!" I screamed. "Do something."

"Like what?" he screamed back, trying to control his horse.

"The spell! Cancel it!"

"Cancel it?!"

Graves cursed. He was ready to argue the futility of trying to negate his spell but decided to *show* me I was an idiot instead. Dropping the reins into his lap, he flashed his hands around in gestures like he'd used to cancel the animated reins.

One grizzly sped after Zachariah, while others closed in on other panicked horses and drivers. Another bear swiped at the side of one fleeing wagon, splintering the wood and spilling more cargo. Horses and drivers, moments from horrible death and nowhere to go, froze in place, staring at the teeth that would rend them apart.

The bears shimmered, like a mirage in the desert. They stopped in mid-attack as their original horse shapes returned, confused, their rider's blood smeared across their muzzles. Each horse glanced around at the others in an expression close to embarrassment, before bolting for the trail and disappearing.

Our caravan horses shied from these savage ones, several trying to flee again. The drivers got their animals under control, calmed them, spoke comforting words that they did not believe themselves.

Zachariah didn't move, reins gripped in pressure-white hands.

The clearing was calm once again, except for the disaster of spilled goods and torn bandits. One wagon had tipped in the pandemonium while two others remained wheel-locked.

"Cutting it close on that cancel," I said to Graves.

He looked at his hands, still in mid-gesture. "I didn't—"

"What in all the jumping hells was that?" Zachariah screamed as he crossed the clearing toward Graves and me.

"It wasn't his fault," I said, bringing my horse forward. Nobody sane would want to be on the ground in front of the lead driver and his clenching fists. "That bandit shot his crossbow at Graves."

"I saw that. Know what else I saw? Bears. *Bears!*" Zachariah seemed unable to speak in less than a full-volume scream. "You get one bolt fired at you, and change their horses into bears?! You couldn't just put them all to sleep?"

Graves opened his mouth, then shut it with a snap. "Huh. I didn't think of that."

"Zachariah," I said. "The bandits attacked first. Graves reacted."

The lead driver sputtered with purple rage which came more from the terror of having a bear chasing him down than from actual anger. The man didn't move.

"Your caravan was protected," I pressed on. "And that is what you are paying us for. Who knows what else they would have done. You saw how nervous they were."

Zachariah took a deep breath, exhaled, did it again, and again, until he wasn't shaking, or at least not as much. He turned toward the drivers. "You two, get those wagons untangled. The rest of you get that wagon back upright and check the horses."

Luckily the horse attached to the overturned wagon was okay. Better to pull that wagon the rest of the way to Grand Gesture myself than chase down one of those bandit horses for replacement. They had a frightening glimmer to their eyes when they'd fled as if all that had happened wasn't so bad, and that blood around their mouths was a taste they could get used to.

I shuddered.

"You two," Zachariah snapped, turning back toward us. "Keep watch for other bandits. There'll be no bargaining for passage at this point."

I rode my horse up the trail, keeping an eye open for bandits left behind. If any had been watching they would be gone by now, assuming they were smart, which was no guarantee. No, we needed to get these wagons out of here. If more bandits *did* come, they would attack from a distance, and Graves would be the first target.

When I returned, the two wheel-locked wagons had been separated, and the overturned one was upright again along with its horse. In all two casks of beer had been smashed, while three others had slow leaks. This last was fixed by turning the casks upside down. Several sacks of consumables had been destroyed when they hit the ground. One of the wagons had a wheel beyond repair and was in the process of having it replaced.

It was lucky none of the drivers or horses had been injured in all that had happened, and the amount of goods lost was light considering a wagon had overturned.

Within the hour the caravan was once again headed along the path. I rode far ahead, watching for signs of ambush and finding none. They weren't the only bandits in these hills, but either that group had been acting alone, or no other wanted to chance being mauled by bears.

"Bears," I shuddered.

At lunch, we took our rations among the other drivers, all of whom ate quickly then realized there were other tasks to be done.

"Huh."

"What?" Graves asked.

"I do believe we are being shunned."

Graves looked around at the drivers who huddled in a group outside one wagon. Zachariah was nowhere to be seen, eating his meal away from everyone.

"I hadn't noticed."

Graves returned to the food without any particular relish. The fact he didn't notice us being avoided told me how used to it he was.

"What the hell," I said. "It's the last day anyway. Soon we'll be in Gesture and can go our separate ways."

"No more caravan jobs, right?"

I shook my head. Next time in Timurpajan, I would have to stop in and see Narvin, talk up the protection job Graves had provided and do some damage control. I was sure Zachariah would sully our names, and it would take a lot of convincing before we got another chance from Narvin.

"I want a real meal tonight," Graves grumbled. "Something hot and with actual taste."

He closed the box and put it aside, the meal half-finished. Couldn't blame him, trail rations were not the best examples of food.

"I think we both deserve a good meal at least," I agreed.

The wagons entered Grand Gesture ahead of schedule, with hours of daylight remaining to unload. We rolled our way through the sprawling streets toward the storehouses. This city was even greater than Timurpajan. Grand Gesture occupied most of a valley between the Bandit Hills and Razor Mountains. Several thousand people lived and worked, played and fought here. Like any town, there were places you wanted to be and places you didn't. The mercantile section where we dropped off the wagons was one of the rougher spots.

Our wagon train was common enough that we didn't draw too many glances, though some stopped as we rolled past, counting wagons. I descended from my horse, giving her a pat on the neck and the last bit of apple from my lunch. She was a great horse, understanding what was wanted without much effort. I would miss her.

Graves stood to one side, fingers twitching, while I headed toward Zachariah.

"Here," the lead driver said, shoving a sack of coins my way. "I trust I don't need to say we will *not* be needing your services for the journey back."

Zachariah turned away.

"This pouch seems light," I said, loud enough for anyone nearby to hear.

Zachariah stopped and turned back. "No. The full driver's wages are in there."

"And the protection?"

"Contract stated the caravan was to arrive intact. There were kegs of beer lost plus several sacks of goods, not to mention the damage to the wagons."

"All of which was less than you would have paid to those bandits."

Zachariah opened his mouth, ready with some retort but then only shook his head and turned to march away again.

113

"I wonder what Graves will do when he finds out you stiffed us. You know he can turn horses into bears, right?"

The driver stopped, not turning back toward me, his hands clenched into fists.

"How many horses will be in your caravan on the way back?"

The man shuddered, pulled a second sack from inside his tunic and tossed it over his shoulder. I caught it one-handed before it hit the ground.

"My thanks, Zachariah. A pleasure doing business with you."

He stormed away without glance or comment.

CHAPTER 9
A MEAL, A BEER, AND TWO CHANCES FOR DEATH

"Can we find that place now?" Graves demanded.

"What place?"

"Where we can settle down for a couple of weeks. Where I can practice magic without interruption."

"Oh, that place," I said. "Nope."

Graves cursed. "I knew you would do this. I—"

"First we get a drink."

"A drink?"

"And a hot meal. That was what you wanted, wasn't it?"

"I...well, yes."

"Good. That pub should do." I pointed at a place we had passed earlier while rolling through town. The sign hung by one hook but they would have to serve food better than caravan rations.

"A pub? Isn't that a bit cliché?"

"Cliché?" I asked, starting toward the promise of beer and beef.

"You know, the adventurers heading to a pub," Graves said, following.

"We're not adventurers. I'm a trader looking to start a business, and you're a wizard learning better control."

"All that sure felt like an adventure."

Bears, bandits, and cultists. Yeah, that was hard to argue with.

"Anyway," Graves continued. "In a story, isn't this where the next chapter would begin?"

"Life isn't a story." Hadn't Dad said the exact opposite? "Whatever. I don't care. I'm thirsty."

Graves half-shrugged. "Cliché."

The crooked sign proclaimed the establishment to be the Shut Up and Drink.

"Charming," Graves said.

"You're the one who likes to observe people in pubs," I said, turning toward the wizard. "Just behave yourself."

"That isn't always up to me."

"Fair point. Maybe you should wait out here."

"Not a chance. I want some wine. Besides, I doubt Armentia would be happy if I was kidnapped outside some seedy watering hole. She might think you'd abandoned me."

"Another fair point."

Not that I would let Graves out of my sight anyway. He had that twitchy need to cast a spell.

"Okay, let's just be careful in there. Do you need to cast a spell before we go in?"

"Mind your own business and I'll mind mine, Spider, thank you."

He pulled the door open and stepped into the pub beyond.

Wonderful. Graves was moving into snappish and rude. He was in definite need of casting, but I was too tired to argue.

The heavy scent of body odour and stale beer assaulted our noses. The place was dim and shadowy, enough so that our eyes needed time to adjust. What presented itself once we could see was a rougher place than expected, even given the pub's name. Where the Sainted Ogre was a place to go for food and drink, a place to meet with friends, the Shut Up and Drink was a place to, well, shut up and drink.

Around the room were many obvious adventurers, wearing much the same leer as Farrobane's boys. Rough people who wanted to get drunk and fight.

So why wasn't anyone fighting? Was it too early?

People drank without belligerence or even signs of outright drunkenness.

"Nice place," Graves muttered.

"Well, we can't leave now," I answered in a low voice only Graves could hear. "Some of these patrons would follow us."

Graves harrumphed.

"Besides," I said. "Look."

Graves followed my gaze toward the huge bouncer at the bar. She was of some race unknown to me, astounding in itself, and was built like a mountain. Nearing seven feet tall if she'd been upright instead of resting on a sturdy crate. Her gaze scanned the crowd and was the real reason everyone behaved themselves. No weapon hung at her belt, and it didn't seem like she would need one.

She reminded me of Lees, though the bouncer was both taller and broader. What appeared similar to the tribal markings worn by trolls covered her arms up to the neck, but her face was anything but trollish. The ridge above her eyes was pronounced but not grotesquely, and her nose wasn't the cucumber-like protrusion of a troll, more flattish. No teeth protruded from her mouth either, no tusks. Against one shoulder rested an elaborate braid hanging from the back of her head. That one item gave her a distinctness beyond her muscled arms and unspoken potential violence.

When her gaze landed on us, it stopped, eyes narrowing in warning. I waved her a greeting, saying we weren't there for trouble. She ignored it.

You can't make friends with everyone.

"So true, Dad."

"What?" Graves asked.

"Nothing,"

Graves followed me to an open table on the right-hand side of the bar. It was closer to the bouncer than the other patrons wanted to be, but we had

117

no desire to cause trouble.

The server who strolled over took our orders with a frowning, disinterested face, then disappeared into the back.

"I hope it's good," Graves said. "I've had enough of barely edible food."

"You didn't like Zachariah's caravan rations?"

Graves grumbled, drumming a tuneless beat with his fingers.

The food and drinks arrived, plunked in front of us with enough force to jostle one limp carrot from my plate. Graves placed a finger on the cold grey meat at the centre, then on the even colder potatoes.

"If this were hot it would be unappetizing," he said. "Cold as it is, this dish struggles to rise to the level of putrid."

"Just eat it."

He scowled at me as if I'd suggested he strip down and perform a dance for the patron's, then waved a hand over his meal. "Heat up."

"Don't—"

Too late.

A flash of amber eyes, a whiff of garlic, and the food in front of Graves remained greasy, cold and unpalatable. His expression of revulsion didn't change either, but some tension left his body, successful casting or not.

After three days of travelling with Graves, I was aware that his spells always had some effect. A creeping unease travelled along my spine, and I was about to comment when the portal opened over our table, the size and shape of a wagon wheel and growing.

Where did this portal of Graves's lead?

At least I hoped this belonged to Graves. Then, remembering the story about him summoning that frost giant, I changed my mind and hoped it was the doing of some practical joking wizard. Finally, I wished I was back in Timurpajan and hadn't heard of the Tower of Wizardry, Graves, or cults.

Wish in one hand—

"Not now, Dad."

A vicious snarl came from the portal and I was on my feet, retreating, but coming up against the back wall.

A creature, a monster really, leapt from the portal, smashing through the table next to ours and onto the floor. It was the size of a wolf, covered in similar grey, wiry fur. The head came together at two beady eyes above a narrow snout. When that mouth opened, it showed an impressive number of sharp teeth.

Not an herbivore then.

From the portal blew a frigid winter wind, swirling snow throughout the room.

"Not again," Graves said.

How did the attempted heating of food bring a portal to who knows where? There wasn't any correlation, not like the horses changing to bears. At least those had been two animals, and that had followed the order to protect Graves.

"Rathagast," the bouncer shouted, jumping to her feet, pointing. "Rathagast."

The entire patronage were on their feet, screaming, yelling and heading for the door with wild, fearful glances behind them. Graves remained seated, staring at the back of the creature which was, of course, between us and the door.

It stepped forward, eyes locked on the bartender in his once-safe spot behind the bar. The man had frozen, dropping a glass he'd been drying to shatter on the floor.

The bouncer came in from the monster's right, rushing the beast as it tensed to pounce on the bartender. She grabbed it by the fur as it leapt, keeping hold of it and spinning, slamming it down against the floor in a splinter of floorboards.

Her eyes locked on the portal and she took a step toward it, then sighed and leapt back at the creature. With a grunt, she grabbed it around the middle and squeezed. The beast howled and thrashed, reaching its head around, trying to snap its teeth on her neck.

"Go home," she muttered.

With a grunt, the bouncer jerked it upward, then swung the beast around and through the portal as it snapped shut. The creature's tail didn't quite make it, the portal severing it to fall on the floor with a meaty splat.

Silence filled the place.

The bouncer stared at the spot where the portal had been, her mouth working, then bent and grabbed the amputated tail.

I pulled Graves to his feet and grabbed our packs, pushing him toward the door in as casual a manner as possible.

"Stop," the bouncer said, one finger the size of a breakfast sausage pointing at us.

"Um," I said.

"Get 'em, Nila," the bartender yelled. "Look at this place."

"Run," I hissed, pushing Graves ahead of me and through the door.

Outside, I grabbed the wizard by one arm and pulled him up the street. To be fair, he didn't need much urging as the massive form of Nila came slamming through the door a moment later.

"Oh, crap," I said.

"We're dead," Graves agreed.

"Not yet. Come on."

We weaved our way around people headed home from work or out to drink, muttering *excuse me* and *look out* every few steps. Behind us the creature called Nila barrelled straight down the centre of the road, everyone jumping out of her way. It would take another minute at best for her to catch up this way.

Still holding Graves by one arm I headed for a side alley, hoping our pursuer wouldn't see the detour. If she did, the alley had a narrow entrance which would slow her as she navigated through sideways. I didn't know this area but assumed the path would lead through to the next street.

I was wrong.

We came out of the alley and into a widened area closed in on all other sides.

"So, you didn't know where we were going then?" Graves asked.

"I made an assumption," I said, examining the walls for a way to scale them. "What kind of alley doesn't go anywhere?"

"The kind where we get trapped and horribly murdered?"

We turned in time to see Nila scrape her way through the alley and stopping with her back to our only exit.

"Rathagast," she said.

Graves and I looked at each other. Nila made no move forward.

"Be ready with a spell," I said in a low aside.

Graves peered at the wall of muscle and stepped back, putting me between the two of them. "What exactly should I cast?"

"I—"

"Rathagast," she repeated, holding the severed tail toward us.

"Rathagast?" Graves said. "That's the name of that...monster?"

"Yes. A creature from my home."

Her voice was deep and rumbling, but at the same time melodious. Not what I expected from someone so huge.

"Your home?" I said. "So, um...you aren't from around here?"

Graves rolled his eyes.

"Where is home?" I tried.

My strategy was simple. As long as she spoke, she wasn't killing us. So keep her talking.

121

"I don't know!" Nila wailed, shaking the tail back and forth at us, like a dog far too excited to see its master.

Okay, so that strategy didn't work. Graves and I each took a step back, wondering if perhaps Nila was a lunatic.

The huge bouncer stared at us, then the bloody stump of tail in her hand. She dropped that arm to her side, took in one breath which would have equalled several of mine, and let it loose in one slow exhale.

"Back home I fell through a hole like the one he made." She pointed one meaty log finger at Graves. "I want to go home, but no one knows where it is. I don't know where it is. But that hole led there." She pointed back toward the Shut Up and Drink.

"Ah, yes," I said. "I understand."

"So, you'll open the hole again?" Nila asked.

"Impossible," Graves said.

Her face clouded over, arms crossed like two trees growing around each other.

"Try not to piss the giant off," I said.

Graves waved a hand to say it was mine to explain, before crossing his own arms and leaning against a wall.

"Well," I started, "um, Nila, was it?"

She nodded, once.

"Graves's magic—that's Graves, and I'm Spider—his magic doesn't work like that."

She uncrossed her arms, looking from me to Graves and back.

"It's all random. Chaos magic it's called."

Nila leaned back against the wall, still blocking the only exit. She looked toward the sky, right fist knocking against the wall beside her. "Have you opened a hole there before?"

"They're called portals, and no," Graves said then stopped, thought for a moment. "Unless... Are there frost giants where you come from?"

She shook her head.

"No, I didn't think so."

"Please," Nila asked. "Won't you try it?"

"It's hopeless."

Her hands clenched into fists the size of hams.

I cleared my throat and when the wizard turned my way I inclined my head toward Nila, widening my eyes.

"Oh, Gods! Okay. Fine. I'll try."

"It can't hurt," I said.

"Oh yes? Remember those words later."

"Hmm, yes. We should do this outside of town."

"In case something like the rathagast?" Nila said.

"Yeah, exactly," I agreed. "Are there other creatures like that where you come from?"

"Yes. It is wise to go outside of town. The next rathagast may not be so small."

I gasped, and Graves made a strangled noise. Nila didn't seem to notice.

"I'm tired, and it's almost night," Graves said, yawning. "Can we do this in the morning?"

"We just came off a caravan," I explained, "and were looking forward to sleeping in a real bed tonight."

Nila stared at us, mouth in a tight line, then shrugged. "Guess I can wait another night. Come on. I can get you a room."

Graves and I glanced at each other.

"No, not at *that* inn. This place is safe and clean and has better food."

Food. We hadn't gotten to eat dinner.

"I could sleep on coffee beans," Graves grumbled.

"Careful what you wish for," I said. "Okay, lead on, Nila."

CHAPTER 10
THAT NIGHT

"**P**lease don't cast anything tonight that will cause our horrific deaths," I said getting ready for bed.

Nila had been right. This inn was cleaner, and the food didn't need spells cast on it. The beds were comfortable too, though Graves and I shared a room.

Graves half-shrugged. "I promise not to cause our horrible deaths on purpose. Is that enough?"

I continued to change.

"You know I can't cast the portal she wants, right?"

"Think of it as a chance to practice."

Graves grunted disdain and sunk his head into the pillows on his bed. Within moments the wizard was asleep and snoring. I lay on my own bed, staring at the ceiling.

Should we take off?

Nila seemed reasonable, but would she remain so once Graves was unable to cast the portal she wanted? She could do us both severe damage without effort.

Getting out of bed, I padded across the room to the window and tried to tug it upward. It was either locked or stuck in place. Same effect.

Trapped? Were we being prevented from leaving?

I headed to the door and pulled it open, looking into the hall.

No, if we were prisoners, the door wouldn't open either. I was paranoid. Not that I could blame Nila if she *had* taken every precaution on what might be her best hope of getting home.

Downstairs it sounded as if people were enjoying themselves. Music accompanied by drunken singing, not that I couldn't hear it with the door closed. It was pleasant singing though, and not out of control. The sounds reminded me of some nights at the Sainted Ogre.

I'd had one beer with dinner but could go for another.

One drink and one song, then back to bed.

I pulled my hood into place, creeping along the hallway and down the stairs into the main room of the inn. The dozen or so tables were full of people enjoying themselves.

"Everything okay?"

The innkeeper we'd met on arriving looked at me from behind the bar. I closed the few steps between us as he slid a beer across the countertop.

"Thanks," I said, picking it up.

The song being played was familiar, about a brave but naive hero determined to rescue a lovely maiden and win her hand. The only problem being, the maiden preferred the company of the dragon he was trying to rescue her from. The hero wouldn't take no for an answer and went through many painful misadventures until learning his lesson.

It was a funny song, though played quicker than the way I knew. They'd added an extra verse which spelled out the moral of the song unnecessarily. The listener should get the message without it being beaten over their head.

In the end, I stayed a couple of hours, drank more beer than I should have and took part in two songs, one of which got rousing applause. I staggered back to the room in a better mood than I had been for a week.

This was what I wanted. Life on the road, going from town to town, bringing things people wanted for trade and building that business up from nothing. I was just missing the entire business half of that.

Keep that ruby in mind, Spider.

Graves moaned and thrashed in his bed. As I laid my head on the pillows, he popped to his feet. His hands twitched, and he gave a grunt of

125

displeasure toward the door and the sounds below.

His hands waved in the complicated manner associated with his casting, the gestures as random as the results they brought. I didn't bother telling him no, had known this time would need to come, even exhausted as Graves had been. I wish I was less fuzzy headed in case something went wrong.

Shouldn't have had that last beer.

"Silence," Graves said.

And all around *was* silent, peaceful.

Satisfied, Graves slipped back between his sheets without making a sound.

Rolling onto my side also produced no sound of skin against sheets, no creak of the wooden bed frame.

"Hey," I tried to say but had no voice.

Then I laughed into the silence.

It could be worse.

CHAPTER 11
ANOTHER DAY

"Damnedest thing," the innkeeper said, sliding plates of breakfast in front of Graves and me. "One minute everyone was singing, and the next no one could make a sound."

"Very strange," I agreed, glancing at Graves who gave no indication he was listening.

So that spell had affected more than *our* ability to perceive sounds and crossed over into people's ability to make them. How wide was its sphere of influence?

"Slept through it," Graves grumbled, listening after all.

"Some took it as a sign from the gods," the innkeeper continued, "and left for the nearest temple. Most made a game of it, finding other ways to communicate."

Graves gave a derisive snort, attacking his breakfast with jittering fingers.

"Sounds like I left too early," I said, starting to eat too.

Nila came down the stairs into the common room, dressed in a tunic of fur and leather, double-headed stone war-hammer swinging at her waist. The innkeeper greeted her and signalled for food to be brought. She lowered herself gingerly onto the thick wooden planks of the bench next to me, the wood groaning but holding her weight.

A server arrived carrying Nila's plate, with more food than ours combined. She picked up a fork, which was a child's toy in her grip, and started putting food into her mouth. She was neat and fastidious in her way of eating which surprised me. So much for preconceived notions.

"The roads out lead east and west," she said between mouthfuls. "North is wide open, which should give us enough space."

Graves looked from her to me and then back to his plate without comment. He finished and got to his feet.

"I'll be outside," he said, picking up his pack.

Graves would be casting a spell before the door was fully closed. I should follow, but whether there or not, the spell would be cast.

"He's cheerful," Nila said, popping a full piece of bacon into her mouth then wiping it with a napkin.

"Graves is worried he won't be able to open that portal."

Nila frowned. "He can try."

"He will."

"Well, let's get to it then."

Nila rose, grabbing a pack I hadn't noticed earlier. The full backpack was like a child's schoolbag on her shoulder. I followed suit, looking around for the innkeeper who waved a farewell. Whatever we owed had been taken care of already, it appeared.

Outside Graves seethed with arms crossed over his chest, glaring at us. He grabbed the pack resting at his feet and turned toward the road. "Can we get this over with?"

"Yeah, sure," I agreed.

There was no sign of Graves's spell. Then I realized he was in far too belligerent a mood.

"You didn't cast a spell?"

"Of course not," he shot back. "Didn't we agree to wait?"

"For the portal spell, yes we—"

"You think I can't wait?" he said, heading for the east road without watching if we followed.

We strolled along in silence for the next half-hour, enjoying the morning sun... Well, I enjoyed it at least. Graves wouldn't enjoy anything right now, and Nila was impatient.

"Is this not far enough?" she asked.

Graves didn't even glance around. He needed to cast but held off in some cockeyed need to teach me a lesson.

The town was a speck on the horizon but still visible. "We should head off the road some," I said.

Graves grunted, turned north and headed onto the plain leading toward the mountains. This close, they towered over us and were still hours away.

Another fifteen minutes and Graves was in the foulest mood ever. Nila had taken to clenching and unclenching her fists, knuckles cracking with each clench until I was unnerved. Graves stopped and threw his pack on the ground.

"Enough!"

"Yeah, sure," I agreed. "Do it."

I *had* wanted to get far from the town but was also glad to see how far Graves could push himself before casting a spell.

The wizard relaxed, his fingers twitching in expectation. "What am I casting?"

"A portal?"

Graves spun toward me. "Just like that? Like it's easy?"

I took a step back.

"Every time I've cast a portal, which is twice, it's been by accident."

I opened my mouth to speak, but Graves had turned again, stomping away several paces.

"Cast a portal, he says. Humph!"

He weaved his hands in familiar patterns, muttering words under his breath. His eyes glowed amber as he pointed at the empty plain. "Portal!"

The effect was anti-climactic. Ten feet from us a door appeared. It was heavy, made of wood and painted bright blue with a glass pane at head height.

It was familiar.

"Um, that's the Sainted Ogre's door, isn't it?"

Graves nodded, a near-smile reaching his mouth, though if it was from the relief of finally casting or amusement at this door being here, I couldn't tell.

"Oh, I hope that's a copy," I said, certain it wasn't. "Gar is going to be pissed about this."

Nila stormed forward, covering the ten feet in two seconds and grabbing the Sainted Ogre's door by its handle. She lifted it from the ground.

"Well, it *is* a portal, of sorts," I said.

Graves stared at the heavy oak door in Nila's meaty fist. Nothing behind it and leading nowhere.

She dropped it to the ground and turned back to us. "Try again."

Graves took a breath, much calmer now. He wore a frown of deep concentration, staring to the right of the Sainted Ogre's door.

He gestured. "Portal."

Magical energy coursed through the wizard's hands and stopped ten feet away, solidifying into...a round metal window that fell to the ground and did nothing.

"Porthole," I said. "Close."

Nila didn't move toward the window but said several low words in what must be her native tongue. Every one of them was surely profanity.

Graves didn't look at either of us but turned to focus his magic in a fresh spot.

"Portal."

For an hour he cast spells, ten in all, one after another, with the same level of success. The door and window were the closest he got to an actual portal, and the more exhausted he became the further afield the results got. He conjured two dozen, multi-coloured butterflies, a man's hat with an unfamiliar sun emblem sewn into the side, an unremarkable chair, and, in one strange result, managed to raise the temperature around us by ten degrees until that spell lost cohesion and the effect dissipated.

Graves stumbled, his knees giving out, and Nila was there to catch him, guiding him to the conjured chair.

"I'm sorry, Nila. I'm exhausted."

Nila nodded her understanding while I stared at the wizard. The casting of ten spells, successfully or not, was incredible, but Graves apologizing and acting pleasant was just short of a miracle.

She turned back in the direction of town but Graves shook his head.

"I need to rest now. Please."

Please? Who was this wizard?

"Let's set up the tent," Nila said.

I pulled the tough canvas from my pack. It was the one extra we'd been able to snag from Zachariah's caravan. When he'd tried to stiff us, I had forgotten to give it back.

In less than ten minutes, Graves had a place to sleep and get his energy back, under a wide leafy tree that would provide some coolness. Nila picked the wizard up with unexpected tenderness and deposited him in the tent, closing the flap behind her as she retreated.

"How long?" she asked, jerking a thumb toward the tent.

"No idea. First time I've seen Graves push himself to the point of exhaustion. To be honest, I've never seen him cast more than one spell at any time."

Nila sat on the grass next to me, both of us staring at the wide open plain that only stopped when it hit the edge of the Giants' Mountains.

"Sorry you didn't get your portal home."

"Not yet," Nila grunted.

No point in telling her it may not happen. That had already been covered and Nila either believed it or she didn't.

"In truth," she added, "this is the best possibility of getting home I've had. I am grateful."

I nodded an acknowledgement to that.

"Nila, can I ask? What race do you belong to? I've never met anyone like you."

She half turned. "Any-*one*? Not any-*thing*?"

I shook my head, keeping eye contact. Each of her eyes was a deep emerald green the size of a hen's egg.

"Huh! Well, that's an improvement at least," she said. "Most people treat me like a friendly monster, at best."

"People fear what's different."

I reached up and pushed the hood away to expose my ears.

"Yeah, I noticed you were an elf last night."

"You did?" I asked, somewhat surprised. "I guess the hood works better when limiting the time I spend with people. Most don't guess without seeing the ears."

"People aren't observant. Too absorbed in their own stories."

So true. Dad had taught me that people believed what they were shown. Show them a human, and they believed in the human.

"To be fair," Nila continued, "you don't act much like the other elves I've met."

"I was raised by a human so pretty much am on the inside."

"Interesting. Still doesn't explain why I'm not a monster to you."

"My father's best friends were a halfling and a half-ogre couple who helped raise me. She's one of the most wonderful beings I've ever met."

"They would make an interesting couple."

"Oh, yeah. On first meeting them you wonder how that would ever work, but after a short time, it's just perfect. Well, I've known them my whole life and couldn't imagine them apart."

We shared silence for a full minute before Nila spoke again. "My people have no name. We call ourselves, well, there's no direct translation, but the closest in your tongue would be the Forever People."

The Forever People. Very nice. It had a certain poetry to it.

"What's your home like?"

"Home," she said, rolling the word around.

What I assumed was a smile creased her face, the first I'd seen since meeting Nila. I hoped it was a smile anyway. It showed far too many teeth and would have made a starving wolf pack decide it was about time to lose a few pounds anyway.

"Our village lies in a wide valley nestled inside some mountains. We hunt and fish, farm and work, sing and create. I was a protector, like my sisters."

The Razor Mountains lined the distance, home of giants. They went on for miles, unexplored, reaching the end of the continent in the north. Ships, travelling along the sea and mapping the continent's outline were met by more mountains lining the edge and showing no way in. Wandering into those mountains only took a person so far before becoming un-scalable by any but the giants.

"Is it possible that your home is in those mountains?"

Nila shook her head.

"But why not? So much is unexplored, only the outside edge really. It could be that your people—"

"No!" she said, slapping one meaty hand in the grass next to her. "No!"

Hmm, time to stop talking.

She drew in a deep breath and let it escape. "Forgive me, Spider. I appreciate your attempt, but it isn't possible."

"Okay, you know best."

Nila sighed.

"But...how are you so sure?"

"Because," Nila said, "your world has one moon, while mine has two."

"Oh. Yes. Well, that *would* be hard to mistake."

Nila let out a bark of laughter, short and sudden. "It would."

"Tell me more about your home."

She glanced sideways at me, perhaps looking for true interest, before turning back toward the plain. "My father was a stonemason, an artist. He would make such wonderful items out of the stone, from sculptures to furniture to weapons. My mother is a warrior as all females should be."

An apologetic shrug.

"No offence, Spider, but this world of strong men and weak women, physically anyway, is backward to me."

"Not all women are weak, not all men are strong. My friend, Lees, she went adventuring into dungeons as the warrior of her group."

Nila smiled again, and I found it less jarring this time, knowing what it was.

"I would like this Lees."

Oh yes, the two of them would get along well. Of course, Lees would need to adjust to not being the biggest woman in the room.

"In any case," Nila continued, "our males are artists, thinkers, teachers. They're more frail than females, so we are the hunters, the warriors."

"You mentioned sisters?"

"Yes, three sisters and a brother," her eyes shone at the mention of a brother. "I am the youngest except for my brother, Dasshin, who teaches the children to read and write, and to play music."

"Everyone learns? Even your warriors?"

"Of course. We're not mindless beasts living to fight and hunt. I even play an instrument like your guitar." She sighed at this. "I've tried to fashion one since coming here but can't find a material strong enough to survive my playing."

What wood could have enough strength for that? The ironwood trees in the far western continent?

"How *did* you come here anyway?"

Nila groaned. "Stupidity. Carelessness. I was hunting alone and came across a glowing portal, like the one Graves cast, only flat against the ground. I stepped on it by accident and fell into this world."

"Fell?"

"On this side, it was thirty feet up. I plummeted through a horse cart and onto the ground underneath, then lay there staring at the portal above, shrinking and disappearing. I was surrounded by weak, pale humans who looked at me like I was a monster."

"People fear what is different," I repeated.

"Oh, they feared me for certain. I was sure I would need to fight my way out, but one man stepped forward and spoke to me. I didn't understand the words, but the tone was amiable. I followed him, and he gave me a job."

"A job?"

She looked toward her feet. "I made sure people paid their debts to him."

"Oh! He was a loan shark?"

"Loan shark?" she worked the words around in her mouth. "Yes, I like that. It fits. In any case, I was learning your language, not so difficult, and learning about your culture, which was baffling."

"Yes, it is, isn't it?"

"I moved on from that job to working as a protector at the pub and sometimes helping unload the caravans."

"You didn't like your job with the loan shark?"

"No. Hurting people for money is wrong, dishonourable. My people have no concept of commerce or personal ownership. It didn't take much to learn though. Money is an equalizer, letting weaker people be strong through its influence."

I hadn't quite thought of it that way before. "Money keeps the caravans moving."

"Yes. You humans are so spread out, like you don't want to know each other. Each person tries to be the most important instead of helping each other for the greater good." Nila looked embarrassed again. "Sorry."

"No, no. That's a fair description."

We were silent, lost in our thoughts before she turned to me again. "What about you? Who is Spider?"

"Me?" I thought about it. "That's what I'm trying to figure out I guess."

She grunted an acknowledgement.

"My father died recently and now I'm finding my own way in the world. I want to build a trading business, but for now I have to take care of our wizard friend."

I explained the story of breaking into the Tower of Wizardry and the seemingly unending debt. I told Nila about how they wanted Graves away from the tower until he could become less dangerous.

"Oh yes? How is that working?"

I imagined that rathagast again and shuddered. If it hadn't materialized where Nila was, everyone in that place would have been slaughtered. She laughed, reading my expression, and I joined her, but something about all of that troubled me.

"Maybe this Armentia could help me," Nila said. "I visited every magic-user here in Grand Gesture, hoping one could get me home. They all said the same: Not knowing where I started from, they couldn't send me back. With millions of worlds, to just pick the right one would be astronomical odds."

"Millions?"

She nodded.

"Millions of worlds?" I whispered, trying to wrap my mind around the concept and finding it incomprehensible. More than *one* world was unimaginable, and now there were millions? It was staggering. "Maybe...maybe when Graves wakes up, he'll be able to open the right portal again."

"Best chance I've got," Nila said, the doubt in her voice matching my own.

How in the hells would Graves open that portal at random a second time? How had he even opened it the first? One chance in millions?

That's what bothered me.

The rathagast materialized in the one place where someone would recognize it and be able to defeat it. What were the odds of being in the same room as Nila and opening a portal to her home? Astronomical.

Graves hadn't even been *trying* to open a portal.

#

Morning passed into afternoon.

We checked on our wizard every half-hour or so to ensure he was still breathing.

The contents of Nila's pack turned out to be items she could use without destroying them. A set of utensils proportionate to her hands, a sturdy metal tankard and a bowl.

She'd also brought containers of stew from the inn, enough for lunch and dinner, so it appeared we were out here until morning anyway.

We ate lunch and waited some more.

Plenty of time for contemplation.

"His magic is truly random," Nila said, returning after an hour's search for firewood with arms full. "I doubt he'll cast the portal while trying."

I'd come to the same conclusion, yet for the last hour, an idea had been tickling the back of my brain. One last possibility—

"So, I will travel with you until he casts the portal again by accident," Nila said, a statement of fact, neither request nor suggestion.

Oh, fantastic. Another person added to a group which was already too crowded. Still, how could I dissuade her against coming with us when this might be her only chance of ever seeing home again?

I couldn't.

"Be warned though," she continued, adding sticks to the fire. "When that portal appears I will jump through, no matter what dangers surround you two."

"Oh, of course. Understood."

Except, she'd had that exact chance back in the pub and hadn't taken it. Why? Because the bartender would have been ripped apart. No, Nila wouldn't abandon us any easier.

Since I was already saddled with Graves for the next year, Nila might as well come along. The three of us *could* be a force to be reckoned with, clearing out dungeons and caverns, selling magical treasure. Graves's magic would only get better with practice while I could open any door or chest. Nila would be the muscle that could snap anyone in two...

Something clicked into place.

"Nila, why didn't you just grab us in that alley and force Graves to cast the portal?"

"Wouldn't work. His magic is random."

"Yeah, but *you* didn't know that. As far as you were concerned, we were two friends travelling together. You could have threatened to break my neck if he didn't..."

Nila closed her eyes.

"Ah, you don't like violence, do you?"

Nila was silent before giving her head one quick shake. "Not if there is another way. To hunt, to defend one's family, there is honour in that, though I still do not revel in it."

"Why didn't you say so?"

She rolled her eyes. What was it about me that brought that response? "Since coming here, my size has kept humans at a distance, and I haven't had to hurt anyone. When I worked for that...um..."

"Loan shark."

"Loan shark, yes. When I worked for him, I used the idea of violence, but when it came to actual harm, I couldn't do it."

"And as a bouncer?"

"Oh, no one caused trouble when I was around. The most I had to do was suggest it was time for someone to leave."

"But you're a hunter, a protector."

"I am." She grabbed at her stone war-hammer, slapping the head of it in one palm before speaking again. "But, I'm also a follower of the moon god, Trileme, a god of peace. In my world, among my people, it is a strangeness for protectors to be so masculine and scholarly."

Nila's world was not so dissimilar from this one, reversed maybe, but still having the same types of games.

"Why do you want to go home if you were strange there?"

"I'm stranger here," she said. "At least at home, I'm not a monster."

"I don't think you're a monster."

Unfortunately, not everyone would share my outlook. Lees had sometimes been treated that way, and she was only half-ogre.

So our little group now consisted of an unreliable wizard, a semi-pacifist behemoth, and a thief who would rather be alone. Some crew. Not ready for those dungeons. Our best tool was intimidation, and dungeon creatures don't intimidate, not with any kind of reliability.

The sound of a prolonged yawn interrupted my thoughts, and we turned to see Graves in the tent's flap, scratching his backside.

"Morning, sunshine," Nila said.

Graves came over to the fire. "Did I miss lunch?"

His fingers twitched in that familiar way that said he needed to cast, but he wasn't his usual belligerent self. Was the secret in exhausting him? Graves had slept longer than any night since we'd come together.

"Yep, but not dinner," I said, gesturing toward the containers of stew.

Graves drummed his fingers against the side of his leg. He turned toward the plain, leaving to cast a spell.

"Why don't you use your magic to heat dinner?" I said.

Graves glanced at me, then at the fire, his mind working as the sleep left his brain. It was an idea I'd been turning over in my head while Graves slept, and when his eyes went wide, I knew he'd seen it too.

"Last night at the pub, when I tried to heat my food, that portal opened."

"Worth a try," I said.

Nila perked up at the idea, hope returning to her face.

Graves took a seat on the chair conjured earlier and accepted the bowl of stew I held toward him. He turned toward the open plain, the need to cast growing in his eyes, confidence too. I started to believe he *could* cast that portal for Nila.

Well, maybe.

"Heat up," Graves said, pointing at the food.

Twenty feet behind us a portal opened, wide enough to drive a caravan through. For all of three seconds, we were excited, until the landscape on the other side registered. Another wide open plain, this one of raging flames and burning pits. A hot wind carrying sulphuric stench blew through the opening.

"Is that hell?" Graves asked.

"I've never seen it personally," I said, my voice a low whisper. "But it's about what I would expect. Can you close it?"

"Are...are you sure you want me to cast *more* magic at it?" Graves stared at the portal, hands twitching in readiness to try.

"What could make that worse?" I asked.

"Well, the portal could become permanent, or the spell could call whatever lives on the other side, or—"

"Never mind. Maybe just hold on," I said, "but be ready."

The hole in reality hovered, shimmering. Nila circled it, stopping at one side.

"It's got no thickness," she said.

I circled in the opposite direction and saw what she meant. The portal had width and height, but no depth. From behind it didn't exist at all. I saw Graves as if I could follow a straight line to him...which I was not prepared to do. No way was I was touching that portal.

"So, not your home then?" I asked Nila.

She shook her head. "Too much fire and burning."

Five minutes later, each of which felt like a full day, the portal began to shrink.

"Spider? Nila? Come here."

Graves was pale. He goggled at the portal while Nila and I rushed to his side.

Inside the far too slowly closing portal was movement. A great, lumbering body made its way toward us, a body of molten fire that was cut from our view at the waist and which we saw less of with each second.

"Faster," Graves whispered.

Portal almost closed, a pupil the size of a pumpkin pressed against the opening, glaring at us. With a muffled pop, like a child's soap bubble, the portal disappeared. We allowed ourselves to breathe once again, staring at the spot where the hole had been.

"Well, that was closer than the blue door," I said, jerking one thumb in the direction of his earlier results.

Nila said, "Try again, Graves."

"But...I just opened a path to hell..." The wizard glanced at me, and I shrugged.

He muttered something that might have been *when did I become the rational one?* and turned back toward the plain.

"Portal."

Ten feet away a plant sprouted and in seconds became a full-grown tree. Graves threw his hands up.

"How is that a portal?" he demanded.

"Like before," Nila suggested. "Heat the food."

"Right, right." Graves hurried to the seat and took the same plate of food. "Heat up."

The result was immediate.

It was also unremarkable except that the spell did exactly as asked. The food in Graves's hand heated to a perfect temperature, the wonderful smell of beef in thick gravy wafting out and making our stomach's rumble.

"Well," I said, "might as well eat if it's going to work. Heat the other two."

Graves cast again, heating the second bowl like he had the first, which Nila was already eating. We looked around for some other effect but found nothing noticeable. Graves exchanged bowls with me, and I started to eat, wondering what the third casting would bring.

Graves sunk onto the chair, looking at the bowl of food. Even cold it wasn't as unappetizing as what we'd been served at the Shut Up and Drink.

"Heat up."

The spoon was halfway to my mouth when the ground underneath me disappeared. A wide portal the size of a house opened under us, and we fell through. Me, Graves, and Nila, our packs, our dinner, the chair and the fire.

Ten feet is a steep fall when you aren't ready. Everything and everybody slammed into the ground at the bottom with enough force to bounce. The chair shattered, our dinners spilled, and the fire flew in every direction, one stick landing on Graves and setting his purple robe to smouldering. Nila, first on her feet, jumped forward to slap it out.

We jumped up, rubbing our sore bodies and staring at the portal. It was too high over our heads for even Nila to reach, and it had started closing.

"Do something," I hissed at Graves.

He came out of his daze and pointed both hands at the shrinking hole. "Stay open."

Another blink and it was gone, this time with a crack of force echoing through this new world.

"At least I didn't fall through a horse cart this time," Nila said.

We looked around, hoping for signs of familiarity.

"It's darker here," she added. "Night already."

"Any idea where we are?" I asked Graves.

"None."

Nila looked up at the sky. "Only one moon. Wherever we are it isn't home."

CHAPTER 12
A WHOLE NEW WORLD?

We were on a wide plain that extended to mountains in the south but continued on in every other direction. It was much like the one we'd been on a minute ago and a world away.

"Now what do we do?" Graves said.

I shrugged, watching those distant mountains. They could have been our own if not in the completely wrong direction.

"This isn't my fault," Graves said, looking first at me then Nila. "You both wanted me to cast that spell."

Nila stared at the moon, full of the same marks and craters as our own.

"Huh! Nila, do moons look the same in every world?" I asked.

"No." Nila's braid swung with the motion of her head shake. "Of the two moons on my world one is large and yellow, the other pale red. Both have features unique to this one."

Understanding filled Nila's face. This moon wasn't different. It was exactly like the one that rose above us every night.

"Same world," I said.

"Must be," Nila agreed.

"It is?" Graves asked then looked at the mountains between us and home, any relief fading. "How do we get back?"

Again I shrugged.

"It's colder here," the wizard complained.

Nila watched the moon another minute before pushing some of the still flaming sticks from our fire together. Adding some twigs and what we could find nearby soon brought the fire back to what it had been minutes ago.

The three of us sat on rocks, staring into the flames.

"What now?" Graves asked.

I poked the fire with a stick, the flames surging. "Well, we have enough dried food for a couple of days, less appetizing as that might be."

Our dinner had spilled when we'd fallen, and if not for the packed rations, it would have been a hungry night.

"Most of our stuff came with us," Nila added.

"Except the tent," Graves said, then gave a groan. "And my bedroll. Wonderful."

"At least mine and Nila's packs came through with us," I said.

Graves looked around. "My pack?"

"In the tent," Nila said.

"Not even a change of robes?" Graves sniffed at the ones he was wearing.

There would be some adjustments, but it could have been a lot worse.

"No clean socks either?!"

Graves was warming to this reality already.

"Is there a way through to the other side?" Nila asked. "Some pass?"

"Possible. Without searching, who could know? All I know for sure is there's a reason those are sometimes called Giants' Mountains."

With that, we started setting up sleeping arrangements. My bedroll would need to be shared with Graves tonight and, oh, how I was looking forward to being punched awake during his thrashing nightmares.

#

Next morning we ate a leisurely breakfast, lingering over that final cup of tea while avoiding the fact we had no idea where to go or what to do.

Some adventure.

The idea of it was fun, but not when others looked at me for direction. When had I become a leader? I didn't feel like one, didn't want to *be* one.

And where was I supposed to lead them to? Each direction lacked the same promise as every other, and I had opened my mouth to say that when a commotion in the distance got our attention.

Shouts of anger came to us first, followed by shapes rushing toward us.

"People," I said needlessly.

Brilliant. My powers of observation were intact.

Nila and Graves didn't notice. The three of us got to our feet and watched the approaching group.

As they got closer, it became obvious one was out ahead of the rest and headed straight for us. This man was bandaged, the wrappings well-worn though still obscuring his flesh. Every few steps he glanced at those closing the distance behind him.

"He's being chased," Nila said.

I was happy to hear someone else point out the obvious.

Soon, the bandaged man was close enough to see his darting eyes and hear his panting breath. I caught him as he barreled into us.

"No," he mumbled. "Don't touch...don't touch..."

Then he collapsed to the ground, still trying to crawl from his pursuers.

Nila stepped forward, getting between the approaching crowd and us, pulling the double-headed hammer from her waist. I rested the man's head against my backpack and moved next to my giant friend. Graves, after a moment's hesitation, staring at the man on the ground, stepped up next to her as well on the opposite side.

The crowd, perhaps thirty men and women in all, came to a hesitant halt ten paces from us, no one volunteering to be in front. They all stared at Nila, muttering, gasping for air from their run. One man was pushed forward from the group to become de facto speaker. He turned, searching for a spot to push back into anonymity. Finding none he faced us, smoothing his tunic.

Not knowing the standard of dress on this side of the mountain we

146

could only assume these were villagers. They wore nothing particularly flashy to say they were more than that, and their weapons were farming implements and sticks.

Yes, villagers.

"Ho, strangers," the man in front ventured, going for the, we're-all-friends-here tone of voice.

I raised one hand in greeting while Nila grunted. Graves kept silent, his eyes drifting to our guest and back again.

"If we could just take that man, we'll be on our way."

A glance at our guest told me he was awake and aware, recovering from the chase. His eyes flashed to me but he didn't have the strength to do more than that.

"Is he a criminal then?" I asked.

"A criminal?" the mob's speaker asked. "Well, no."

One of the mob muttered.

"I mean, not exactly."

The same man muttered again.

"It should be evident that he is a danger," speaker said.

"That's not a very believable ventriloquist act," I said to the man who was muttering. "Your lips are moving."

Nila huffed a breath which I took as a laugh. The mob facing us didn't enjoy it as much, all glancing at the mutterer.

"If you want to speak why don't you step forward?" I asked.

The mutterer stepped forward, joining the original speaker.

"This man came into our village," he said, "trying to infect us."

The man on the ground spoke, his voice low. "Looking for water. Food."

I turned back. "Says he was just hungry."

The crowd murmured.

"It should be obvious that he is diseased. Unclean," the speaker said, disgust clear in his voice.

"Well, now," I said, speaking in my best negotiating voice. "I suppose it is at that, but what are you planning to do with him?"

"Kill him!" one man in the mob said.

"Hang him!" another yelled, brandishing a noose.

"Hang him from what?" I asked.

The mob looked around for a stout tree with limbs appropriate for a lynching but found none.

"Drown him?" one suggested.

"Isn't he diseased?" I asked.

"Yeah!" several villagers shouted, latching on to the words, simple and true.

"Then won't you taint your water supply?" I asked.

"Um…"

The mutterer closed his eyes. "Can we focus here?"

Nila grunted and bared her teeth. Several villagers took steps backward, and one looked scared enough to bolt.

I turned my attention back to the leader, a smile on my lips that didn't reach my eyes. "Yes, let's focus."

"Thank you. Now, if you would just give him over, we will allow you to return to your breakfast."

"Hmm, how about you leave him with us instead?" I countered.

The mutterer and the speaker looked at each other, then at the mob. Any potential backup had moved several paces back. Mutterer turned back to us with a simpering expression.

"Friends—"

"Oh, we're not your friends," I said. "We don't much like people who think thirty against one is fair odds."

Mutterer gurgled his first response, then tried one more. "But…he has the rot."

Graves nodded, taking an extra step away from the man without saying a word.

"I don't care if he has a fetish for merfolk," I said. "Leave him with us."

The mutterer grimaced at the idea, though his mob appeared happy with the arrangement.

"Green flash," Graves mumbled, pointing at the spot between mob and mutterer.

I gritted my teeth, expecting any effect from an earthquake to a demon. Instead, we got what Graves asked for, a harmless flash of green light.

When mutterer glanced behind him, his mob was fleeing across the plain. He and the original speaker turned back to us, speaker looking like he wished he was with the mob but had missed his opportunity.

Mutterer gave a brief bow before turning and following the rest at an unhurried pace. We lingered like that for another minute until sure the villagers weren't going to do anything stupid.

The bandaged man's eyes had closed. I checked to ensure we hadn't rescued a dead man, but he still breathed. A vague, sickly-sweet smell came off the man.

"That's the creeping rot," Graves said, pointing at the man and taking another step away.

"Is it?"

"I saw it when I was a child, back at my father's home."

"Let him rest for now," I said. "What else can we do?"

Graves's eyes lingered on the man. I couldn't blame him. The creeping rot was a horrible disease, spread by touch. It killed the flesh, leaving it with an appearance like paper after a fire. It had been stamped out years ago, on *our* side of the mountains at least.

Then again, so had the Cult of the Sightless Eye, and they were making a comeback.

As it turned out, we had nowhere to be, and plenty of time for allowing this man to recover. He slept for several hours while we debated what to do next. Graves kept looking at him as if the disease might jump from under the bandages and attack.

I'd touched the bandaged man, caught him when he stumbled. No parts of his skin were exposed but—

"Thank you, my friends," a soft voice said.

We turned toward the bandaged man. His eyes were open though he made no move to rise. Graves took yet another step away.

"If you keep doing that you'll be a speck on the horizon soon," I told him.

The wizard peered at his feet as if they were guilty of acting on their own. He forced them to take one step toward the bandaged man and shook his head. This was as close as he would get.

"I am Coron," the bandaged man said. "A priest of the goddess Wagarial."

I looked at my companions. Graves gave his half-shrug and Nila shook her head once.

Coron sighed.

"You have the rot," Graves blurted, more accusation than statement.

"I do. I was working with unfortunates in the north. There is a hidden colony of those with this disease."

"And you *went* there?" Graves demanded. "Knowing this?"

"Of course. They are as deserving of help as any other."

Graves had no answer to that.

"I had hoped that Wagarial's powers would protect me, or at least cure me."

"No such luck, huh?" I asked.

Coron shook his head. "I am travelling back to my monastery."

"They'd be able to cure you there?" I asked.

"Yes. Many of my order live there, and the head priestess has great healing powers. She will cure me."

"She's healed this disease before, has she?"

Coron nodded, staring at me with a sadness in his eyes, already knowing.

"We'll take you there," I said.

"What?" Graves demanded. "No! We've saved him, done our good deed. Let him go his way."

"Graves."

"I have no intention of dying that way, Spider."

"Fair enough," I said. "You and Nila wait for me here."

"I'm coming," Nila said.

"I have to go. You don't."

"I'm coming," she repeated.

Graves threw his hands up. "Have to go? Why do you have to...?"

He took a step away from me, his mouth dropping into an open gape. I pulled up my sleeve and showed him the circle of papery, flaking skin, no greater than a thumbnail in size. Graves took another step away, shaking his head. He turned toward Nila who stared back without a trace of expression, then all around him before clenching his fists at his side.

"Fine. Fine!" The wizard pointed a finger first at me then at Coron. "But I'm not coming near either of you until you're cured."

Fair enough, and better than I could expect from Graves. He'd experienced the creeping rot in person and knew what the end result would be if we didn't get to Coron's monastery.

Our new friend ate the food we offered, regaining some of his depleted strength and stamina. The disease coursing through his body not only rotted the skin but weakened his entire system, and that chase across the plain had taken whatever he'd had left.

With a helping hand from me, Coron got to his feet, swaying like a drunk sailor on a ship. Nila came forward with a stout walking stick, holding it toward the priest.

"My thanks," he said, staring at Nila as if he'd never seen anyone like her, which was probably true.

"Do you not have ogres on this side of the mountain, no trolls or giants?" I asked.

"Trolls?" Nila asked. "Really? I can see the comparison to giants or ogres, but trolls?!"

"I'm asking more about the presence of other races than making a comparison."

Nila grumbled. "Fine."

Coron shook his head. "The ogres died out generations ago. Is that what race you are?"

Nila shook her head. "I'm not from around here."

"I see." Coron cocked his head to one side. "Another dimension?"

"Another...?" Nila shook her head.

"Dimension. Another plane of existence. Another world."

"Yes! Yes, that's right. What do you know of other worlds?"

"Just theories I'm afraid. Many worlds existing side by side but distinct from each other."

"Is there a way back?" she demanded.

Coron thought about that. "It seems to me that if you travelled in one direction, you should be able to travel in the other. My head priestess would know more on that."

It was against the odds, but still more hope than she'd had a moment ago. Now there were two reasons for going to this monastery.

Nila and Graves packed the camp, such as it was, while I explained to the priest our own story and where we had come from.

"There are settlements on the far side of those mountains?" he asked.

"Settlements. Cities. Towns. Whole civilizations and races."

"Fascinating."

A glint shone in his eye making me wonder if we weren't similar. The priesthood gave him a means to travel the lands and see what he wanted while trading did the same for me.

This world was indeed fascinating.

CHAPTER 13
ON THE ROAD AGAIN

Coron led the way, striking out in the direction of his monastery, a three-day journey from here. I stayed by his side, chatting and learning as much about this side of the mountains as possible. It was obvious he didn't know of any way through to our side of the mountains, but maybe he could be of help in other ways.

This side of the mountains went for miles in every direction except south, encompassing cities and civilizations, as ours did. The mountains ringed the land in on all sides, opening only in the west to a vast ocean too rough to sail on.

Was it possible to set up a trade route with this side of the mountains? Perhaps falling through the portal hadn't taken me further from my goal after all. Yes, that was worth some thought, but before that, I would need to be healed.

Throughout the morning, Nila followed behind us, but at Coron's urging not *too* close. He wasn't sure if this disease could jump to races like Nila's, had no way of knowing in this land without ogres or contact with the mountain races.

Graves needed no urging. He stayed at least ten paces behind Nila, his eyes boring a hole in the back of my head. Every couple of hours he would cast a spell, nothing that forced us to hurry on or fight for our lives at least. I wondered for the briefest of moments if Graves could cast a spell to cure the disease but pushed it from my mind. We weren't that desperate yet.

Coron needed rest often to recuperate his strength, and when we halted for lunch, the priest slept beneath a tree the entire time. Though, maybe it was more a deep meditation because when he woke he had perfect knowledge of all that had been said and done while his eyes were closed.

"You know," Graves said by way of conversation, from the far side where we'd stopped for lunch. "It occurs to me we are getting farther and farther from that couple weeks restful practice you promised me."

I turned toward him, a retort on my lips but stopped short. He had just cast a spell and was in his most amiable stage, trying to get past his fear of the disease. This was his way of saying he was still with me.

"True," I said. "Maybe once this is done we will find a place to sit and think for a while."

"Sure we will."

"Why not? As long as we have the coins to support ourselves."

All expression retreated from Graves's face, and the wizard slipped into silence, digesting this idea. There would be no response, at least not for now.

Nila and Graves went through the task of packing up camp again. Graves, in particular, didn't want either myself or Coron touching any of our belongings.

"What can I expect from this disease?" I asked the priest after he'd woken and got back on his feet.

"You can expect to be cured at the monastery," Coron said.

I smiled but continued waiting for an answer.

Coron nodded. "Early stages of the disease has a person losing appetite and energy. As you see, I sleep a lot. That continues through the duration of the disease."

"Okay," I said, having noticed a decrease in energy and wondered if it was my imagination or not.

"The skin starts to flake and die in layers, in the way an onion will sometimes go bad. The skin underneath itches with a persistence which borders on maddening."

His fingers twitched, ready to scratch.

"But, if the afflicted person starts scratching they will rub away the top layers of skin and what's beneath will begin to die. With the flaked, dead flesh in place, it slows the process for the inner layers."

"And this covers your whole body?"

"Every inch of it. Were I to scratch the dead skin away I would lose a quarter of my body's weight. The bandages I wear are as much to hold me together as to protect other people."

I found my hand rubbing at the patch of dead skin on my right arm and forced it to stop.

"You would do well to bandage that," Coron said.

"How long?"

"Until death?" Coron asked. "Well, for some, like that community in the north, the disease takes years. Others find it accelerated. Ten days for me—and I am in my fifth before you ask."

"Ten days?" I whispered.

No point in asking if the rot was accelerated in me. The disease had already spread from that patch on my arm to halfway up my shoulder. So, five days until I looked like Coron.

And he was right, it itched.

That afternoon we passed from plain to forest. It was nice to be out of the sun and into the cool cover of trees.

With an extra mouth, our food wouldn't last us the three day's journey. Coron didn't eat much, though he did force himself to keep up his energy. It was obvious the man didn't find any food appetizing.

"We need food," Nila said.

I looked at her backpack, and she gave her head a quick shake. "Nothing edible."

None of us had expected this to be an adventure. It was supposed to be a short trip outside town for Graves to try casting portals. I had expected us to return to Grand Gesture once Nila saw the results or lack thereof.

"What do we have?" I asked.

"Barely enough for dinner, and only that if we're frugal. When we stop, I can set some traps, though I don't know what there is to trap."

"Small creatures," Coron said. "Rabbits and mattas."

"Mattas?" I asked. "What's a matta?"

"Other than this disease? Nothing at all," Coron said, then a grin broke across his face. "What's a matta with you?"

Nila groaned. "Saw that coming."

I shook my head. Graves, who had heard the exchange, only shot visual daggers at the bandaged priest's back.

"Seriously though," Coron said. "There are rabbits and some edible roots. Berries too."

"We can see the berries for ourselves," Graves said, heading to a bush by the side and pulled a thick red one from it. "Any other obvious information to give us?"

Graves raised the berry toward his mouth and popped it in.

"Well," Coron said, in a slow drawl, "I can tell you that one is poisonous."

"Gurk." Graves spat the berry to the ground.

He glared around at Coron who had come to a stop, leaning full weight on his walking stick. The bandaged man was in obvious discomfort yet still wore a pleasant expression on his face.

Graves stomped on ahead of us while Coron moved to where the wizard had departed. He picked a berry from the bush and placed it into his mouth, chewing.

"Hmm, my mistake. Not poisonous after all."

He winked at Nila, then started along the trail after Graves.

"I like this guy," she said to me.

As we travelled that afternoon, Nila and I gathered berries in our bowls, which had held the stew we never got to enjoy. By the time we stopped for dinner, we had a fair amount, though berries wouldn't do much to fill us.

"I thought those were poisonous," Graves demanded.

"Oh, no," Coron shook his head. "Just the purple ones."

"I had a red one."

"Really? It looked purple to me."

Coron made his way to a tree and leaned back against it, sliding down with the help of his stick.

"There is a trading post between here and the monastery, where supplies can be purchased," Coron said through a weak yawn. "I wouldn't be welcome there, but the rest of you could enter. Even you Spider, so long as you keep that hand bandaged."

I looked at the place where the rot had started for me, flipping my hand over to the unblemished side and back again. Already that entire arm under my tunic was wrapped to prevent flaking, and there were other spots on my body itching with maddening insistence, where I was afraid would show signs of rot when I had time to look. Graves was right about one thing—I had no intention of dying this way.

Nila set off with some lengths of thin cord for snares and a small knife. Well, small for her. In my hand, her knife would be a machete. With luck, those traps will net us some breakfast before morning, if not then we would see how many berries it took to fill a person.

Graves had gone off searching for the edible roots Coron had spoken of. He'd been listening in when the priest described how and where to find them, though the wizard would acknowledge nothing of the sort. He'd left the camp, his fingers twitching and ready to cast.

I set to getting a fire going, not wanting to admit how tired I was from the day. Once the camp was set up and ready for the night, I allowed myself a chance to lean back and close my eyes.

Silent, fitful dreams waited behind my eyes.

"Spider!"

Not so silent after all.

"Spider!"

My eyes shot open as Graves came rushing back into the camp, eyes wide and wild.

"What is it?" I asked, then realized. "What did you cast?"

"I was hungry, casting a spell for food, and my mind was on the bacon from the inn—"

"The bacon you turned back into pigs?"

"Yes, that bacon," he said, frustrated. "What other bacon...? Never mind. Anyway—"

A crashing noise came from the forest.

"What did you cast?" I repeated, getting to my feet.

"Well, like I said, I was thinking of bacon. I conjured up—"

At that a great boar charged from between the trees and stopped, staring at Graves and myself. It was as massive as that one from the cage below the warehouse in Timurpajan and even looked to be the same breed.

The pig's eyes found me, one a deep black and the other a baleful red.

"No! It can't be."

The boar squealed in recognition and charged

"Is that any way to treat the guy who freed you?" I asked.

As the pig reached me, stomping our blankets and bedrolls put out for the night, I dodged right.

"I thought we were friends, brother boar."

It rushed at me again.

Hmm, guess not.

True, I had freed it from the cage, but I had also taunted the poor beast and given it a slap on the ass.

"Hey there," I said in my most amiable voice. "Remember those two guards you stomped?"

The boar destroyed our fire as it passed through, not even registering the flames or heat. It squealed in fury and frustration as I dodged again. This time I slipped on a blanket and fought to regain my balance. The weakness of my disease had taken its toll, and there wouldn't be enough energy to dodge a third time.

Off to my left Graves weaved his hands, ready to cast. Negating the spell wouldn't help this time. He hadn't created this boar, he'd only brought it here.

The creature scuffed the ground with one hoof, and I could swear it was smiling, knowing it had me now. Wild muscles bunched as it took the first step to charge.

All my hopes were on Graves's spell.

With my recent luck, the boar would be duplicated or grown to monstrous size...*more* monstrous size.

To my left came a pop, a flash of yellow smoke, then silence. Graves wore confusion on his face, staring at his hands that had misfired.

Great.

Then Nila was there, soaring through the air and into the boar. The two hit the ground in a writhing mass of fur and braid, muscle and tusk. The two wrestled until Nila got both feet between her and the pig, kicking out. The boar flew a few feet and slammed into a tree, jumping back to its feet and glaring at the giant opposition before it. Nila howled. The pig stopped, took a step back, head cocked to one side. Realizing it had found one wilder than itself, the pig took a last glance at me, snorted its disgust, then turned and bolted back into the forest.

We three stared at where the boar had disappeared, while Coron remained reclined against the tree, his ability to sleep more to do with exhaustion.

"Damn," Nila said. "I'll never catch it now."

With the danger over, it occurred to us that the boar was also potential food, though I'm not sure I could have eaten this particular pig.

"So." Nila turned to Graves. "Tried to cast food? Or pissed off a boar in the woods?"

"Well, um...food actually."

She looked into the trees then back again. "A little underdone for my taste."

She smiled at Graves and the wizard, for one instant, returned the smile. For whatever reason he accepted her. Maybe because they were both capable of destruction without trying.

Nila stayed awake late that night after our meagre dinner hoping the boar might return, but no further sound of the beast could be heard. It had well and truly escaped the cultists this time, and I was glad for that, even if it did try to kill me.

I drifted to sleep, imagining the confusion the boar's disappearance was going to cause and had better dreams for it.

In the morning we were *very* lucky. One of Nila's snares had netted us a rabbit. Spread between four people it didn't amount to much, though Coron only nibbled.

"You should eat," Nila said.

She was staring at me rather than the priest. The food in front of me was untouched.

"No appetite?" she asked.

I shook my head but forced myself to eat.

"How far is this trading post?" I asked.

"We'll reach it by evening," Coron answered.

"Evening? Will they be open?"

"Oh yes. Always. They are a trading outpost but also do business in...less legal items."

"Black market?"

Coron rummaged in the pocket of his travel robe, pulling out some coins. He jingled them then passed the handful of unfamiliar currency to me. Hopefully, this would buy enough food to get us to the monastery.

Speaking of the monastery, I did some quick calculations in my head. "Aren't we cutting it a bit close for getting you home, Coron?"

The priest gave one quick nod, adding nothing and I dropped the subject. He knew. When we met him, he was already on day five of the disease, plus the three we would spend travelling brought us to eight. He said the disease took ten days, but what if it advanced quicker in some people?

Cheerful thoughts.

No, there were two days of wiggle room in his disease, and that would be enough. It had to be.

Our journey was quiet that morning. Coron had explained what the coins were worth and how little we could expect to get with them, but even caravan rations sounded like a delicacy now.

Nila had fashioned a spear using a straight-ish stick she'd found, her dinner knife and some trapping twine. It would have worked well if she could find anything to throw it at, but the forest was quiet. It seemed all the animals were smart enough to hide from us hungry bipeds.

CHAPTER 14
THE TRADING OUTPOST

The stop at noon was lunch in name only. It was more of an opportunity for Coron and myself to rest. We'd gathered berries along the path that morning, but these only stopped us from starving. Images of Lees's spiced potatoes danced in my memories. Would I ever taste them again? Well, I *did* know the recipe so could always make them myself if we were stuck on this side of the mountains.

"No."

Nila turned, one eyebrow raised.

"Sorry, didn't realize I was speaking out loud."

She shrugged.

"I was just thinking, having humans on both sides of these mountains couldn't be a coincidence. There must be a way through."

"Or used to be," Nila said.

I lapsed back into silence and so did Nila, keeping her eyes open for signs of food to hunt.

"It's like everything's gone into hiding," she said.

Something came to me that should have come sooner. This disease was muddling my mind as well as making me weak. I saw in Nila's eyes the conclusion I'd reached.

"We aren't the only predator in this forest," I said.

She shook her head.

Afternoon wore on and became evening, bringing with it a desire for something more than berries.

"The outpost," Coron said, through attempts to catch his breath, "is just ahead. Maybe...five...minutes."

The smell of burning wood carried to us here. That meant a stove or fireplace, and possibly hot food.

"Are you okay?" I asked.

"Yeah," he gasped and leaned against a tree for support. His hand holding the walking stick gripped tighter, pressing it into the ground.

"I'll...wait...here."

Nila shook her head.

"That might not be a good idea," I said. "There's something else in these woods, scaring all the wildlife off."

Coron went silent, head drooping.

"What is it?" Graves asked. "What's out there?"

"No idea."

"Oh, that's just great."

"I'm not a fortune teller," I snapped.

The wizard took a step back, and I closed my eyes. "Sorry. I'm tired, and this itch is maddening."

Graves took a further step away. I ignored it.

Coron's head popped up. "There *is*...something out there...but I can't...sense what." He gasped in several breaths. "If I wasn't so...distracted...I would have—"

"Is it close?" Graves interrupted, the first time he'd spoken directly to Coron all day.

Coron listened more and shook his head.

"Nonetheless, you can't stay here," I said.

Coron started forward again. I offered him my shoulder, but he shook his head with a smile of thanks.

"When we get to the outpost, Graves and I will go in for supplies," I said.

"Sure you don't want me to get you a fair price?" Nila asked.

I imagined her there with hands on hips, smiling.

"No... I mean, yes, that would be ideal, but I can handle traders. You may be needed more outside."

Whatever was in these woods, it wasn't as simple as a wolf or bear. That wouldn't quiet an entire forest or scare all the animals into hiding. Nila would be most intimidating for this creature if it came around.

The path we'd been following curved and came into an open area housing the trading post. The full moon had risen, painting the clearing and building with its light.

"Aw, hell," Graves muttered.

The building itself was more or less still there, though it looked as if they'd gone through battle. Windows were broken, as were all of the barrels and supplies that had been stored outside. Two wagons were overturned, their horses missing with bloody smears where the unfortunate animals should have been.

The outpost itself had a fire at the end away from the entrance. Flames shot from the missing windows, helping the moon light the clearing.

"The food," Coron said.

We understood. Whatever happened here had already happened, but we still needed that food. Nila and I both shot forward, Graves moving to follow us after glancing at Coron and realizing he would be alone with the bandaged man.

"Stay with him," I shouted, and the wizard stopped.

We burst through the front door which hung from one hinge and into the shadowed interior of the trading post. Fire raged in the back half of the building, behind double doors. No danger of burning yet, but no help with seeing. We started scrounging for anything we could find through touch.

"Light."

A glowing orb hovered above our heads, and I turned to see Graves in the doorway.

"He's just outside the door," Graves said, seeing the expression on my face. "I didn't desert him."

I nodded. In truth, the light was most welcome until we saw the inside.

Dead men lay everywhere, draped over tables, dead on the floor, all torn to pieces by whatever stalked those woods.

"Coron," I called. "Come inside. You don't want to be out there."

Nila glanced around. "Inside didn't help these guys."

That was true too, but we would take our chances.

A counter stretched the entire length of the outpost, floor to ceiling shelves behind it with all manner of products from books to tools. Judging by the tables and chairs arranged on this side, the counter acted as a bar too.

Coron staggered into the building, dropping his walking stick and leaning against the nearest wall. He slid down it, unaware of the grim surroundings.

"Graves," I said, snapping his attention away from the bodies and back to me.

"It's like the bears," he said.

It *was* similar.

"Bears?" Nila asked.

"Oh, we had a problem with some bears on the last caravan ride."

"Ah."

"Magic bears," Graves added.

"Oh, I want to hear that story later," Nila said.

"Graves, do you think your magic can do something about that fire?"

Yes, we were that desperate.

The wizard turned toward the double doors leading into the outpost's back half, presumably a storage area. Smoke came from a gap at the bottom and light from the flames inside outlined them. He half-shrugged and moved forward while Nila and I returned to our search.

"Found a sack of nuts here," Nila said, throwing it onto the counter.

Nuts sounded like a feast, and where there were nuts, there would be other food. Most of the sacks and barrels had been torn open or smashed, whatever they'd held either gone or spilled.

"Don't eat..." Coron gasped. "Any...open...don't..."

"Coron?" Nila asked, but he was already unconscious, head sagging against his chest.

What Coron said made sense. Without knowing what had caused this damage, it wouldn't be safe to eat anything exposed. We could infect ourselves with something worse than the rot, something that *couldn't* be cured by a healer.

"Uh-oh," Graves said.

We spun toward the wizard who retreated from the double doors. They no longer glowed with the flames of the next room, but both doors bulged against some internal pressure.

"Graves, what...?" I started.

Before finishing that thought, the bulging doors slammed open. A deluge of water rushed through, knocking Graves off his feet. I wondered about the water not exiting through the broken windows of the back room, then the wave hammered me down as well. Nila set her feet in a solid stance, grabbing the counter for balance. The water rushed against her, up to her thighs, her eyes wide and nostrils flaring at the experience.

Graves went hurtling past me, headed for the front door as I managed a one-handed grasp on a table. That didn't last, and I followed close behind him. The flood reached Coron, bouncing him off the door frame then out the exit.

At the door, Graves managed to grasp the frame for a second before I shot into him feet first and we flew out the door together in a tangled,

167

writhing bunch of bruised arms and legs. Outside we rolled toward Coron, Graves spinning to avoid just that. We ended up lying in the sodden grass outside the outpost, Coron still unconscious.

I got a hand under me which decided *not* to hold my weight and deposited me face first into a puddle.

"Gods!" I muttered, rolling onto my back and looking at the unconscious priest.

"Fire's out," Nila said from the doorway.

Graves tried to disentangle himself from the soaking robes which weighed him down, slipping onto his backside. Then, with as much grace as a troll dancing a jig, he managed to get to his feet.

Lying on the ground, bruised and battered, I started giggling.

Graves spun on me, indignant.

It was the perfect reaction, and I rocked with laughter.

Nila snorted.

Graves peered around at the wet carnage. All the dead bodies which had been inside and much of the furniture and supplies now littered the outpost's lawn. It looked like a slaughterhouse.

He gave his half-shrug. "Careful what you wish for."

Still laughing, I got to one knee. Graves stepped toward me, one hand out before remembering my condition. He stepped back again. I waved a hand, pretending not to notice his change of mind.

"Thanks," I said. "I can do it."

Somewhere deep inside I found the strength to get upright then went to Coron, pulling him up and throwing him over a shoulder.

The man weighed so little.

I brought the priest back inside. From the jumble of furniture against the inside wall, I pulled a chair with arms, something Coron could lean on without toppling. Graves and Nila stood in the doorway.

"Do we still have that sack of nuts?" I asked.

Nila nodded. She'd had the presence of mind to not only hold onto them with her free hand but to hold them above the water. We continued our search of the soggy interior. Behind the counter, a few canisters of unknown goods sat on higher shelves. Nila jumped over and grabbed the closest one.

"Jerky," she said.

My mouth watered. I didn't care if it was orc jerky at this point... Well, okay, maybe not orc. The other canisters held similar items. It wouldn't provide a fancy meal but would fill that hole we each felt.

"Huh!" Nila said.

I turned toward her.

"Check this out," she said, tossing something small toward me.

I caught it one handed and saw it was a ring that might have once been someone's wedding band. Nothing remarkable really.

"Is that gold?" Graves asked.

"Too light. Something cheaper. Won't buy us any meals I'm afraid."

I held the ring out toward Nila, and she raised one hand.

"Won't fit any of my fingers," she said.

I looked at Graves who shook his head. He wouldn't touch the ring now that it had been in my hands, not until it had been boiled in vinegar anyway. I slipped it onto my hand for safe keeping.

Graves groaned. "You ever listen to those stories where a ring is cursed?"

I pulled it off my finger without a problem and slid it back on again. "Can you tell if my precious is magical?"

"Why did you say it like that?"

I shrugged. "It just seemed appropriate."

"In any case, no. I can't tell if it's magical unless you want me to—"

A cough came from our right. I turned, expecting Coron to be moving but it wasn't him.

"Someone's here," Nila said.

We searched the interior, pushing toppled benches and kegs aside, tossing splits sacks of goods. Under one pile was a man, blond hair dyed red with his own blood. Three claw marks had been raked down the right side of his face, obliterating one eye and most of his nose.

We crouched in front of the man, leaning him against some open sacks. One of his arms was gone from the elbow.

"Gods!" I said. "What—"

"Wolf..." the man gasped.

"Wolf?" Nila said. "A wolf did this?"

The man shook his head. "Wolf..."

"A pack of wolves?" Graves asked. "Dire wolf?"

He shook his head again, fading. The man wouldn't last.

"Let him talk," I said.

"Were...wolf."

Graves spun toward the open door as if expecting it to be there. The door was empty, and the man on the floor was dead.

"Werewolf," I repeated.

Graves rushed over to close the door. It hung by one hinge but he was able to wrestle it into the frame, sealing us inside.

"That didn't help these guys," I pointed out.

"Yeah, well, neither will an open door."

True enough.

"It's been here already," Nila said. "It won't be back tonight."

"Are you an expert on these monsters?" Graves said, the start of panic in his voice.

"We have them in my home realm too."

Graves opened his mouth, then shut it and nodded, accepting Nila as the closest to an expert that we had.

"Okay, let's get a dinner going," I suggested. "We'll think better on a full stomach."

We had nuts, jerky, some dried fruits and vegetables, and best of all an entire keg of beer. Not as tasty as what Lees made, but at that moment it sure gave hers some competition.

Coron roused, looking around with a drowsy, heavy-lidded expression at the water and destruction. He raised one eyebrow then was back to sleep, not even questioning why he was wet and bruised. Tomorrow he could eat while we hiked, but for now, sleep was more important.

Nila cleaned out the iron stove at the room's centre, getting a fire started, the smoke going up through the chimney. We would have to hope the smell of fire wouldn't attract the monster stalking these woods, but what other choice did we have? It was either get dry or get sick.

The skin under my bandages felt like pasty liquid, a sickly-sweet smell of dying flesh wafting out from between layers. I shuddered to touch them, imagining what it had to be like for Coron.

He was down to two days left.

Our bedrolls dripped with water, as did any changes of clothes and the packs themselves. We arranged ourselves around the stove on chairs that dried quicker than the floor would. It wasn't a comfortable sleep, but it was better than sleeping outside without a tent.

The back room had once held storage. Those black market items? We wouldn't know for sure now. All that remained were blackened shelving and one charred lantern, which must have been the starter of the blaze.

We took turns keeping watch so this beast didn't surprise us in the night, though I accepted Nila's assessment that it wouldn't be back.

Better safe than sorry.

THE WAYWARD SPIDER

My father hadn't spoken in a while, maybe because there were others to talk with now. Whatever the case may be, it was comforting to hear his voice, even if only inside my head.

"That's not even one of yours," I mumbled, drifting to sleep.

Shouldn't surprise you. I was a thief you know.

I chuckled to myself and slept a dreamless sleep.

CHAPTER 15
A TRIP THROUGH THE WOODS

I woke to the smell of coffee, sure it was a dream or imagination. But it wasn't.

"Found an intact bag," Nila said. "Outside."

I didn't care if each bean had passed through that werewolf before brewing. The coffee woke me, and even Coron drank a full cup of it. That wasn't all though. A smell of something meaty frying turned out to be jerky heating in a pan on the stove. It would never replace bacon, but for now, it was delicious. We each had three strips, and when Coron didn't want his, a fourth.

Nila sighed, enjoying the coffee she sipped from her metal tankard. This was the happiest we'd been in days...well, content might have been a better word.

The bedrolls and packs had dried overnight, and we had salvaged enough food to keep us going. The situation was improving, assuming we weren't horribly killed by the werewolf come nightfall.

"Hey," I said, "you didn't wake me for my turn on watch."

Nila shook her head. "We managed. You needed the sleep more."

Graves agreed. It was daylight, and he'd been outside to cast a spell and back again.

I glanced around at our little group, finding my sentiments disconcerting. I'd never wanted to be around other people, never had much use for them outside of Dad, Gar, and Lees, yet somewhere in the past few days, these three had wormed their way into my life. They'd gone from a chore weighing me down to people I cared about and who cared back.

I wasn't sure I liked this. Worse, I wasn't sure I didn't.

We packed our now dry belongings and the supplies and got going, wanting to be far outside the werewolf's territory by the time night came. The slowing factor was Coron and to a lesser degree, myself.

After an hour of hiking, we came to a bend in the road, the rough path continuing north.

"We need to pass...through the woods...," Coron gasped, "to get to...the monastery."

"Well, that's just great," Graves said, back to his usual pleasant self. "Would have been nice to know—"

"Graves," I said, and the wizard drifted off to a grumble.

"So, is there a path?" Nila asked.

"I don't...think so."

"You don't think...?" Graves said. "Haven't you passed this way before?"

"No."

"You... Then... What?" Graves sputtered.

"Are you sure the road won't take us there?" I asked.

"Eventually," Coron agreed. "In a few days."

"Ah," I said.

Coron did not have the luxury of days.

"And...we need to get out...of these woods...before night."

No one needed a reminder.

Graves threw his hands up. "Well, if we're going to stroll through the trees, let's just get started."

The wizard wasn't happy, and I couldn't blame him. We'd been travelling a two-people-wide path through the woods, easy to see. Now we were starting at an unavoidable, stumbling shortcut through the trees.

No sense overthinking something you'll end up doing anyway.

We got moving.

Unease dogged our steps the rest of the day, even though we knew the werewolf couldn't be coming until night, and even then, maybe miles away. The nervousness came from what we *didn't* know. What else could be in these trees that would make a werewolf appear tame?

Lunch was a rushed affair, eating on a tree downed with age while Coron napped. As soon as we woke the priest, he was itching to go, though he could have used much more rest. He stumbled over roots and rocks, often needing the trees for balance even with the help of his walking stick.

He came to a stop, dead on his feet. "You should...leave me here...."

"What?" I said. "No."

"I can continue...on my own. You're in...danger."

"We're always in danger," Graves mumbled. His eyes were wide, glancing all around us, jumping at every sound.

"We're not deserting you," Nila said, voice firm.

"Thank you...my friends," Coron said.

Then he collapsed.

"I'll carry him," I said.

Nila shook her head. "You're not much better. I'll do it."

"You can't do that," Graves chimed in. "The rot."

"It's a human disease. Maybe I'm immune."

"And maybe you *can* catch it, but the priestess can't cure you."

True concern was etched on his face. Nila considered.

"Wrap him in a bedroll," she said, "but keep his face free to breathe."

I did as she asked and placed him on Nila's shoulder. Graves still didn't like it but could see no one would listen. He turned and headed in the direction we'd been going.

The rest of that day was spent in deeper silence, no one interested in conversation, concentrating on the exhausting task of putting one foot in front of another.

The sun was low in the sky when we broke through the final line of trees and out onto another open plain. Even the air changed, was sweeter and less stifling, with a slight breeze. Nila placed Coron on his feet and the priest, now awake though no steadier, looked at her with mournful eyes.

"You shouldn't...have done that," he said.

Nila shrugged in way of answer and started marching in wide circles, taking great strides and working leg muscles which hadn't been stretched since morning.

Coron oriented himself while working his way out of the bedroll.

"The monastery...is that way," he said, pointing in a direction I think was west but wouldn't have bet my clean socks on if I had any.

The man was ready to pass out again.

I shook my head. "We need a place to make camp for the night."

"How about there?" Nila asked.

She pointed at a boarded, one-room cabin, tucked back into the tree line. A simple porch with two rough rocking-chairs occupied the front.

"A hunting cabin?" I asked.

"Maybe," Coron said.

A cabin sounded better than sleeping on the unforgiving ground again and would be some protection if we weren't out of the werewolf's territory yet. With unspoken agreement, we all headed for the abandoned structure. Coron swayed with each step, even though he'd spent the last hours unconscious. I wasn't particularly steady either and was sure Graves and Nila were ready for sleep too.

The door swung open and we were looking down the shaft of a loaded crossbow.

Not abandoned after all.

The weapon swung toward Nila and rested there before lowering.

"Git inside, you idiots," the old man on the other end said.

He was human, like everyone else we'd seen on this side of the mountains, and at least into his seventies. He was also built like a beer barrel, with arms like a troll. This guy wasn't someone to challenge to an arm wrestling—unless Nila was up for it.

With the business end of the crossbow he gestured toward the open door, but his eyes scanned the woods and plain.

Coron staggered through, followed by Graves. Nila gave me an arched eyebrow, and I returned a *do we have any better options* kind of expression. We followed. The man backed in and slammed the thick door closed behind us. He put the crossbow down and slid a thick length of timber into place to secure it.

Inside, the cabin was sparsely furnished with a table, two chairs and two beds, all made from the same rough wood. On one wall was a fireplace with a pot of something delicious over the flames. There were two windows, one on each side of the cabin, each of them boarded with planks of wood.

Coron slid into one of the chairs and leaned against the seat back. Graves headed to the fire, warming his hands.

The man turned toward us, a glint in his eyes.

"The werewolf?" I asked, gesturing at the windows.

The man jerked his head toward me, mouth opening. "You seen it?"

I shook my head. "Saw its handiwork, though."

The man cocked his head to one side, and we told the story of what we'd found at the outpost, skipping the part where Graves almost drowned us in the middle of a forest.

"Ah, poor folk. I knew most of 'em. Hunters 'n trappers, traders 'n rogues. Not all good, but no one that bad either."

We nodded, having nothing to add to that epitaph.

"That monster, it's come every night fer the past couple weeks," the man said, "sniffin' 'round outside, but never tryin' to get in. Leastwise, not yet."

"During the full moon?" I asked.

"Durin' any moon. That full moon stuff's just stories."

He moved to the fire and threw another log on, Graves shifting to get out of the man's way.

"Warm enough yet, lad?" he asked, clapping one hand on the wizard's shoulder.

Graves grunted his thanks, and the man turned back to the room. He gestured to the other empty chair which I took. Nila inspected the window boards while Graves was happier at the fire.

"I'm Xareb, by the way."

I introduced each of us, ending with Nila.

"Thought y'were the beast fer a minute there," the man said. "Was ready to shoot ya."

Nila grunted.

"No offence," he said, holding up one hand.

"How could I take offence?" she grumbled.

Xareb grunted now, sounding much like Nila. "Got no problem with non-humans. Not used to seein' 'em around here is all. Most folk 'round here are humans."

"Sounds boring," Nila said.

"Are there many people around?" I interrupted.

"Less and less, 'cause of that creature," Xareb said. "Lots of cabins out here fer people not wantin' to live in cities with all their rules."

That was something I could appreciate.

"Used to live here with my son. He disappeared, him an' his dog."

The last was said in a low voice, staring at the floor.

"Barex and Pup, that was his dog, went 'splorin some caves he'd found an' didn't come back. I..."

Xareb looked at his crossbow and the ready bolt. The tip was made of silver. The man gave the impression of being uneducated, but that didn't make him stupid.

"For the werewolf?" Nila asked.

He nodded, a flash of steel in his eyes. "They woulda been the beast's first victims, disappearin' 'bout when it showed up. Pup woulda defended Barex to the death, and my son never woulda left his dog neither."

Silence filled the cabin until Xareb roused himself. "Ah, you must be hungry. Only got two bowls, so you'll need ta share."

He returned to the fire and pulled the lid off, allowing a rich aroma to waft through his cabin and make our stomachs rumble.

"We have our own bowls, Xareb," I said. "No need to dirty yours."

Graves got out of Xareb's way again, moving to beside me. "We're leaving after dinner, right?"

"Want to leave already, lad?" Xareb said, without turning from the pot he stirred.

"I..." Graves said.

"Suit yerself. The beast roams them plains too, though."

Graves looked at me. Then back to Xareb.

"Make you a deal, though," the man said. "You help destroy this monster what killed my boy, and you can have s'much food as y'like, and a place to sleep."

Graves rolled his eyes at me, but the scent of that food and thought of a soft place to sleep had already made his decision. The wizard grumbled and returned to the fire's warmth.

"Nila?" I asked.

"Too late to leave now," she said. "Besides, Coron needs sleep."

I'd come to much the same conclusion, but my head was kind of fuzzy and I didn't trust it. It was comforting to hear Nila agree.

"Of course we'll help, Xareb," I said.

179

Without looking around, Xareb started scooping stew into the two bowls he held and passed them to Graves and me. Nila pulled her own larger metal bowl from the pack. It was filled as well.

Coron continued to sleep in the chair, head down.

"He's got the rot, does he?" Xareb asked.

I agreed, and the man shrugged as if that happened to everyone eventually.

"That doesn't bother you?" Graves asked. "This disease?"

"Long as he keeps bandaged."

Graves sputtered in confusion and outrage.

"Lad, I gots a werewolf comin' to visit every night. The rot don't hold much intimidation fer me right now."

I could have laughed at that, if not for the solemnity with which Xareb said it. No, he'd lost his son, and there was nothing funny in that.

Nila was halfway through her bowl, teaching me the value of shutting up and eating. Graves had started as well, and I joined in, lifting the spoon to my mouth.

The heavy door was assaulted from outside, something immense and strong slamming into it, the wooden beam creaking in protest.

A second attack followed, but we'd already started moving. I deposited my spoon and bowl onto the table with regret, while Nila got to her feet, grabbing for the stone war-hammer at her waist. Graves stood ready, a step behind us where he would have the chance to cast, mind and lips working.

Coron continued to sleep.

A third impact to the door, the beam groaning and starting to splinter.

I pulled the two daggers at my back, aware of how inadequate they would be not being made of silver.

The next barrage cracked the beam, the door flying inward to slam against the wall. In the opening seethed seven feet of hairy, snarling nightmare.

Xareb scrambled forward, trying to get at his crossbow, and getting a backhanded slap from the werewolf instead. Nila barrelled forward, slamming into the creature shoulder first and propelling it back out of the cabin.

Graves and I rushed to follow them onto the cabin's front yard, watching Nila jump backward and away from the beast. It had landed ready, swiping one swift arm out, only narrowly missing her.

"Don't let it scratch you," I warned.

Nila shook her head.

The werewolf howled, glaring at each of us with red, haunted eyes.

Xareb pushed past, raising his crossbow to level at the creature's heart.

"Do you have more bolts than the one?" I asked.

"What?"

"More than one? What do you do if you miss?"

The crossbow wavered. "What d'you suggest?"

"Wait for a guaranteed shot."

Xareb thought about this and gave one quick nod, crossbow aimed at the werewolf's frenziedly moving torso and heart.

Graves and I went left, me in front as an obstacle to give the wizard an opportunity to cast. Nila went right, war hammer raised, a fierce bellow in her throat. No one would ever suspect this woman didn't like violence. Xareb crouched in a straight line with the monster, awaiting that perfect shot.

The werewolf came our way, slavering and growling, the smell of mangy dog preceding it. Graves stepped back, hands working. I readied myself to take the attack, reminding myself to stay clear of those claws. One scratch and the rot would be a blessing by comparison.

"Freeze!" Graves yelled, like a city guard chasing a fleeing thief.

A flash of amber eyes and magical force shot from his hands, passing so close by my head that there were actual stars. The temperature around us plummeted, bringing it down to a brisk, winter air. Steamy breath plumed from the werewolf's mouth, and it stopped, confused by the change in its environment.

"Almost," Graves muttered.

With a shake of its head, the werewolf returned the attention to us, a deeper growl in its throat as it coiled to spring on me.

"Graves!" I yelled.

As the monster started its leap, Nila was there behind it. She grabbed one arm, twisting it behind the creature's back while snaking the other around its neck.

The werewolf writhed and bucked, lifting Nila from the ground, though the two were similar height. With a twist of shoulders, Nila was brought up and over the werewolf to be slammed into the ground at its feet.

"Graves," she shouted. "Again."

This time I ducked.

"Freeze!"

If the temperature declined much more, we would be rooted to the spot, frozen solid. The werewolf was wearing fur and would survive that change better than any of us.

When I turned again, I found sharp teeth poised to take a bite from me. I backpedalled, making the noises any creature makes when sure they are about to be eaten.

The werewolf didn't move.

It *had* frozen.

The spell had worked as requested when we needed it most.

Graves wore a stunned expression to match my own.

Over on the porch, Xareb saw his opportunity, aiming his crossbow at the unmoving creature's heart. His finger tightened.

"No!" Coron said, appearing in the doorway. He bumped our host's arm, sending the silver bolt shooting into the dirt at the werewolf's feet.

The man rounded on the priest. "Why? That beast killed my son."

Coron shook his head, sinking into one of the rocking chairs. "No. I think...it *is* your son."

Xareb spun toward the beast. "My son? How?"

"You said...werewolf...came around...after...he disappeared?"

"Yeah, him and Pup. And?"

"Too much...coincidence... What if your son...was cursed?"

Xareb stared at the werewolf, dropping the empty crossbow to his side. Hope leapt into his eyes for the son he'd resigned to death.

We all approached the beast, looking at the open mouth of sharp teeth, the eyes which moved in quick jerks. It breathed but was completely paralyzed.

"Can you do anything?" I asked Coron.

"I can try."

He sat cross-legged in front of the werewolf, chanting, beseeching his god. The ritual took fifteen minutes, and at the end, Coron collapsed.

"That's...all...I can..."

He was already unconscious, or at least I hoped that's all it was. His bandages were soaked in sweat.

"Whew," I said, relieved to find a pulse at Coron's neck.

"Look," Nila said.

A pale golden glow surrounded the werewolf, growing with each second until the beast was engulfed and the brightness forced us to turn away.

"Barex?" the father said, stepping toward the light. "Barex, can y'hear me?"

The werewolf let out a sharp bark as the glow receded. Nila raised her hammer, bracing for a renewed attack, while on my other side Graves's fingers twitched in readiness. I took a step back, wondering where I could drop Coron to help my friends.

The glow receded leaving an after image, like looking into the sun for too long.

"Barex?" the man said, hope in his voice.

Another bark.

"Xareb," I warned, "maybe you should—"

A furry shape on four legs bolted from the night, jumping up to place front paws against the older man's chest.

"Pup?"

Pup gave a happy bark and licked Xareb's face. The dog was only a fraction smaller than a wolf, though a lot less than a werewolf.

"Where did the dog come from?" Graves asked. "Where's the werewolf?"

"The dog was the werewolf," Nila said.

"But...where's Barex?" the man asked. "Where's my son?"

Pup dropped back onto all fours, giving a whine filled with such sorrow that the answer was clear. How had the dog become a werewolf though? That was something we couldn't know since Pup wasn't talking.

That night we slept inside, sharing the beds and eating the stew. Pup curled in a ball in front of the fire, while the old man remained outside on a rocker and waited for morning. He would be off at first light, the dog leading him to Barex's final resting place.

CHAPTER 16
MONASTERY

When we woke in the morning, both man and dog were gone. Except Coron *didn't* wake. He breathed and gave every sign of being in deep slumber, but we couldn't rouse him.

"Let him sleep," Graves said, scooping leftover stew into a bowl for breakfast. "Removing the curse exhausted him."

I looked at the wizard who half-shrugged.

"Like when I tried to cast all those portals and slept through the day. Some spells take more out of the caster."

"We need to get him to the monastery," I said. "It's his last day."

"I'm not touching him," Graves said.

I shook my head. "No, I'll carry him."

Nila snorted. "You'll never make it."

"I'm fine."

"Sure you are," she said. "That's why you lean against anything when you stop moving."

"I..."

"You wrap him up. I'll carry him again."

The tone in her voice said that she wouldn't take any argument on this. We took enough stew with us for lunch, but nothing more, making sure plenty was waiting for Xareb when he returned.

We left the cabin, closing the door behind us. The morning's brightness had us squinting after the dimness of the boarded-up cabin.

"Oh, gods!" Graves said, staring at me with eyes wide and taking half a step back.

"What?" I reached up and felt the papery texture of my face, all along the right-hand side. Flakes of skin fell.

"Don't touch it," Graves cautioned.

Nila set Coron down and rummaged through her pack, pulling spare bandages out.

"Better not touch me," I said in a low voice. "Just toss them here."

Already several spots under my leather tunic and pants were wrapped, but this was the first sign of it on my face. I hadn't thought of myself as vain, but this was a greater impact than all the rest of the disease's effects.

When I'd finished wrapping my face, Graves circled around me from a safe distance.

"Looks good," he muttered. "Didn't miss any spots."

I hoisted my pack. "Come on. The sooner we get there the better."

The day passed without incident. No werewolves. No dead bodies. No spells gone awry. Not that it was pleasant in any way. The sun beat down, sapping what strength I had and making me wonder how Coron had made it as far as he did before meeting us.

After lunch the monastery came into view, up on a hill like a mirage.

"Is it real?" I said in a low voice to myself, staggering toward it.

"Yep," Nila agreed. "I see it too."

"Huh, maybe not to myself."

Nila stopped, and I did as well, staring at her while I swayed. She reached out a hand that could have palmed my head, the way a child would a ball.

"Fever," she said.

"Fever? What fever? Coron doesn't have one."

Why was I needing to argue about this?

"Coron is unconscious," Nila reminded me, turning toward our wizard, several paces behind. "Graves, you need to guide Spider."

"I'm not touching him."

Nila said nothing, staring back at the wizard who fought to meet her gaze. She raised one eyebrow, and he glared down at his feet, muttering.

"Okay!" he spat, coming toward me. "Spider, grab my robe."

Before offering the robe to me, Graves inspected it, making sure there were no rips where our skin could meet by accident. I grabbed the robe, protesting the need and staggered after the other two.

Fifteen minutes later we entered the monastery and stopped in its entry, wondering what our next move was. Surely there was a bell rope to announce our entry.

"Bell rope. Bell rope. Bell rope," I muttered.

Why would anyone think I had a fever?

I don't have a fever. You have a fever.

Graves shook free of my grip, glaring at his robe like something that needed burning. Which was just what he was probably thinking.

The entry wasn't that big, but open doorways led in each direction. Straight ahead would be the room for prayer time and holding services, assuming they did things the same in this religion as they did on our side of the mountains.

"Greetings travellers."

A woman in immaculate white robes was suddenly in the door to our right, taking us in. She made no movement, only watching with the eyes of someone concerned. Her eyes fell on the bundle Nila carried, Coron's face sticking out from the bedroll.

The priestess gasped. "Coron?"

"Yes," I said. "He has the creeping rot."

"Ah, yes. He has problem curing that one, particularly on himself."

"He had no trouble passing it on though," Graves said.

She gazed at me. "Come in, please."

"Coron's in his last day," Nila said. "He needs attention soon."

"I see."

The priestess moved with the unhurried but steady stride of someone used to these happenings. We followed through the door straight ahead, passing from the entry into a somewhat wider room with an altar.

"Place him there," she said, gesturing.

We followed the priestess, passing rows of pews, five to a side, all facing forward. Nila dropped the still sleeping Coron onto the flat altar.

"He won't wake?" the priestess asked.

"He cured a werewolf last night," Nila grumbled.

"A were..." The priestess spun toward Coron. "No wonder he's still asleep. He must have drained any energy he had left. He's lucky to still breathe."

I knew how he felt. It would be nice to lie down and sleep for a month or so. My eyes closed. I swayed.

"Spider?" Nila said.

It was the last I heard before falling over backward.

#

When I awoke, I found myself in a bed.

Across the room was a second bed with Coron in it. The man slept, still wrapped in the same dirty bandages he'd been wearing when we'd arrived.

Had they been unable to cure him?

Reaching up, I found bandages still wrapped around my own head and could see the ones on my right arm.

"Leave those alone," a voice said with gentle firmness... Or was it firm gentleness? My mind was muddled.

Off to one side was the priestess, watching me.

"The rot has been reversed in yourself and my brother, but it takes time to draw it out."

I started to speak, but she raised a hand.

"Save your energy. You will be weak and dazed for some time yet. The disease coursed through you quicker than it did Coron, perhaps due to your elfin anatomy."

Reflexively, I reached for my hood and found the entire tunic had been removed.

"There are few elves left on this side of the mountains. The story is that most returned to your side ages ago."

I sat up straighter, or attempted to at least, collapsing back into the pillows. The priestess was right, I was weak.

She waved the unspoken question aside. "Yes, there is a way back, but not until you've rested. Your friends can make preparations."

"Nila? Graves?" My voice was a rasp, but I needed to ask. "How—"

"They're fine. No rot in them."

I cleared my throat and said with little volume, "Why couldn't Coron cure himself?"

"We each have those tasks we are better at, but the rot is not one of Coron's," she said. "He went to the rotter communities in the north to get better, trying to help those poor people."

"He almost died."

"It is our purpose, to help others. None of us want to die, but we will do what needs doing."

I liked this woman.

The world in front of me blurred and shimmered.

"Sleep," the priestess said.

And I did.

Next time I woke, Nila hunkered at the foot of my bed while Graves occupied the chair beside it. The wizard wore a priest's robe of white which was out of place on him. Nila wore the same one-piece tunic of fur and leather but recently cleaned.

"'Bout time," she said. "Must be nice to sleep all day."

Graves drummed his fingers against one leg. He wasn't twitchy so must have just cast.

"Purple's more your colour," I managed.

"Oh, I had that robe burned," Graves answered, "along with anything else you two might have touched."

"We have new bedrolls," Nila added. "Everything else has been sterilized and blessed."

It was surprising how much of my energy had returned. I wasn't ready to run but could now reposition myself in bed.

"How long was I out?" I asked.

"Day and a half," Nila said.

Graves nodded. "We came in yesterday after lunch."

That wasn't bad, not that we had anywhere to get to.

"Oh! There's a way home," I said.

Nila shoulders slumped.

Oops.

"But not one to your home, Nila?" I asked.

She shook her head. "Same answer the wizards gave. Without knowing which world I'd come from..." She waved a hand to show the rest of this story was well known, with an obvious ending. "When you're rested and healthy we'll head for the passage back."

"It's inside the caves," Graves said. "Where Xareb's son must have been exploring."

"Really? Then...there's other werewolves living there?"

Graves shook his head. "According to the priestess, if Pup had been turned by another werewolf then there would have been a whole pack in the area."

"Then how—"

"The caves are cursed," Nila said.

190

"But they *do* have a way to our side of the mountains." Graves was excited, animated.

"Excellent," I said. "Now, do we go back right away?"

"Why not?" Graves asked.

"Well, it seems there is a whole world here, and nothing pressing for us back home."

Except a cult chasing me for stealing some cheap goblet. Maybe by the time we head back, that will be cleared up. Norn would have gotten word to the king by now.

A whole civilization to set up trade routes with, once we knew how to get back and forth.

"I'm not interested in more adventure. You promised me a place to practice my magic." Graves looked off across the room at nothing in particular. "But that place could be on either side I suppose."

"No difference to me," Nila said, "but shouldn't we confirm there *is* a way back first?"

That did make sense. Knowing where the passage was didn't mean we had to take it right away. We could travel around. There must be something worth trading on this side, something unique and profitable that we could take back with us.

My gaze landed on the other bed and its occupant. "Has he been awake?"

"Off and on," Graves said. "Mostly delirious."

"Not the first time he's had that disease," Nila said.

"What? Seriously?"

Graves nodded again. "He can't cure it and goes north to practice. He comes back infected at least once a year."

I reached up and touched the bandages around my head.

"One more day," Graves said. "You aren't contagious, but the healing spell needs time to re-attach your skin."

"You'll have some scarring where you scratched," Nila added.

My right arm would be the worst for that, which was fine. At least I'd managed to resist scratching at my face. Though, now that I think about it, there were some flakes of skin that fell before the bandages went on. I'd find out tomorrow, I guess.

In the morning, as promised, my bandages came off. The monastery possessed mirrors, and I was able to inspect the scarring on my face. Not too long and off to the right, but still there. The ones on my arm were more noticeable, especially with my shirt off.

"You're pale," Nila said. "You need sun."

"I'm an elf. Elves are pale."

"Even for an elf, you're pale."

"You are quite pale, Spider," Graves agreed.

"Wish I'd had my shirt on when you two arrived."

"You could reflect sunlight," Nila added.

"Oh yes," Graves said. "Like the mirror."

"Could use you to send messages across a distance."

"Are you two done? Next time we need money you should do a comedy act."

"Hmm," Nila said.

Graves scratched at his chin.

"Almost transparent really," Nila said.

"Like the belly of a fish."

"Now we're done."

Graves agreed.

I grumbled to myself, getting back into my tunic. If the two of them *did* decide to do an act, I would be busy that night. Still, the fact Graves was joking gave me some hope.

Once I was dressed, we went searching for Coron who was gone from the other bed. The priest ate in the dining room, showing his first real appetite since we'd met him. He leaned to one side in the chair, balanced against the arm. It was obvious he still hadn't fully recovered.

He was more handsome than expected. No idea why but I thought he would be plain, maybe even ugly, under the bandages, but he wasn't. He would have been in his late thirties or early forties, with a strong jaw and wavy brown hair.

"Good morning, friends," he said and gestured to the empty chairs.

We joined him, starting to eat the food that had been laid out. It was all delicious, but the cheese was like none I'd ever tasted before. The texture was smooth, with a hint of saltiness and when my teeth sank in the cheese gave off a squeak.

"Phenomenal," I said.

"Our monks make it," Coron said. "An activity to clear their minds, yet people come from miles around to purchase it."

"I can see why," I agreed.

This cheese certainly fit the description of unique and tradeable. It would need to be transported with some speed, but we could have it to Grand Gesture in a couple of days. In colder months we could transport it through to other cities too. Hmm.

"Humph," Nila said.

Graves looked up from his food. "What?"

She gestured toward me with her fork. "We're going back after all."

"Have either of you tasted anything like this?" I asked, sure that I must have missed it in my travels.

Both shook their heads, Graves returning to his breakfast with a grumble about me making up my bloody mind.

"We could load your packs with this cheese before you leave," Coron suggested.

"That would be great."

Coron cleared his throat.

"Our monastery makes no profit," he said, looking down into his plate. "Save for the sale of this cheese which keeps us operating. We...rely on the kindness of those we help."

Nila glanced my way, giving a sideways nod toward Coron. It was true, they had indeed saved my life, as well as feeding and sheltering us.

"I hate to bring it up considering—"

"Considering we saved your life first?" Graves said.

"Yes," Coron replied, so low it was close to inaudible.

"Graves," I said.

"You *did* save my life," Coron said, looking at me.

"We saved each other, plus the monastery has fed us, replaced our bedrolls, given us a place to sleep, and is now stocking us with food to start a trade route."

Graves rolled his eyes, and I suppressed an urge to slap him.

"Without them, we wouldn't know the way back either," Nila pointed out.

Half-shrug.

I pulled out our pouch of coins, pouring it into my lap to separate into two equal piles. The one pile went back into our pouch as travelling money, the other I deposited in front of Coron.

"They aren't much use as coins," I said. "Not on this side of the mountains, but for the base worth of the metals?"

Coron thanked us, and the coins disappeared into his robe.

"I did want to thank you for helping me get home," he said. "I usually take a direct route and arrive in a few days, but this time I met with trouble. Intolerance of the rotters has risen in recent times."

I glanced at Graves who continued to eat, not looking the least embarrassed.

"So it's true," I said. "You've had the rot before."

"Several times. I am unable to cure it, but I keep trying, and I help these poor people in other ways."

"Maybe your god doesn't want the rotters cured," Graves said.

Coron stared at the wizard, letting an obvious anger diffuse. "My god is one of peace and love. All people are equal in Wagarial's eyes, even intolerant asses."

Graves either missed the inference or didn't care. He finished eating then wandered outside to cast a spell.

Coron watched him go, shaking his head sadly. "Any other disease or affliction I can help but not the rot."

"Why not?" I asked.

"I...That is..."

"Sorry, Coron. I didn't mean to pry."

"No, it's just... You see, both my parents died of the disease. I want very badly to help these people, but for some reason, I am not allowed to."

"Oh, Coron, I'm—"

"We can leave in the morning," the priest said, changing the subject.

"We? Are you coming with us?"

The priest joining us would be a welcome addition. If I had to travel with an ever-growing group then having one that could heal certainly made sense.

"I'll bring you to the caves on my way back."

"Back?" Nila asked. "To the rotter community?"

"Yes," Coron said. "There is still much to do there."

Strangely, I was disappointed. What happened to the elf thief who wanted to travel alone?

"You don't look strong enough to travel," Nila said.

"I'll be better by morning and will get more strength while we walk."

After breakfast Graves cornered me alone in the hallway.

"You know," he said, "some of those coins you gave away were mine."

I turned to the wizard, ready to give a retort, but he was in his pleasant spot, having recently cast a spell.

That, and he was right.

"I apologize, Graves," I said, pulling the pouch out and holding it toward him. "You are correct and I should have consulted you first."

Graves considered this, nodded once and strolled away without reaching for the pouch.

CHAPTER 17
BACK AGAIN

In the morning we packed our bags with supplies, including one whole backpack filled with delicious cheese.

"I'd like to say my thanks to your head priestess," I said.

"My sister has asked that I bid you farewell. She is in meditations and will be for several days."

"Your sister?"

"Yes, Karon is my true sister, from birth. A sister in two ways. We came here as children when our parents died. The followers of Wagarial took us in, trained us, gave us a purpose in life."

A purpose in life? Yes, that is essential. What is *my* purpose though? I thought it was trading and thieving, but somehow, it's become leading this group. Is this a permanent change? Are the two mutually exclusive? This was something needing serious thought, and luckily time to think was something we had plenty of.

The caves were close to Xareb's cabin, a full day from the monastery. We would impose on the man's hospitality again if he would have us. I was anxious to hear what he'd found about his son, hoping the man had found closure and could start the process of healing.

The day was beautiful, the sun wonderful on my face. For the first time in memory, I travelled with my hood down.

Once again, we had no incidents and had come to the conclusion that going to or from the monastery was about the only good luck zone for us. Hopefully, that would continue on our return trips.

Would it be the same group coming back though? Neither Nila nor Graves had a goal to be traders of cheese. Nila might be interested, at least until she found her way home, and Graves would be fine if he was comfortable and had time to practice.

Time will tell.

"Time always does, eh Dad?"

But the voice didn't sound like my father now. It had come to sound more and more like my own. Had I outgrown the need for him?

Something else to think about.

We arrived at Xareb's cabin after nightfall.

"Xareb," I called from a distance, remembering the crossbow. "Xareb, we've returned."

No response. We approached and knocked on the door.

Nothing. Not a sound. Pup should have at least barked a warning.

The door was unlocked.

Inside everything was as it had been when we'd left close to a week ago, except the fire had gone out, and the pot of delicious stew was congealed and inedible.

Xareb had never returned.

"We must find him," Coron said, stalking toward the door.

Graves yawned, obviously wishing only to sleep, but said nothing. Now that Coron had been healed, our wizard held no hostility toward him, or at least no more than he had for everyone. Coron, for his part, ignored Graves as much as possible.

"Can we find the caves in the dark?" I asked.

"I... I've never been there myself," Coron admitted, glancing at the door then back. "Karon told me how to find them, but..."

"As much as I want to find Xareb," I said, "we won't do him any favours getting lost in the woods tonight. We should sleep and set out at first light."

Coron turned and scowled at the door again. It wasn't in the priest's nature to not jump to someone's aid. I worried about our host too, but there was something more, something potentially worse. What if Xareb, Pup, or *both* of them returned in the night as werewolves, or something else?

A watch was set. We wanted neither to surprise the old man or be surprised *by* him.

Graves yawned again, louder. After a quick meal, he cast a spell without much result and crawled into bed, asleep in seconds. We watched in groups of two so beds wouldn't need to be shared, and I fell asleep to a conversation of Nila and Coron comparing gods.

Next morning we headed out, moving through the woods at a brisk pace. The caves were not easy to get to, up inside the mountain wall that separated us from home and off any path a person might follow. How had Xareb's son ever found these?

In all, there were ten cave entrances, each one leading to who knew where.

"My sister only told me of the cave that would lead you home," Coron admitted, pointing at one particular entrance.

"Let me guess," Graves said, "we aren't taking that route yet."

His voice was harsh, accusing, the man in need of casting a spell.

I shook my head. "We aren't abandoning Xareb."

That man had seen enough tragedy in his life.

Nila crouched, examining the dirt, then stood and moved toward the caves. She passed one entrance and stopped at the next. "This is where Xareb and his dog went."

"Oh yes?" Graves said. "And how can you be so sure?"

"If I explained tracking to you, would you understand?"

Graves stared at her before dropping his gaze.

Nila stepped in close to him. "Cast a light spell for us to see in there."

He nodded, pointing toward the cave entrance. "Light."

A boulder outside of the cave floated a foot off the ground and hovered there.

"Well," Nila said, looking at the floating rock. "It's lighter."

Graves sighed, and we pulled a couple of torches from the packs.

Inside, the cave was high enough for each of us to move upright in single file. Though Nila would rub shoulders against the stone unless she moved sideways.

"Nila leads the way," I said. "Then Coron. I'll take the back."

We entered the cave. Two steps in the temperature cooled by several degrees, though not unpleasantly. A breeze pushed past, fluttering the torches and telling me this cave had another exit. This was a place for finding forgotten treasures, or at least would have been in old tales.

We went slow, taking our time, with me examining every step for traps or a place where one of us could twist an ankle. While a cave might be the perfect hiding spot for treasure, it was also the sort of place where anything could live. There's a reason Xareb and Barex hadn't come home.

An hour of crawling through that cave gave us all a healthy respect for the place. Several spots had offshoots to choose from and tighter passages where Nila got the worst of squeezing through. It would take an expert mapper a lifetime to sketch all of these caves if the rest were similar to this one.

"Straight," Nila said at one junction. "They headed through here."

Her tracking skills were impressive, pointing out barely noticeable signs of Xareb and Pup. The cave walls were thankfully starting to widen.

Drip.

And the rocks were becoming slick with cave water.

"Stop!" Coron said.

We all halted in mid-step, looking for the danger. Coron stepped forward and inspected the moisture on the ground, then looked at the ceiling.

Drip.

"Come on," he said, "but let me lead."

The priest squeezed around Nila with some effort and a little contortion on both their parts then headed forward, keeping an eye on the roof. Several times he slipped in the moisture and Nila grabbed his arm to keep him from falling.

Drip.

The area widened as we went, and the steady sounds of cave water grew from ahead. Coron tensed at the sound.

Drip. Drip.

At least Nila was able to move straight again without rubbing her shoulders against the walls. She stretched her aching muscles as we headed forward.

"Stop here," Coron said.

We did.

Drip. Drip. Drip.

The sounds of water had grown until we should have been able to see the source.

Drip. Drip. Drip.

Coron stepped forward one step, two steps, and gestured for us to do the same.

Graves breathed his annoyance at all the skulking.

"There," Coron said.

We stepped up next to the priest and saw what he pointed at. About eight feet from us, a figure with a dog pressed against his leg.

"Xareb," I called, stepping forward.

Coron put a hand out to stop me. He shook his head.

"Look at them," he said.

Neither Xareb nor the dog had moved, as motionless as statues.

"Xareb," I repeated, though heard the doubt in my own voice.

Drip. Drip. Drip.

"What happened to them?" I asked the priest.

Coron took another cautious step, and we all followed. Out of the gloom came another figure, close to Xareb and also with no hint of movement.

"Must be Barex," Nila grumbled.

Drip. Drip. Drip.

All three stood in poses which would have been casual if they'd been moving. As it was, the stances were awkward. Barex had one hand up as if warding off sunlight. Xareb held his out in greeting.

Drip. Drip. Drip.

The drops were enough to drive a person mad.

"What is it?" I asked.

Coron looked at the ceiling again. "Petrification water."

We all followed his gaze but couldn't see the source of dripping ourselves. Drops came at random intervals, dropping at equally random spots.

"It's a natural phenomenon in some caves," Coron explained. "The water seeps through stone for so long it takes on similar properties."

"What can we do?" I asked.

"If only we had barrels to wear," he said, "but the blankets will have to do."

We looked at each other then back at the priest, not following his thoughts...or maybe not wanting to.

Coron continued. "Spider, Graves, and I will hold the blankets overhead to stop the petrification water from hitting us."

"And me?" Nila asked.

"They'll be heavy," Coron gestured toward the two men and dog. "When we get there, you'll need to drag them back where I can cure them."

Nila nodded her acceptance. At least it wouldn't be a tight squeeze.

"If anything goes wrong—" Coron began.

"Goes wrong?" Graves cried.

"Yes. If anything goes wrong, remember I can cure you."

"Which is why you'll stay here," I said.

Coron started to argue, and I held up a hand.

"How do you cure us if you're the first one turned to stone?"

"Turned to stone?" Graves cried again. "I'm not going in there either."

I pulled a blanket from my pack and turned to the wizard. "I can't ask you to do this, but I won't be able to hold this blanket over Nila by myself."

Graves looked at Nila then the statues of Xareb and his family, then back at me. His teeth were gritted, and the flickering torchlight made him appear angrier than he was.

"Fine," he snapped, grabbing one end of the blanket.

Or perhaps exactly as angry as he was.

Coron took the packs, arranging them against a cave wall behind us, out of the way. Graves stretched the blanket above us like a shop awning. Before crouching underneath the makeshift shelter, Nila went to her pack and removed some lengths of rope, slipping them over one shoulder.

Half-step by half-step, we three shuffled forward into the open cavern, Coron holding both torches out to give maximum light. Nila moved in a crouch, low enough to keep underneath. The first drop hit the blanket and seemed to have no effect. Then another, and a third. The blanket stiffened, gaining weight with each drop. Graves let out a groan, though whether from the extra weight, or the knowledge that petrification was inches away, was unknown.

It took less than ten minutes to reach the trio of statues since none had gotten far into the room. Nila grabbed the still form of Pup.

"Forget the bloody dog," Graves said. "I'm not doing this a second time."

Nila said nothing but took the rope from her shoulder, tying one length around Xareb's ankle and another around his son's.

"Ready," she grunted.

"Wait," Graves said, balancing the petrified blanket on one hand. He pointed at the forms of the father and son. "Light."

Good thinking. If the statues could be made lighter—

Both Xareb and Barex glowed with a soft luminescence, the way certain moss did. We could see better, but neither of them was any lighter.

"Oh, come on!" Graves groaned.

"Ready," Nila repeated.

Not enough room to turn, we backed through the area in the same manner, inch by inch until we had reached Coron and safety again. Once there, we dropped the heavy blanket where it shattered.

Nila deposited the dog by Coron, then kneeled at the ends of her rope and started pulling Xareb across the room. At first, I was sure he would be petrified to the floor, but Xareb came, scraping stone on stone, causing sparks.

In five minutes the old man rested next to Pup, and Nila knelt to perform the same task with Barex, reuniting the stone family.

"Are you sure you can heal this?" Nila asked.

"Of course," Coron said. "Curing petrification is one of the first healing spells learned."

How much petrification happens on this side of the mountains if that spell got priority?

"I wonder whether I could do it?" Graves said.

I placed a hand on his shoulder and shook my head.

Graves half-shrugged the idea away, still in his pleasant state from casting his 'light' spell.

"Reason I asked you, Coron," Nila said, holding up her hands, "the water on the ropes..."

Her hands had become the same grey stone as the walls, and it was creeping upwards. She didn't look completely worried, and I wished I held her confidence in the priest's spells. Yes, he'd cure Pup of being a werewolf, but all I could focus on was that he wasn't able to cure the rot. Were there other afflictions he had trouble with?

Spell wasn't the right term though. It was more a prayer to Wagarial for the god to work through him. What happened if the god wasn't listening though, as gods so often were not? Did the priest need to try again later when his god wasn't busy?

The stone had travelled up Nila's arms and reached toward her torso. "Any time now."

Coron guided Nila to the other statues, then hummed a deep, melodious tune of what almost sounded like recognizable words. Could I not understand because it was another language, or because they weren't meant for my ears?

That same bright glow as when Coron cured Pup filled the cave, and I turned away. The priest stared on. When I looked back, Nila was flexing her fingers again and swinging her arms.

"What a relief," she said.

"Father?" an uncertain voice said. "Pup?"

Xareb jumped forward and grabbed his son in a rough bear hug while Pup barked at both of them, tail wagging. A touching family reunion.

"Ah, my friends," Xareb said after a minute or so of cherishing his son's life. "Thank you."

"Yeah, I thank you too," Barex said, "but let's get outta this cave. I've spent enough time here."

Neither questioned why they were glowing, perhaps attributing it to the cave waters. In either case, they lit our way back to the entrance and outside. By then another hour had passed, and Graves stomped away to cast a spell.

"So soon?" I muttered.

Nila watched him go, getting a grip on her stone war-hammer.

A roaring bang and a flash of amber light.

When Graves returned, the hem of his white robe was smouldering. Nila stepped forward and poured water from one canteen onto it.

After all these days of travelling together, I still found no pattern to Graves's magic results. Sometimes it succeeded, and sometimes it didn't. There were times when it only kind-of did what he asked, and others when it was catastrophic. Nothing matched to a particular mood for Graves, and it didn't matter if he was more rushed or relaxed, tired or refreshed.

The trio of Xareb, Barex, and Pup didn't stay, leaving in the direction of their cabin. The father kept touching his son as if unsure the younger man was actual flesh returned to him. Coron had gotten their promise to stay away from these caves, but who knew if *that* promise would hold. If Barex was as curious as me, it wouldn't be long.

We rested on nearby rocks, spreading out food for a quick lunch. Nila continued stretching her arms as if afraid they would turn back to stone if she didn't keep moving. Graves watched the spot where Xareb and family had disappeared earlier, head cocked to one side.

"Something wrong?" I asked.

Half-shrug. "Barex had been turned to stone, right?"

"Yeah."

"Well, why was the dog a werewolf then?"

We all stopped eating and glanced around at each other, then at the other caves behind us.

"Those caves remain largely unexplored," Coron said. "There could be

206

all manner of curses in there."

"Wonderful," Graves said. "So, instead of getting home we might become werewolves."

I had to agree with our wizard on this one. We would have to be extremely careful.

After lunch, Coron led us back, counting cave entrances before stopping in front of one.

"Here we are," he said. "Seventh from the right."

I turned to the opening then back to Coron. "You sure you won't come with us? At least for a while."

He shook his head. "I have much to do here, but maybe one day."

What more could be said except goodbye? Even Graves shook the priest's hand before turning and heading into the cave.

"Remember," Coron called after us, "don't trust anything in there."

"We remember," I said, giving a final wave.

CHAPTER 18
THE WAY HOME?

I led the way, followed by Nila, with Graves bringing up the rear. Like every other cave, this one was pitch-dark, our torches lighting the way. Graves had started to cast his light spell again but dropped his hands with a quick shake of his head, perhaps remembering the last two attempts and wondering what other unintended results could be had.

Inside the cave, it was cool and damp, though the water coating these walls wasn't petrifying. We followed the passage for an hour, and it never wavered in size or shape, remaining wide enough for Nila to pass through and high enough that she didn't need to stoop. There were no branching passages either, just one continual winding path to follow.

"Maybe we're in the wrong cave," Graves grumbled.

We had to hope we weren't. The torches had started to dim, and we only had one spare. That might get us back, but there wouldn't be enough light to explore other caves unless Graves was able to cast his light spell successfully.

I held up a hand, slowing. "Let's take a break and—"

The ground slipped from under my feet, the slickness of the stones robbing me of balance.

"Spider!" Nila called, a moment later grunting with the impact of falling herself.

It was too slippery to stand, trying only landed me on my back again.

Graves cursed and fell.

I slid forward on the water, struggling to get some control as the floor curved down. Then Nila's foot collided with my backside, propelling me further forward.

"Sorry," she said.

The torch fell from my hand into the water and was extinguished. We were in total blackness and judging by the air against my face, my momentum had increased, as had my speed.

I was sliding down the cave's steep decline.

Mental pictures of slamming into a stone wall at the end of this slide played inside of my mind.

"Slow!" Graves shouted. "Stop!"

Whatever spell he tried wasn't working, but they did give me the fear of a bear sliding down the path behind us, bewildered and angry.

"Light," he yelled.

A green globe shot out above us, showing the stone walls shooting past at incredible speed.

"Gak!" Graves said. "Worse. Much worse."

We followed this slide helplessly for several minutes until it rose upward in a slight ramp, sapping some of our speed. Then I was out over empty space and plummeting downward. Somewhere above Graves gave a shriek, and in between us would be Nila.

The green globe kept pace with our fall, showing a vast open area. To our right was the cave's wall, rushing past. I didn't want to know what was at the bottom, my fear of a stone wall replaced by fear of stone floor.

Hitting the water drove my senses from me and tumbled me end over end, then the weight of Nila slammed into me and drove me deeper. I swam sideways, trying to get out from under her and back upwards.

My head broke the surface, and I gasped. Beside me, Graves tread water inside his white robe, which was impressive, but costing him energy as he fought to not become entangled. He pulled off the backpack and dropped it, then grabbed the back of his robe and pulled it over his head, letting it sink too.

Nila was nowhere to be seen. We both twisted in circles, the light globe hovering overhead.

"Nila," I called. "Where are you?"

Nothing.

"Nila," Graves said. "Nila!"

A pause.

"She's too heavy," I said.

"Nila," Graves said again.

The tone had changed. He wasn't calling for her, he was casting a spell.

"Nila!" he commanded.

The water around us foamed, and Nila shot to the surface, coughing and spluttering. For one brief instant, she was above the water, then splashed down again, making huge waves that threatened to submerge us.

"Can't swim," she said, slapping the water with her great hands and dousing us in her panic. "Can't swim."

"Nila, it's okay," Graves said.

She continued to splash but didn't sink.

"Nila!" Graves yelled.

It was unusual to hear the wizard speak above his monotone, even in his annoyed and fractious stage. It got Nila's attention.

"My spell will keep you afloat."

She stared at him, eyes wild. Her thrashing slowed and then stopped. Sure enough, she stayed at a constant level in the water.

I looked around us, not seeing any kind of shore to swim to. There must be something though.

Then again, just because we want something doesn't make it fact.

Nila bobbed, not at all comfortable with having nothing but water underneath. Also, given the unpredictability of Graves's magic, the spell could cut out at the worst time.

We needed to find land.

The pack was a water-logged weight on my back, pulling me under. Each second of treading the water felt like a minute. I couldn't keep my head above the surface. I was under water for a second. Then five. Then just under.

I pulled the straps of my pack free, allowing it to fall away from me and resurfaced.

"There goes the cheese," I muttered.

Nila splashed in the water like a baby. Only, where a baby splashes with joy, Nila gave the impression of wanting to cause physical harm to the water.

"Stay here," I said, swimming to my right.

Nothing. More gloom and water.

I swam in a circle around the other two, keeping an eye on the distant horizon, getting more desperate with each stroke. My circle became a spiral until something other than water appeared.

"Here," I called. "This way."

Nila splashed, getting an idea of how swimming worked. Once she had the basic understanding, her great hands were able to shove at the water and propel herself forward. Graves came along behind her, keeping a healthy distance to avoid her flailing fists.

Now that the shore had been discovered, it only took a couple of minutes to get there. I dragged myself onto land and collapsed onto my back. Behind me Nila came out of the water, patting at the dry earth with both hands like it might all be an illusion. Graves followed and curled into a ball.

We lay there panting and gasping. Each of us had dropped our packs to stay afloat, and Graves had even lost his robe, lying on the shore in underwear, socks and sandals. At least Nila's hammer was still attached to her belt. She probably hadn't thought of detaching it while fighting to stay afloat.

"Well," Nila said after several minutes. "The sliding part was fun at least."

I gave a weak laugh, glad she was able to make a joke. And she was right—the sliding *could* be fun, knowing there was no stone wall at the end to kill us. Too bad we couldn't get back to the top and try it again, couldn't get back to that side of the mountains at all.

There would be no return trip until Graves perfected his ability at casting portals.

That world was lost to us.

\#

We rested by the edge of that cave lake for close to an hour before having the strength and will to move again. Nila stared at the water, afraid to turn her back on so treacherous an animal. For my part I stared at the lake, knowing the packs we carried now rested at the bottom. Would all that delicious cheese be ruined? Maybe not, and there was other food in the packs, other supplies to be salvaged.

"I'm going to swim to the middle," I said. "Maybe I can dive down and get the packs."

Nila's expression told me she thought I was crazy. Graves had no comment, looking away from us toward the water.

I stripped to my breeches, happy to remove the wet leather, and waded in. At least there were no jokes about my paleness this time.

The water was truly a lake, extending into blackness on all sides. It could go for miles for all we knew. I judged where we'd come down and swam to the spot. After taking several deep breaths I dove, kicking downward until my lungs ached from lack of breathing. No bottom, no packs touched my fingers, only more and more water. I turned and kicked for the surface, lungs demanding to breathe.

Bobbing in the water, I got my air back.

"Nothing?" Nila called.

"Not yet."

I upended and tried again, sure that I'd gotten further with my mad kicking this time, and still didn't find the floor of that lake. If I could have cursed underwater, I would have.

The packs were gone.

My head broke the surface again, and I swam back toward shore, lying there and gasping once again.

"So, nothing then?" Nila asked.

"Nothing."

I stared up into the darkness of the high cave, my mind churning.

"What was the point of all that?" I said, more to the ceiling.

"Of what?" Nila asked.

"This whole side trip through the portal. The werewolf. The rot. The cheese. All of it."

Nila shrugged. "There needs to be a point?"

"In those stories the bards tell, there certainly would be."

"Stories need to make sense," she said. "Life doesn't."

I grumbled and sat up.

She took a deep breath. "If there is a point to everything then it's known only to the gods. Maybe in the end, when we look back, it will all make sense."

Graves stood, staring out at the lake. "Maybe we went through all that just to bring cheese to whatever lives down there."

The way he said it gave me a chill. "Lives down there?"

"Well, yes. Something must live there. Fish or other creatures."

Yes, there would be something living in there. I hadn't thought of that while wading in. It could be a big sort of something too, considering the size and depth of the lake.

"Hey!" I said to Graves, an idea striking me. "Do you think you could bring the packs up? You know, the way you pulled Nila up."

Graves thought about it and got to his feet, aiming both hands out toward the water.

"Come to me."

He eyes glowed their familiar amber. Magic shot out toward the spot where we'd splashed down...and that was it.

"Nothing?" I asked.

He half-shrugged.

"No look," Nila said, pointing.

The water was roiling, like something was being pulled through the water toward us.

"You did it!" I said, thumping Graves on the shoulder.

Then it surfaced.

The biggest, ugliest fish I'd ever seen, all huge eyes and needle-teeth, skimming just above the water and coming straight at us. This fish was big enough to swallow any one of us whole.

"Graves," I said.

The fish opened its mouth, shooting a forked tongue ahead of it, eyes locked on us.

"Graves!"

Nila stepped forward, hammer at the ready.

The fish wasn't slowing. At this rate, it would barrel into us like a runaway wagon. A wagon filled with sharp daggers and a desire to eat us.

"Graves, negate it!"

"Oh!"

The wizard waved his hands. Nothing happened.

"Run!" I yelled.

Graves waved his hands again. "Negate! Turn off! Whoa! Go back!"

His eyes glowed, and the fish dropped back into the water. I'd never seen a fish look surprised before, but this one seemed to manage it.

Suddenly I wanted to be far from the water's edge.

"Want me to try again?" Graves asked.

"Nope. Let's get out of here," I said, trying to sound nonchalant.

Nila backed away from the lake, hammer still raised.

Graves cast his light spell, replacing the fading globe that had followed us down the slide. At least there was no amusing re-interpretation of what he asked this time.

Only one choice of direction was available, and we followed it. I allowed myself to dry as we hiked, carrying my clothes, and got dressed further up where it felt safer. At least I still had my knives and lockpicks. Everything else in the packs could be replaced.

"You suppose we could have come out on the wrong shore?" Graves asked.

Nila rolled her eyes. "We better not have. I'm not getting back in that water."

"Hells, no," I said. "Let's not worry about that until we have to."

"Yeah? When will that be?" Graves said.

"When we get to a dead end."

"This could go on forever."

The point he brought up was both valid and grating. "Assume we're good until we discover otherwise."

Graves half-shrugged, as if none of it mattered much to him in the end, and maybe it didn't. Except for a lack of food, the wizard could have everything he wanted here. Lots of time and space to practice. Water to drink.

Could he conjure food? Nope, that didn't work out so well last time, but with practice...?

In the end, any worries about where we were heading were unfounded. The cave sloped upward, the surroundings becoming brighter until we broke through into the sunlight of mid-afternoon.

Nila glanced at the sun. "We're back on your side."

"But, where are we?" Graves asked.

Nila took another look at the position of the sun, compared it to the mountains.

"That way," Nila said, pointing to the southeast.

"What is?" Graves said.

"Where we were when the portal appeared."

Graves followed the direction as if he could see for miles.

"The tent! My bedroll and pack," he gasped. "Oh! A change of clothes!"

Well, there's a fine turn of circumstances. Now Nila and I would be the ones without bedrolls and packs. Irony was a pain sometimes, but at least we would have *something*, assuming it was all still there of course. We'd been gone long enough for someone to come take it all.

That would be more painful irony.

Graves headed off, all skinny limbs and determination inside his underwear and sandals, trying not to show how aware he was of his near-nakedness. Nila and I scrambled to catch up.

All we had left were my lockpicks and daggers, Nila's stone hammer and the remaining coins in my hip pouch. It would be a cold night if Graves's pack, with the spare flint and tinder, *was* gone. Unless we could return to Nila's friend in Grand Gesture for a room.

Let's see if we couldn't get our wizard less revealed first.

"How far?" I asked Nila, shuddering.

"You cold?"

"No. It's just..." I looked at Graves's skinny butt bobbing. "Not appreciating the scenery."

Nila chuckled. "Hours."

I sighed. Maybe Graves would get tired of being in the lead.

But he didn't.

The sun had set behind the mountains, but at least it was warmer than the other side, and as it turned out, we did have some luck. Our campsite was where we'd left it, and undisturbed it seemed. Graves bolted forward when the tent came into sight, disappearing through the closed flaps. A minute later he reappeared in one of his purple robes.

"That's better," he and I said at the same time.

Graves sniffed at the fabric of his robe, relishing the clean scent. He dragged his pack out and dumped it onto the grass.

"The wagon rations," I said. "I'd forgotten about those."

Three meals worth, if we were frugal.

"Ah," Nila said, retrieving the flint and tinder pouch from the pile.

She set about the task of starting a fire for the night.

"Oh no," Nila groaned. "We lost my traps."

We groaned with her. There would be no fresh meat for us until we replaced her equipment. For tonight, we would need to be happy with dry rations while we rested and made our plans.

Hopefully, tomorrow would bring us better luck.

CHAPTER 19
OPTIONS

Breakfast was less than phenomenal—a shade over edible. We were lucky to have it, so no one complained about eating rations, not even Graves.

"Where next?" Nila asked.

We crouched around the fire which burned low. The coins in the pouch didn't jingle as much as we would have liked and, even though we all knew what was in there, I tipped it into my hand.

"Well, we have enough for a couple of days if we get to a town, but—"

"Let me guess," Graves interrupted, "we'll need to find a job to make more."

I shrugged.

"What a surprise," he said, getting to his feet. "We always seem to be moving farther away from that place where I can SIT AND PRACTICE!"

These last words were shouted directly at me. The wizard's hands had clenched into fists at his side. I stared back at Graves before replying.

"You're right," I said.

"YOU DON'T... Oh. Well, yes..." Graves stammered, ready for an argument that wouldn't come.

I *had* promised him that, several times, and we'd done anything but. I knew how it felt to always be moving away from your goal and could empathize. He was missing one point though.

"Do you realize everything you've accomplished in the last couple of weeks?" I asked.

Graves didn't answer.

"Casting a light spell on a caravan wagon with no distractions isn't any test of your skills but casting one while sliding down a path to who-knows-where is useful and an actual, practical test."

Graves had no answer, but his hands stopped clenching.

"When I first met you, a light spell was as likely to conjure a horde of zombies as it was to brighten things. Now you can conjure it with ease."

"Sometimes," he admitted.

True. There was that floating rock, plus Xareb and son glowing in the dark, but why fight my own argument?

"I don't remember ever conjuring a horde of zombies," he said.

"Well, the day is still young," I said.

Graves made a noise that might have been a half-laugh, then turned and stalked off to cast his morning spell.

"You handle him well," Nila said when Graves was out of earshot.

"Thanks. He is right though. I did promise him."

"Maybe he should get that chance and see it's not as interesting."

"Hah! Not a bad idea. Next time we have the spare coins."

Nila snorted like I'd said the next time unicorns flew out of my nose... And yes, yes. I know unicorns don't fly. Just painting an interesting picture here.

"So, where to?" I asked. "Back to Gesture?"

"Nah," Nila shook her head.

"Time to move on?"

"All that travel on the other side made me think. If I'm stuck here, I want to see more than one town."

"I'm sure Zachariah has poisoned our name back there anyway, at least where the caravans are concerned, and probably more."

We were silent, a muffled implosion of air from Graves's spell carried to us. Neither Nila nor I even turned. It was funny how quick we'd become accustomed to it.

"We need money so Graves can practice and conjure that portal for you."

"That's what *we* want. What do you want?"

"Me? I want to start that trading business."

Nila's words echoed back inside my head: Maybe he should get that chance and see it's not as interesting.

But I did still want that trading business. I *did!*

"Well?"

"Not that easy. First I have to build some capital, and before I can do that, I need to watch after Graves for the next year."

"And doing a fabulous job of it so far," the wizard said, returning from behind us.

That didn't sound as sarcastic as it could have at least.

He came and settled on the rock opposite us.

"To the east is Persinia," I suggested. "About a day's walk along the road."

Persinia was one of four sister cities arranged into a square called The Box. It being closest to the Bandit's Hills, it was also the wildest of all four, holding a necessary abundance of town guards, a thriving trade business, and an impressive amount of illegal activities.

"I'm sure we can find something to do for money there."

Graves gave his half-shrug, in his post-casting, agreeable mood. Nila nodded.

It didn't take long to strike the camp and pack everything we owned. The tent folded into a compact package but wouldn't fit inside Graves's pack, not with the bedroll and what food we had. Nila slipped the thick canvas roll under one arm instead, carrying it the way another person would carry a coat.

Following a diagonal route, we started our journey toward Persinia, meeting with the road after about an hour. A couple of hours after that, we were into the low hills surrounding Grand Gesture's valley.

These hills held less chance of bandits since they had nowhere to disappear if all went badly. People passed through this way between Gesture and Persinia often, and it was considered to be a safe route.

So, of course, we were ambushed.

CHAPTER 20
NOT THESE GUYS AGAIN!

We came around a bend, and there they stood, ten feet ahead as if just another set of travellers headed in the opposite direction. The difference being that they *were* just standing in the road, blocking it actually. There were fifteen in all, wearing the beaten leather of people who had been blocking paths as a career for their entire lives. Four at the back held crossbows, ready to snap up and shoot. The rest had drawn swords, standing in a rough semi-circle.

"Bandits," I muttered.

"Here we go again," Graves said.

Anyone with sense would have taken one look at Nila and decided somewhere else was where they needed to be. Like, say, one of the cannibal islands as a dinner guest.

These bandits, it seemed, had no sense.

So on to plan B then, which was counting on Graves and his magic, may the gods be merciful. If he could do something to the bandits, anything... No! Not *anything*. Turning them into bears, for example, would make a bad situation worse.

"Where *have* you been?" a voice said.

Stepping from behind the sword-wielders came a man in light brown robes. He spoke as if we were expected and should have been here long ago. Beside him came a woman in chain-mail and the perpetual scowl of a career criminal. Someone who would slit a throat for fun and maybe some coins.

Aptly enough, throat-slitter held a knife against the neck of some complete stranger, a tall, thin man with wild fear in his eyes. He looked to be about as far outside his element as a person could get.

The robed bandit held up one hand with a fist-sized globe which pulsed an unnatural blue light. The more he held it toward us, the brighter it glowed.

"Oh yes, that's the elf," he said to throat-slitter then turned back. "We've been waiting for you."

"Cultists," I groaned.

How were these guys everywhere now?

"Let me guess," I said. "If my friends give me over they can go free."

"Did I say that?" the robed man asked. "No, these two will make fine sacrifices."

"Every bit helps break down the veil," throat-slitter said.

The cultists behind muttered their agreement.

"The veil?" I asked. "What veil?"

The priest opened his mouth to speak then shook his head. "I'm afraid we are pressed for time. If you'd arrived earlier...ah, never mind. Let's just say it won't be your concern for long."

"Right, of course," I said. "Well, that *spells* it out, I guess."

"Subtle," Graves muttered.

Nila stepped forward, shielding Graves and me from view and growling at the group to draw their attention. She threw the canvas tent on the ground and lifted her stone hammer in one motion.

The robed man sighed. "Unfortunate. I'd hoped for the troll to be alive, but that isn't so important."

"Troll?!" she shouted.

With a gesture, the crossbows were raised and aimed at Nila.

Throat-slitter's hostage made an *un-unh* noise in his throat, begging us not to mess with these guys. He made eyes toward the crossbowmen, which were too prominent to need pointing out.

I stepped from behind Nila, murmuring. "Can crossbows hurt you?"

"Of course. My skin is tough, but it isn't armour."

"Hold on," I said, hands raised toward the cultists.

"Don't shoot the elf," the robed man said.

"No! Wait, we'll come peacefully," I said.

Robed man raised a hand and the crossbows were pointed somewhat away from our hearts.

"Anytime with that spell," I whispered to Graves.

"I already cast it," he said.

"Well, where is it?"

"I don't know. Nothing happened."

The only proof of his spell was a droning noise coming from all directions. It was unnerving, but little else. Only Nila and I seemed to hear it anyway.

"Cast another," I hissed.

"Come out where we can see you," Robed man said. "Or we shoot the troll."

Nila growled again.

Graves stepped into view.

"Drop the pack and keep your hands where I can see them."

Graves unslung his backpack and threw it next to the tent, then raised his hands in surrender.

"Don't try casting anything," the head cultist said. "I assure you, crossbows are quicker than chanting a spell."

"Graves?" I said.

A smirk reached the corner of his lips. This was something he enjoyed, proving someone wrong.

One bandit put his sword away and started forward, shackles in hand. As he neared us, a cocky sneer on his own lips, Nila snaked a deceptively quick hand out and grabbed him by the throat, lifting him from the ground while moving in front of Graves and me. His sword clattered to the ground. Crossbows fired. The hapless cultist became a shield to catch the bolts that would have otherwise struck us.

Graves cast a second spell.

The crossbowmen started reloading.

"I thought you hated violence," I said.

"Unnecessary violence," she answered. "Trileme condones passive violence to protect one's clan mates."

"Oh, for the love of..." Robed man hissed. "Do I need to do everything myself?"

The sword-bearing cultists started forward while the ones in back continued reloading their weapons. Before anyone took two steps, the wind increased, blowing in from all directions. Overhead an ominous green cloud grew, swirling like a maelstrom.

Everyone stopped.

"What is that?" I asked in a low aside to Graves.

"No idea."

The first spatter of rain struck, a fat drop of bizarre, bright-green liquid.

I groaned. A backfire spell that just did something weird. Exactly what we needed.

One cultist laughed.

"Is this your best, wizard?" the robed man asked.

More drops fell, hitting exposed skin with a sound like frying bacon.

"Hey! It burns," one of the cultists said, a twist of smoke rising from the point of impact.

The spattering increased to a drizzle.

Nila crouched and grabbed the tent, rolling it out in one quick snap to hold over us, like a canvas umbrella.

"Acid," she said.

The cultists fled in every direction as drizzle became downpour. Two of the crossbowmen set off their weapons by reflex. One bolt buried itself in a second cultist's back while the other lodged in Nila's upper shoulder.

She cursed in her native tongue but held the tent steady.

The rain came straight down, hitting the ground with such ferocity that it bounced in all directions, including toward us.

"Ow!" I said, looking around for better shelter.

"Ow!" Graves agreed.

Nila knocked us to the ground, sheltering us with her body and pulling the tent over her back.

The occasional drop made it through Nila's defences to burn a hole through our clothing. It sunk a quarter inch into our flesh, cauterizing the wound afterwards.

What was it doing to Nila?

Her eyes were closed against what must have been agony, but she didn't move. Only when there'd been silence for a minute, no more drops against the tent, no more screams, did Nila remove the shelter.

"You two okay?" she asked.

We both jumped to our feet, staring at her with concern. I was afraid to ask, knowing her other side must be destroyed.

"What's wrong?" she said. "Oh! The acid. Nah. Told you I had tougher skin."

She turned to show that her back, while smoking and inflamed, was unscarred. Her leather and fur tunic didn't fare as well, its back side completely eaten away. With nothing to hold them in place, the front parts fell into the dust.

Nila turned toward the dead cultists, pulling the crossbow bolt from her shoulder.

Bits of skin and cloth clung here and there, but little else. They'd taken the full brunt of the heavy caustic acid storm and showed it. The rain had eaten leather armour from their bodies and the skin underneath from their bones. Grinning skulls sneered back.

Not even Throat-slitter in her metal armour had survived. She would have withstood the storm best, but not by much. The acid had made its way between the spaces in her chain-mail to the softer flesh beneath.

Nila crouched over her corpse. "Huh! Didn't harm the metal."

She grabbed the chain-mail shirt and pulled, shaking it free of the previous owner. It was nowhere near her size, but with some improvisation Nila attached the armour to what remained of her tunic, fastening it at the back. It did little to hide anything on that side, but she seemed to wear clothes for our own modesty rather than hers anyway.

Our tent, the bedroll, the pack and everything inside it were all beyond salvation. We were back to only the clothes on our backs, and those being acid-eaten in far too many places.

No food, no supplies, no sleeping arrangements and now, no clothes. The few coins we had would be even more limited now with needing to replace everything.

"This globe was tracking you," Graves said.

He nudged it with a foot. The globe rolled toward me, glowing brighter blue.

A chill snaked along my spine. "Can we destroy it?"

Graves picked it up and threw it against some rocks. The sphere bounced off like a child's toy.

"Nope. I could try magic on it."

I looked at the handiwork of his acid storm and shook my head. "Forget it for now."

Graves slipped the globe into a pocket of his tattered robe. "Even if we could destroy it, that doesn't mean there aren't more."

"Good point," I agreed. "Nice spell by the way."

He half-shrugged.

"See, practical application."

"I was trying to teleport them away."

"Huh. Well, at least you didn't turn them into bears."

We turned our attention to the cultist's hostage, a man who had dissolved as thoroughly as the people holding him.

"I wish we could have saved him," I said.

Graves gave an, *oh well, what can you do*, motion.

Nila knelt in front of the hostage's body, starting a low, throaty chant. This was an unseen side of her, but then again, we hadn't had any dead to pray over before now.

"Wonder who he was," I said.

"A king's agent."

I turned to Graves, and he looked back.

"How would you know that?" we both said at the same time, then, "I didn't say that." Followed by, "Yes, you did." And, "Stop saying everything I say."

We continued to stare at each other, bewildered.

"You fellows did a good job on this lot."

Graves's lips hadn't moved, and I was sure mine hadn't either. Nila continued to chant.

We lingered like this for another heartbeat before Graves turned, moving to one side as he did. Revealed in the space was a transparent version of the man on the ground, or what he'd looked like before the acid rain anyway.

"Good show," he said. Or I mean, *it* said...no, I *did* mean he. I...

"A ghost," Graves said.

The figure was riveted by his scoured corpse. "Yes, I suppose I am."

Graves backed away from the spectre, stopping next to me, then took another step back so I was in front.

"Are you here to haunt us?" Graves asked.

The ghost brightened, turning away from his human remains. "Hmm, yes, I guess I am at that."

"Want to give it...um, him, any more ideas, Graves?"

Graves tried his best to get further behind me. I moved aside, and the wizard squeaked his outrage.

"There's unfinished business I need your help with," the ghost said.

I looked at Graves who mouthed the word *no.*

"I can promise a reward," he said, "for bringing a message to the king."

"The king? King Vernion?"

"Well, I didn't mean the troll king. In any case, I have a message for him. His ears only, you know."

"If it's his ears only then why do you need us?" I said.

"Um... Good question. Well...in case he can't hear me."

"So, the king's ears and ours?" I asked.

"Yes, that's right. But you'll need to forget it all afterwards. Safety of the realm you know."

"Right. What sort of reward?"

Graves groaned, said in a low voice, "Don't do it."

"Well, I don't know exactly," the ghost admitted. "Whatever the king is willing to give."

"Sounds iffy."

"Okay, well, I had some coins in a pouch. Will you take that as down payment?"

I turned toward the man's corpse and shuddered. "Feels ghoulish."

"It is a pretty grim," the ghost admitted, "but I give my blessing."

Well, if the previous occupant gave his okay...

"My name is...Amp, by the way," the ghost said, sticking a hand out to shake, dropping it when he realized the futility of the gesture.

"Amp?" I asked. "Odd name."

"Yes, well, it's short for...um, Ample. I was always enough for the job. More of a codename really. As a king's agent, I should have an interesting codename after all."

"Right. Of course."

"Anyway, all my friends call me Amp."

"Uh-huh."

"Oh!" he brightened. "You can too, of course."

An odd request for friendship considering we were responsible for his death, and a horrible one at that. Was it the shock of finding himself dead?

"How did the cultists capture you?" I asked.

He waved one ethereal hand, dismissing the thought. "All part of the job as king's agent. Fear of death and all that."

"Don't you mean, *no* fear of death?" Graves asked, coming forward a step.

"Oh, is that how it goes?" The ghost waved that away too. "I'd been on these cultists trail two days, ever since the king's nephew was kidnapped."

"Prince Rupert?" I said.

The ghost nodded.

This was bad. Rupert was next in line for the throne.

"We don't know why he was taken," Amp continued. "There was no ransom demand. All the king's spies and agents are on the hunt for him, but only I, the king's best agent, saw the clue."

The ghost had puffed up under his own self-importance.

"What clue?" Graves asked.

"After the disappearance, I noticed someone suspicious in the castle and followed them. He led me to the Cult of the Sightless Eye."

Amp eyes widened as if that revelation should have been accompanied by thunder and lightning.

"Yeah, we met them," Graves said.

"Anyway," he sighed, "another cultist must have taken Prince Rupert elsewhere."

Amp stared at the dead bodies all around.

"I was about to attack when that woman grabbed me from behind in an unbreakable grip like steel."

"Did you tell anyone at King's Corner you were following the cultist?" I asked.

"No time. Deeds, not words, you know. I did what needed to be done, as any good agent would. Now the king needs this information about the cult."

Nila finished her prayer and looked around. "Who were you talking to?"

"Nila, this is Amp," I said, gesturing toward the ghost.

"Don't see anyone," she said.

Graves and I glanced at each other, feeling crazy, then back at Amp, sure that the ghost would have disappeared while our eyes were off him. It would have been perfectly chilling, just like a story told around a nighttime campfire.

But, no. Amp was still there.

"You see a ghost," Nila said. "What's his dying quest?"

"Dying quest?" Graves asked.

"Yeah, if you see a spirit then the gods have tasked you with performing a dying wish."

"Listen to the she-troll," Amp said.

I shook my head. "She's not a she-troll."

"What?" Nila demanded. "She-troll?!"

"Sorry," Amp said, speaking quickly. "I've never seen a she-troll and assumed."

"He apologizes," I told Nila.

"Humph! I'm a bit tired of that."

"You're the king's agent but haven't seen a troll?"

Another wave of his ethereal hand. "It is your fault I can't complete my task, maybe that's why you've been tasked with my dying quest."

Graves groaned again.

"I could just conscript you into service. As king's agent I do have that authority, I think. Don't I? Yes, I do."

"And how would you enforce that exactly?" Graves asked.

"Well...I...don't know, but won't you do it anyway? Please?"

I turned to Graves who threw up his hands, knowing what was coming.

"Fine," I agreed.

"Don't forget the coins," Amp said.

Forgetting the coins would have been nice, but we needed them too much.

"Graves?"

"Nope."

I didn't think so. Bending over the dead man I felt for his pockets. A pouch, eaten to nothing on one side, with one silver coin and a bunch of coppers. Not much.

"There's more where that came from," Amp said.

I added the coins to our own stash and returned it to my tunic. Now we had enough to pay for a meal and get some clothes, though not great examples of either.

"I'm never going to get to just sit and practice, am I?"

"Practical application, Graves. Remember?"

"Oh yes!" he said with mock enthusiasm. "I can do some card tricks for the king."

"That's the spirit."

Graves cursed under his breath.

CHAPTER 21
BLABBERGHOST

"The official name of the area isn't *The Box* of course," Amp said as we followed the road toward Persinia. "That's what everyone calls it because the four cities are more or less equidistant from each other, all joined by the roads. It looks like a box on maps."

"Yes, I do know that," I said.

"The four cities are Persinia, Alora, Farminat, and what is called King's Corner, which is also not the proper name. It is, in fact, the Castle Blackstone and is the seat of government for King Vernion, housing his castle, the various branches of cabinet, and everything that keeps the roads in a state of repair. These four together are 'The Box.'"

"I know that too. I've travelled quite a bit."

"Even King Vernion calls it this," Amp said, not listening.

"What's he saying?" Nila asked.

"Absolutely nothing," Graves said. "In a million words or less."

Nila grunted.

"The four cities of The Box are ever expanding toward each other," Amp continued. "One day they will all meet and become one massive megacity."

"Mostly he's giving some kind of historic monologue," I added.

"Doesn't sound like a secret agent," Nila said.

Amp had been talking without break since we left the ambush spot, flitting from topic to topic, adding commentary on anything that was said. His monotonous rambling faded to a background noise, like bird's chirping but less soothing. In truth, the concept of silence had been forgotten...well, not by Nila.

We hiked the rest of that day, arriving in Persinia toward twilight. The three of us shambled into town, as stylish as River Rats. Our clothes had continued to deteriorate as we travelled, the holes enlarging, and Nila's makeshift tunic was giving the impression it might have reached its limits and would perform a spontaneous indecent exposure any second now.

The clothing shop was in the process of closing as we stepped through the door. The man behind the counter glanced at us then shook his head.

"Sorry, no discards today."

"We're paying customers," I said.

The man scanned each of us in turn, one eyebrow raised in clear disbelief. I dropped the coins on the counter in front of him, saving what I hoped would be enough for a room and meal.

The shopkeeper inspected each piece of currency.

"That is just rude," Amp said. "There is nothing wrong with those coins. Why when I get to King's Corner...blah-blah-blah."

Amp didn't actually say blah-blah-blah, of course. This was just what Graves and I had started hearing once we determined the ghost wasn't saying anything of importance, which was most of the time. A defence mechanism of sorts against wanting to push daggers into our own ears.

The coins disappeared below the counter with a sigh. "Follow me."

He ushered us to the back of his store where a rack of bargain items hung. The material was cheap and scratchy and wouldn't last us given our lifestyles.

"Is this the best you have?"

"No, of course not. This is just the best you can afford, which is coincidentally my worst."

I pulled the trading outpost ring off my finger and held it out. I'd mostly forgotten about it. "Will this help?"

"No," Graves said.

I turned to him. "What? Why?"

"Why, what?"

"Why did you say no?"

"I didn't."

I looked at Nila who shrugged. Amp was nowhere to be seen.

I shook my head and turned back to the tailor, holding the ring toward him.

"No," Graves repeated.

"Okay, I heard you for sure that time."

The wizard stared at me, baffled then looked at Nila.

"He didn't say anything, Spider."

The tailor plucked the ring from my fingers, turned it over once and handed it back. "Sorry, just tin or bronze. Not worth my time to sell it."

With a sigh I slid the ring back onto my finger, looking at my companions sideways. What game were they playing?

"Spider," Amp said.

The ghost had reappeared, and just when I'd started hoping he'd moved on to the next life. I ignored him.

"Spider," he repeated. "Spider."

Graves groaned.

"Sorry, friends," the shopkeeper said, "but there's only so much I can do. I'm running a business here."

"Spider, Spider, Spider!"

"What?" I hissed.

"What?" the shopkeeper answered.

"No, not you. It's..." I turned to Graves to avoid appearing completely insane. "What is it?"

"Are you talking to me?" Amp asked.

"Yes."

"Oh, right. Got it. Don't want to seem—"

"Amp."

"Right, well, ask this villain why he has a unicorn hide curing in the back."

I turned to the shopkeeper, putting my amiable, traders face on. "Are you *sure* this is the best you can do?"

"I already explained—"

"Oh, I know, but it's not like we're asking for unicorn hide or anything."

He stared back at us, no change in his expression but faint beads of sweat broke out on his brow. Everyone has a tell.

"Unicorn hide is illegal," he said.

"*Very* illegal," I agreed.

"The king has put a death sentence on people dealing in unicorn," Amp chimed in.

"In fact," I added. "Last I heard the king had enacted a death sentence for dealing in unicorn."

"I think you should leave now," the shopkeeper said, looking over his shoulder toward the back rooms. "I need to close up and get home."

"Fair enough," I turned toward the front door. "Come on Graves, Nila."

"What about me?" Amp said.

"I hope the town guard isn't passing by," I said. "Wearing these clothes, they're sure to stop us."

Graves and Nila turned to follow.

"You want me to keep an eye on him then, Spider?" Amp said.

"Of course, if we're stopped, I may need to tell them about a back room where they could find some unicorn hide."

"No!" the shopkeeper said, moving forward to stop us. "Okay, okay. How did you...?"

I turned back to face him, the picture of innocence.

The man turned toward another part of the store. "Follow me, please."

We followed him to racks of much better clothing, more in line with what we'd been wearing earlier. This was quality, comfortable, and would last us for the foreseeable future. Not his best stuff but we weren't greedy.

"We'll take two sets of each," I said.

"Two?" the man protested then glanced toward the back room again.

Unicorn hide was rumoured to have magical protection for the wearer, which was so much dragon dung. It was very durable though, and rare.

Troubling to see such a creature killed for clothing. If we weren't so desperate...

"Yes, two, and a backpack to carry everything in."

"Fine," the shopkeeper said through gritted teeth.

I ended up with two matching sets of leathers while Graves got a couple of robes, one his standard purple and the other brown. Tonight I would take time to hide some lockpicks in the seams of my tunic. Zadi's imprisonment had taught me that much.

Fitting Nila was more of a task for the shopkeeper. She wanted fur and leather like she'd had, but the shop didn't have anything in stock, not in her size anyway. In the end he took what she already wore, added parts of a huge leather tunic he couldn't have hoped to sell anyway, and made an exceptional piece of clothing. It was a one-piece tunic of fur, leather and even incorporated the chain-mail in a couple of strategic spots.

"Best I can do."

Nila did deep knee bends and lunges, then a couple of high kicks which threatened to do exceptional damage.

"I like it," Nila said.

The man smiled, starting to usher us toward the front door.

"Not so fast," I said.

"Oh, what?" he demanded. "I've done what you asked."

"You have, and we thank you, but that unicorn hide is a terrible thing."

"You tell him, Spider," Amp chimed in. "There are reasons for laws, to protect these creatures. Why when...blah-blah-blah."

The man looked over his shoulder again, deflating with a sigh.

"I do agree," he said in a low voice, avoiding any eye contact. "And I will take care of it."

I narrowed my eyes at this rather vague assurance.

"The creature is already dead," he continued. "I can't do anything about that, but I can donate any profit from the sale to the unicorn preserves. Will that do?"

I looked at my companions. Graves was uninterested while Nila nodded her acceptance.

"What?" Amp said. "Call the city guard! Oh, the king will hear about this man when I...blah-blah-blah."

We left the shop with our bundles and Amp's incessant chattering in our ears.

Next stop, a meal and a room.

\#

What was left of our coins got us a room with two beds, and an expectation, for me, of being punched awake by Graves in the night. After some haggling, where Nila glared over my shoulder, the innkeeper threw in dinner and breakfast as well. Nice guy. Quite reasonable. As it turned out, neither the rooms or the food were the greatest, but both were better than the alternative.

And come tomorrow we would be broke and counting on the king's gratitude for bringing him Amp's information.

Speaking of Amp, the ghost became more agitated once the sun had gone down and we'd all retired. He paced, for want of a better word, muttering to himself. Given the lateness and trying to sleep, his voice refused to fade to a blah-blah-blah.

"Amp! Please!" I begged. "We need to sleep."

He didn't hear or wasn't listening. At some point, his mutters dissolved into wails, like a ghost from some campfire story.

Right now I was jealous of Nila's ability to sleep, and inability to hear Amp. At least I wouldn't need to worry about Graves's night thrashing.

The wizard jumped from our bed, already casting.

"Graves, wait—"

Too late.

"Silence!"

I held my breath. It had worked once before, more or less. Maybe...

Nila's bed jumped, throwing her upwards. She bounced off the ceiling and landed on the bed in a sitting position, glaring and fully awake.

"Graves!" she said.

"I... Ah..." he stammered. "Sorry."

"He was trying to get Amp to quiet down," I explained.

She grumbled a reply and rolled back into bed, her back to us.

"Should I try again?" Graves asked me.

"No," Nila replied.

#

In the morning, Graves and I slumped bleary-eyed at the breakfast table, drinking cup after cup of coffee to get our brains moving. The one backpack with all of our possessions, which amounted to a change of clothes for Graves and myself, rested on the bench between us.

"I don't sleep," Amp said.

"We noticed," Graves answered. "Apparently neither do we."

"No! I mean, I can't," Amp said. "I want to, but I can't sleep."

"Can't eat either," Graves pointed out. "Or drink, or scratch your nose, or—"

"Graves," I said.

"Oh, right," he said. "Let's not upset the dead guy who kept us awake all night."

He was more peevish than usual this morning.

"It's all true," Amp agreed, "but for some reason, I miss sleeping most. Isn't that strange?"

"Well, if you missed eating most," Graves grumbled, "at least we could eat while you wailed."

"What's he chattering about?" Nila asked.

"He can't sleep."

She grunted. "Can't drink or scratch either."

"That's what Graves said."

"I know. I can hear *him*," Nila said. "Tell the ghost to focus on his new abilities."

"Nila says... Hold on, *he* can hear *you*."

Nila chuckled and said nothing.

"What stuff? Like going through walls?" Amp said.

I looked at Nila, waiting for her to answer, then shook my head. I needed more coffee.

"Yeah, stuff like that," I agreed.

"Listening in on conversations?" Amp gasped. "I could truly be a king's agent."

I turned toward the ghost. "What was that?"

"Oh, I mean, I could truly be the king's best agent. Yeah."

I stared at Amp, then over at Graves whose fingers were twitching. "Why don't you meet us outside?"

"I don't need you to watch after me," he snapped. "I can cast my spells on my own."

I looked at him with one eyebrow raised.

"Maybe I'll just wait for you all outside."

Graves headed out the door. I prayed for no floods or swarms, no boars or bears or giants. A calm, normal spell.

He returned three minutes later, looking over his shoulder.

"What did you do?" I asked.

He shook his head. "Ready to go?"

I glanced at Nila.

"Oh, I can't wait to see this one," she said.

We exited the inn, me pulling our sole pack over one shoulder.

Outside, as far as the eye could see, people were doing a strangely synchronized dance. Everyone stepped to the right and clapped, a sound like thunder with some two hundred people doing it in unison.

"What did you do?" I repeated.

"I was trying to give myself more energy," Graves said. "Then everyone dropped what they were doing and started dancing."

"This is the best one yet," Nila said.

Everyone did a kick to the right.

The looks on their faces were utter bewilderment. A couple of people laughed. One man was yelling like he'd been possessed. A squad of six town guard shuffled left, then right, making sounds like a metal drum as they danced in full armour.

"Let's get out of here before this wears off and they start looking for someone to lynch," I said.

Amp shook his head. "Madness."

The area of effect was about ten blocks and only outside of buildings. At least that's how far we were when we reached the edge of the city and found some people who were not dancing. Would that have been ten blocks in each direction? Forty blocks of people dancing? No wonder the claps were so loud.

Last we heard before passing through the gate and onto the plain was a coordinated "hey-hey-hey-hey" chant, punctuated by claps.

"You have to do that one again sometime," Nila said.

"Madness," Amp repeated.

CHAPTER 22
ON THE ROAD AGAIN... WAIT, I'VE ALREADY USED THAT

No bedrolls, no tent, and no money for a room meant we would need to make it to the castle before dinner. By then we would all be ravenous since we also had no food, but we would make do with what came from foraging. Still, nuts and berries only went so far in feeding three people, especially when one of those wasn't human.

Hmm, nope. Scratch that. Nila may be the most obvious non-human, but under the hood, I was an elf, and Graves made me wonder how someone who housed such power could be classified as human.

Let me try again. Nuts and berries only went so far in feeding three people, especially when one of those had a greater appetite.

Yes, that's better.

The road followed a straight path from Persinia to King's Corner, bisecting The Box since the two cities were opposite corners from each other. Trees and bushes lined each side, though cleared back several feet so as not to impede traffic. We collected sour apples from the trees overhead as we went, doing our best to ignore Amp's constant yammering.

"Hey!" the ghost said. "What if those people just dance forever?"

I turned toward Graves who thought about it. "No, I don't think so."

"Don't *think* so?" Amp said. "As a king's—"

Graves stopped and glared at the ghost. A crackle of amber energy flashed from his eyes, not as impressive as the one Armentia had shown but close enough for Amp. The ghost shut his ethereal mouth for the first time since leaving Persinia.

He sped ahead of our group. With the ghost's back turned, Graves gave me a quiet half-shrug and continued on. I wanted to laugh but was afraid that might start Amp off again.

More walking.

As a child, my father and I had travelled often by foot, though in later years he'd had caravans or horses to do that part of the work. Graves wanted a place to practice, and I was thinking my feet could sure use the rest.

"The roads between Persinia and King's Corner are maintained by the king's engineers." Amp drifted back to start another dissertation on something kingdom related. "This takes a great amount of gold each year to keep the four cities connected. As well as the...blah-blah-blah."

He'd been quiet a whole thirty minutes.

"Nice while it lasted," Graves observed.

The mumbling, wailing spirit of last night was gone, replaced by the millstone of incessant monologue. "After we drop him off with the king and collect the reward he'll be someone else's problem."

"And then—"

"Yes, yes. Then we'll find that place for you to practice, depending on how much reward the king pays."

Graves let himself drift back a few steps to beside Nila. They would travel like that for hours sometimes without saying a word, sharing some unspoken bond. They'd come to a point where Nila would simply say 'time' when Graves was becoming too petulant, and he would then go off to cast a spell without comment. It was a charming system to watch.

"Spider," Amp said from immediately behind me.

I jumped a foot. The ghost was silent and able to sneak up on either Graves or me with ease.

Graves muttered something. Nila laughed.

"What, Amp?"

"When we get to the castle you'll have to follow my lead."

"Fine. You're the king's agent and all."

"Yes. Right. The king's agent."

He said this last in a low, wondering, voice.

"Something wrong?" I asked.

"No, no. It's just...well, Spider...would you say I'm a good agent?"

I looked at the ghost then back toward the road. "Well, I barely know you and haven't seen you in action so I might not be the best judge."

"Oh. Right. Of course."

There was something odd about this ghost but, having never been one myself, I chalked it up to just that. He was doubting himself though, that much was obvious, and it wouldn't help us once we reached King's Corner.

"However," I added, "you are dead, and still have the sense of duty to complete your final mission. So, yes, I would say you're a good agent."

"Ah! Yes, thank you, Spider. I hadn't thought of that."

I gave him a nod.

"Interesting story about the castle...blah-blah-blah."

At least in a couple of hours, we wouldn't have to hear the unending dissertations on whatever popped into Amp's head. Would he move on once this final quest of his was finished?

Lunch that day consisted of all the berries, nuts, and apples we'd gathered. We'd started using my spare tunic as a pouch to collect the food, and by the time noon came around, we had enough for even Nila to enjoy.

"A steak would be nice," she said.

"Mmm, with some spiced potatoes on the side."

"And a glass of wine," Graves added.

"I'd be happy to taste those berries one last time," Amp said.

Graves and I must have reacted because Nila asked what Amp had said. We told her.

"There'll be a day when we'll all wish to taste these berries one last time," she said, popping a whole apple into her mouth.

After that observation, lunch held more satisfaction. We each closed our eyes and savoured the taste of berries and nuts. Amp drifted away up the road, my gaze following him. Nila couldn't see the ghost but she'd gotten skilled at reading our reactions.

"Must be hard," she said.

Graves gave his *oh-well* half-shrug and continued eating.

"Nothing we can do for him," I said. "He's dead and we can't change that."

"No. True."

"Once Amp delivers his message, he can rest," I said.

"Maybe."

"Maybe?" Graves looked up.

"Depends if that finishes the work in his mind."

Graves groaned. "If not then he'd better be staying at the castle."

Nila grunted, looking uncannily at the spot where Amp floated some forty feet away.

After lunch, we travelled in silence, except for Amp of course. With the meal finished he picked up where he'd left off on his talk about something or other. In fact, the closer we came to King's Corner, the more Amp was infected with nervous energy, speaking faster.

Graves had drifted back out of earshot of the after-lunch lesson, and I envied him... I also toyed with slowing until the wizard caught up and shared in my misery. In the end, I was charitable and endured.

After an eternity of listening, King's Corner came into view.

CHAPTER 23
KING'S CORNER

The huge castle-city never failed to impress, with its high stone walls and drawbridge to keep out the uninvited. The gate outside the drawbridge was manned by guards, checking identification on every person wanting entry. Major traffic entered this way, wagons with deliveries, squads of soldiers and such.

"On the castle's far side are several apartment buildings housing much of the workers," Amp explained.

No point in telling him again that I already knew all this. These smaller buildings held everyone not high enough in the pecking order to rate a room inside the castle.

Dad had wanted to do trade here but hadn't been able to get an audience. The castle used their own internal staff, self-sufficient except for what they brought in from other cities in the form of taxes, paid in food or fuel, weapons or services. Vernion was a fair king, not taking more than a city could afford, enough to keep the roads going, as the motto went.

"Around back is another way in," Amp said. "We can bypass security that way."

Amp drifted to the right, headed away from the main gate.

"The security of the castle is run by a man named—"

"Hold on!" I interrupted before the ghost could get into full lecture mode. "Why do we need to bypass security?"

"Well... The gate guards won't be able to see me, so I can't vouch for you."

The ghost continued on toward the back of the castle.

Graves made no move to follow on his own. Lacking any better options, I fell into step behind Amp. If we'd *had* other options, I would have questioned more, but it's amazing what the possibility of hunger and a need for coin will help a person overlook.

We followed the length of the city wall for fifteen minutes before turning a corner.

"The entry on this side is farthest from the road, used by scouts, agents and other castle staff on official business," Amp said. "It's only open twice a day."

"Okay," I said, lacking anything else to add.

"The guard there is a worthless drunk, and often unconscious."

"Drunk?" I asked.

"A blight on the city. I've reported him, but nothing is ever done."

"No one listens to you?"

"Never." Amp spun toward us. "I mean, not in matters of the city guards. That's not the place for a king's agent, you see."

Amp turned away again and rushed forward, outdistancing us before another question could be asked. When we caught up, he floated at the open entry door, scowling.

"Drunk and unconscious."

Sure enough, a guard was leaning back against the wall, chair on two legs, with his own legs braced against the open doorway. We heard his snoring before we'd seen him anyway. Behind the man a rack of shelves with ready to go packs waited for scouts to come and grab them.

"Just sneak past him," Amp said.

"How?" I demanded. "He's blocking the doorway."

"Well...move him. He's drunk. He'll never know."

Graves was relaying everything Amp said to Nila. She rolled her eyes.

I was irked, both at Amp and at myself for following the ghost, but we'd come this far, and I wasn't about to be stopped by a drunk guard. Drawing myself to full height, I stomped forward, shooting one foot out to tip the chair the rest of the way. The drunk guard flipped over backwards.

Amp gasped.

"Awk!" the guard said, hitting the floor and sprawling.

He tried to rise and wobbled, collapsing again to look in bleary-eyed confusion at our group. He reached for his sword, missed it, tried again and gave up.

"Hold it..." he slurred. "Hold it right...there."

"Inspection," I shouted. "On your feet soldier."

The guard fumbled about, getting his feet under control and rising, swaying.

"We've had reports of you drunk on duty."

"Drunk... I... Me?" the guard trailed off into mumblings. "That fink, Amp... Amp..."

"Never mind who reported you. We were sent by your captain...um..."

"SilverStump," Amp said.

"You've got to be kidding me," I said, turning to the ghost.

Amp shrugged, a fascinating motion for someone ethereal.

"Captain SilverStump," I said, turning back to the guard.

"My own brother?" the drunk wailed.

I looked at Amp who shrugged again.

"Yes, your brother," I said, making it up as I went. I draped an arm around the man's shoulders and pulled him aside, away from the door. "He sends a message to save your drinking for off hours. Next inspection might not be by his...um..."

"Lieutenant?" Amp suggested.

"*Loyal* lieutenant," I said.

"Yes sir," the miserable guard said.

While the guard's back was turned, I motioned Nila and Graves to enter. They moved through the opening and into the castle beyond.

I leaned forward, though the guard's breath could peel bark off a tree. "Okay, finish out this shift, but tomorrow, no more drinking on duty."

The man raised his hands, looking like he would fall over again soon. "No, sir."

We turned back toward the door.

"Hey, where's the other two?" the guard demanded.

"What other two?"

"The two that were with you."

"I'm alone."

"No... I..."

I held up three fingers. "How many do you see?"

"What? Three!"

I tsked. "Only one, I'm afraid."

"I need to sit."

"Good idea."

I helped him back to his seat, arranging to be on the inside. He leaned back in the chair with his head against the wall and was asleep that quick.

I frowned at the guard. "Now why does it annoy me that he'll be drunk on duty again tomorrow?"

"I know, right?" Amp said. "Why can't he take his duty more seriously?"

"You're too into the part," Nila said.

Graves nodded. "You should have been an actor."

I rolled my eyes and changed the subject. "Where to?"

Amp led the way, following a circuitous route through the hallways which brought us to a back corridor and door. Outside that entry stood two guards, a muscular man and an even more heavily-muscled woman. Neither were quite as massive as Nila but still impressive.

"The throne room is through there," Amp said.

As soon as we came into view, the guard's hands dropped to their swords.

"Hold it there," the woman said.

Her voice was smooth and even and might even have been pleasant at singing. A scar ran down her left cheek, a puckered white ridge that was probably long forgotten by her.

We stopped, hands raised in a peaceful gesture.

"Amp?" I muttered.

"Yes?"

"What now?"

"Oh! Right. Sorry, I'd forgotten that I wasn't entirely here—"

"Amp."

"Right. Tell them Marmalade."

"Marmalade?" I muttered.

"Yes, that's the password...or, at least it was a few days ago."

Both guards had drawn their swords, ready to attack.

"Marmalade," Graves shouted. "Marmalade!"

The guards stopped and re-sheathed their weapons.

"Could have been quicker about it," the female guard said, rolling her eyes.

"Yeah," the male agreed, "and nice job shouting the password. Now we'll need to change it."

She groaned. "Oh, I hadn't thought of that."

"Sorry," I said.

They waved us forward, glaring as we passed.

On the other side of the door was the king's throne room. We came in through a side entrance, off to the right of the throne, rather than through the room's main doors where people came and went for an audience with the king.

"Who in the hells are they?" a voice said.

CHAPTER 24
IN THE THRONE ROOM

All eyes in the throne room were on us, and in a blink, we were surrounded by all the king's guards. Dozens of swords and an equal number of crossbows were aimed in our direction.

In the middle of the room scowled King Vernion himself on his simple wooden throne, hereditary crown of the land on his head. On the king's right was his royal vizier, a wrinkled man in the robes of a career sycophant, and on the other a man in shining chain-mail, his left arm ending in a stump enclosed by a brilliant silver sleeve.

The king's glare was levelled in our direction, demanding, challenging.

"You heard your king," SilverStump said. "Speak up. Who are you?"

"Well, Amp. What's the message?" I whispered, not taking my eyes off the swords pointed toward us.

Silence.

"Amp?"

For once our ghost had nothing to say.

Nothing at all.

I groaned, seeing it all in one rush of insight. This was all an elaborate revenge plot by Amp against those that had caused his death, and we'd obligingly stumbled right into it. I would turn to see Amp with an expression of expectant glee on his face.

Only, it wasn't glee on the ghost's face. It was doubt. Fear. He looked all around us, unsure what to do. "I..." Amp began. "Um..."

"Hey!" Graves hissed at Amp. "Get your thumb out of your ass, or we'll all be ghosts in a minute. Then I will kick that ghostly ass of yours all over the afterlife."

"Um..."

"King Vernion," I said, bowing. "Forgive this intrusion. We have an urgent message from one of your agents."

The king leaned forward, hopeful in spite of himself. "One of my agents? About Rupert?"

"Yes, sire. We met your man on the road, but he was killed by cultists."

At the mention of cultists, the king's face tightened. "Which agent?"

"A man named Amp."

"Amp?" the king asked, looking from SilverStump to the vizier and back again. "Do we have an agent by that name?"

Both men shook their heads.

"All of our agents are accounted for, sire," SilverStump added.

This was not going well, and Amp was no help.

With some haste, I told a quick version of how we had come to meet Amp, not keeping the part about us following a ghost out of it. Why not? They already thought we were potential dangers, better they think we were lunatics.

"They're lunatics," the vizier said.

Much better.

I glanced at the ghost, who floated with eyes closed and head bowed. He sighed. "Tell them it's Ampersand."

"What?"

"My name," the ghost said, not looking at me. "Tell them it's Ampersand."

"He says his name is Ampersand," I relayed.

The vizier groaned and SilverStump cursed.

"You do know him then?" I asked, expecting the worst.

The king gestured for his vizier to explain.

The man stepped forward, wringing his hands. "A fastidious man in the accounting department, with delusions of grandeur. Always wanting to be an agent or spy. Last week it was an ambassador."

"Ah," I said.

Amp drifted apart from us, eyes anywhere by in our direction. He had to know this was how it would end, or had he deluded himself he was truly the king's agent?

"He is an amateur historian, giving dissertations to anyone unlucky enough to catch his eye," the vizier continued. "And is called Ampersand because there is always something more to come in a conversation with him. It only ends when the other party walks away."

"So, not short for Ample then?" Graves asked, glaring at the ghost. "Because he is more than enough for any job?"

If not for the circumstances of the missing prince, the throne room would have erupted in laughter. Then again, if not for those same circumstances, Ampersand would not be dead, and we wouldn't be here. As it was the vizier turned away, his face hidden inside his cloak, while SilverStump hid a grin behind his...well, silver stump.

"Ample," the king said. "No, I'm afraid not."

"So, we've been following an accountant?" Graves demanded, staring at the ghost.

Ampersand floated, nodding once, then spun back toward me. "The message. Tell the king that the Cult of the Sightless Eye has Prince Rupert."

"Right. The message." And the hope of that reward.

I relayed his words to King Vernion and was rewarded alright, with another eye roll.

"We know all that," SilverStump said. "We discovered their inside man who told us much before dying."

"Then, there's no reward for delivering this message," I said, staring directly at Ampersand.

The ghost's face was slack with shock, shaking his head back and forth.

"No," the vizier said.

I could hear Graves's teeth grinding in fury.

"I see," I said, every muscle tense. "I am sorry we could not bring better information to you."

The king clapped his hands and the guards, which still surrounded us, stepped back. They remained on guard against sudden movements, but it seemed we were no longer considered a total threat.

"You brought me the only light moment I've had in days," the king said, "and for that, I thank you."

The guards may have lowered their weapons, but that didn't mean we were free to go. The king looked at his vizier and made a gesture toward us. The man bowed.

"The cult has some plan in place," the vizier said. "Their inside man wouldn't tell us what before he died. They've kidnapped Rupert because he is the heir, of this we're sure."

SilverStump grumbled his agreement.

"But, why?" I asked.

King Vernion stared at me without expression, one eyebrow raised in question.

"Forgive me, your Highness, but you have other possible heirs," I said. "And you aren't sick. This kidnapping won't cripple the kingdom."

"No."

Though it might cripple King Vernion not to get his favourite nephew back. The man was exhausted like he hadn't slept since the prince disappeared.

"And this cult doesn't seem the type to demand ransom," I continued, reasoning, half to myself.

"They do not."

"So, why?" I repeated.

"Good questions," the king said. "Ones we have asked ourselves, but we have no ideas."

He shook his head, staring at us. Was he searching for some glimmer of guilt? Some tell that would say we were other than what we appeared? He nodded, coming to a decision.

"The daughter of the dwarf king has also been abducted," King Vernion continued. "As has the ogre chieftain's son."

"The major races," I said. "All heirs."

"Yes."

"The elves?" I asked.

The king looked to the man in armour next to his throne.

"A runner has returned, your Majesty," SilverStump said. "No elves have been taken."

"I am sure," the vizier chimed in, "that is to do with the uncertainty on who is next in line for that throne. Magistrate Salu has no heir and will choose a worthy successor when the time comes."

The king leaned forward. "I *will* have my nephew back and destroy this cult forever. I have actual agents scouring the lands, as do the other leaders. You came wanting a reward? Very well. Find my nephew. Bring him home, and I will reward you."

SilverStump and the vizier both leaned forward, undoubtedly to advise their king on the wisdom of trusting strangers who had broken into the throne room.

I didn't care. That one word, reward, had grabbed my attention. Graves let out a low groan, seeing my expression.

The king waved his hands, ending the advisor's chatter and turned to the muscled man on his left. "SilverStump, if nothing else I believe our friends here have discovered a hole in your security."

"Ah! Yes, your Majesty. I will fix it immediately."

THE WAYWARD SPIDER

Vernion waved another hand and our audience was over. Several of the surrounding guards, along with SilverStump ushered us from the throne room, through the hallways and out the front of the castle.

"Unless you get luckier than is possible and find the prince," SilverStump said, "do not *ever* come back here."

With that, he turned and stomped back inside.

CHAPTER 25
PLANS & CONFRONTATIONS

Ampersand sighed.

I spun toward the ghost, surprised to find him still with our group.

"You lied to us!"

He was quiet, not meeting the glare of either Graves or myself. "Would you have done what I'd asked otherwise?"

"No!" Graves said, face reddening and nostrils flaring. "And with good reason."

The ghost was fading, losing his form and becoming transparent. "I...I had to get the information to the king."

"Information he already had!" the wizard shouted.

"I didn't know," the ghost wailed.

If it were possible Ampersand would have been in tears.

"Graves," I said.

"No, Spider!" He rounded on me. "We could have been killed back there. Again. I am so tired of having crossbows pointed at me."

"I'm sorry," Ampersand said. "I really am. I thought the information was vital." Then in a lower voice added, "I wouldn't want anyone else to throw their life away for no reason."

Graves shut his mouth with a snap and ground his teeth, turning from the dead accountant.

"Ampersand," I said gently.

"Don't! Please, don't call me that. It's just a joke, a name they created to ridicule me."

Graves made a noise somewhere between anger and frustration, and I realized I didn't know his true name either.

"Call me Amp, please."

"Ask him what happened," Nila said. "How did he get where we met him."

The accountant started and looked around at the one person who couldn't hear or see him. "You really want to know?"

"She wouldn't have asked if she didn't," I said. "I'll relay it all to her."

"Oh, thanks a lot," Graves muttered to Nila, back to his monotone. She ignored him.

"I... Okay. Well, Prince Rupert had gone missing, and the castle was in a state of frenzy. I saw someone suspicious skulking around, someone I didn't know. You see I know everyone in the castle. I like to talk to people and I—"

"Amp," I said.

"Oh yeah, right. Well, there was this guy I didn't know, and he was heading somewhere in a hurry. I mean, everyone was rushing, but he seemed like he had more of a destination in mind. It struck me as odd and I followed."

As the ghost talked his shape became more defined.

"I pursued the man out the side gate, the drunk's station, and tracked after him, thinking he would head for wherever the prince was held. If only I could rescue Prince Rupert, then I would come back and be the hero. Everyone would take me seriously then—"

"Amp," I repeated.

"Right. Right. Instead, he just followed the road toward Persinia."

"And you didn't tell anyone where you were going?"

"No time," Amp replied. "In any case, he knew I was following the whole time. And when they caught me, they wouldn't believe I was just an accountant."

"Ironic," Graves said. "I have one question."

"Yes?"

"Why are you still here?"

Amp looked at his hands, as if expecting to disappear. He didn't.

"Huh! I don't know," he said. "I guess I still have some task left to do."

"Wonderful," Graves grumbled.

"It is, isn't it?" Amp said, enthusiasm clear in his voice. "So, what's our next move?"

"Whatever it is," Graves said, "it better result in our sleeping indoors. We have no tent or bedrolls."

"Hold on, maybe we do," I said. "But only if we move quickly. Amp, what's the most direct way back to the drunk's gate?"

"I... ah... Follow me."

The ghost took off, heading left around the castle and zipping along the stone wall. We kept up as best we could, me explaining the plan as we sprinted. However quick Amp was in life he was faster now. He led us back to the gate, the drunk guard slouched in the same position he'd been last time we'd seen him.

Nila grabbed both guard and chair, lifting and swinging him out of the way in a gentle arc. Graves and I grabbed two of the smaller packs and one large one just as the sound of stomping feet, metal on stone, approached from inside the castle. We rushed from the entry as Nila replaced the unconscious guard and joined us in retreating the way we'd come.

"Tek!" SilverStump roared.

The sound of scraping chair legs followed by Tek hitting the ground.

"H...hello...lo, brother."

"You've embarrassed me in front of the king."

"How...how did I emb...um...do that? I've... I've been here."

SilverStump ground out several expletives, then, "You are being moved to the stables."

261

We continued on our way, SilverStump's tirade fading into the background.

"I did it," Amp said. "I finally got that drunk replaced."

"Good work," I said, coming to a stop.

"Maybe *that* was your final task," Graves said, staring at the ghost, who hovered, not disappearing. Graves sighed.

I handed the large pack to Nila then opened one of the smaller ones. Inside was a bedroll, two day's rations, plus flint and tinder. Replacing all that we'd lost. Nila's held all of that plus a tent, and two extra day's rations.

Things were looking up.

"We'll be okay for a couple of days," I said. "But—"

"No, let me guess," Graves said, annoyed and cranky, in need of casting a spell. "But we'll need to do something to make money. I've heard this tune before."

"Time," Nila said.

Graves gritted his teeth and made a tight fist, then turned away.

"Yes, go cast your spell," I said. "We can talk more rationally afterwards."

It was the wrong thing to say.

He spun on me, a glint coming into his eyes.

"Graves?" I said.

He muttered a word and flicked a spell in my direction. I dove. The magic followed my path, colliding with me but without any effect. Nila guffawed, and Graves nodded his satisfaction.

My tunic was now a bright orange.

"Oh, very nice," I said. "Every thief just loves to stand out in a crowd."

"Trader," Graves corrected, bending to close his bag.

"You could have turned me into a bear!"

He stepped past me. "I told you, the magic rarely has the same unforeseen effect twice."

I gritted my teeth. Being the brunt of a joke wasn't fun...but it *had* broken any remaining tensions, so I could take it. Even Amp brightened when he looked in my direction.

"Hey, the colour will change back," I called, "right Graves?"

No answer.

Of course it would.

People passing by stopped to stare at my brilliant clothing, nudging each other like the circus had come to town.

Well, there's always that change of clothes in the other pack.

We continued toward the road, passing between two extended buildings which held many one-person apartments. The housing for all lower level people not rating a room in the castle. Amp sped ahead, stopping at one door.

"Your room?" I asked as we came up beside him.

"It was."

"Anything you need?"

"What could I need? Can't touch anything, use anything. I... Wait. There are coins in my desk."

"Coins?" I looked from Amp to the others and back. "Would you mind...?"

Graves rolled his eyes. "In the names of all the gods, Spider. You. Are. A. Thief!"

"Trader."

"Fine, trade for the coins."

"No," Amp said. "Your friendship is enough. But the door key is on my body."

I'd been relaying the information to Nila so she wasn't left out. The hulking woman stepped forward, placing one slab-like palm flat against the door, just above the lock. With one shove it was off the hinges and lying on the floor inside.

"Unlocked," she said.

"I could have picked it, you know."

She turned her back to the open doorway. "Would have been conspicuous in that tunic."

"I...I just..." I stammered.

Nila winked at me then cocked her head toward Amp's room. With her there anyone passing would decide to find another route, especially if she smiled at them. Graves stayed with her, casting a spell which resulted in a two-foot square area of snow outside the door.

No, we weren't conspicuous.

Inside was the well-kept and orderly room of Ampersand the accountant, exactly what one would expect. Neatly made bed. Shelves of meticulously alphabetized books, further organized by subject.

I crossed to the desk and opened its one drawer. Inside was the expected stack of blank papers and writing paraphernalia, all neat and tidy. To the right was a row of coins, arranged in order of denomination, from lowest to highest.

"This should help," I said, pocketing the money. "Thanks."

Amp floated on the far side of his modest room, in front of the bookshelf.

He sighed.

"I'm afraid we can't carry all of that," I said.

Amp didn't respond.

"You know you can stay here. You don't *have* to leave."

Amp turned and shook himself. An action like a cloud dancing. "No. Let's go."

With that he drifted for the door, not looking back on the life he left forever. It showed a strength that wasn't evident in Amp, and it was admirable. On impulse, I grabbed a book off his shelf at random and slipped it into my pack. It was a well-worn volume that had seen many readings. Hopefully a favourite of his.

CHAPTER 26
TRACKING THE TRACKERS

"Got what we need?" Nila asked, pushing the half inch of melting snow with one foot.

I patted my pouch, making it jingle. "It's not much, but if we're frugal—"

"Argghh!" Graves slapped his hands over his ears. "Don't say it."

"We can bed down outside of King's Corner," I said, turning to Nila. "And continue on to Alora in the morning or Farminat."

"Why don't we stay here?" she asked, gesturing toward the open room.

I glanced at Amp and shook my head. He needed to get out of King's Corner, away from his previous existence.

Nila grunted. "So we're not going after the cultists then?"

I wanted to, I really did. That promise of reward from the king and all.

"I don't see how we could. The ones under Timurpajan will have been cleared out, and we have no idea where these others are. If we did, we could have just told the king."

Graves came to such a quick halt I almost walked up his back. He reached into one pocket and pulled out the fist-sized globe he'd taken after the acid storm. It still glowed blue.

"I can reverse the magic, have it track the trackers," he said.

"Are you sure? Can your magic do that?"

He half-shrugged. "The real question is, will it?"

Yeah, a great big what-if hung over that idea.

Graves shook his head and stuffed the glowing sphere back into his pocket.

"What is it?" I asked.

Graves shook his head again.

"You can't do it?"

"I don't *want* to do it," he said. "I don't want to find the cult. I want to practice my magic!"

"We need to find the cult," Nila said.

"Yeah, yeah. We need to find the cult, rescue the prince and save the day because we're heroes."

The level of sarcasm on that last word bordered on being its own art form.

"No," Nila responded. "We need to find them before they find us. They're hunting Spider and have found him twice already."

Graves tried to speak a couple of times, stopping and restarting before any words came out. "Well, yeah... There's that too, obviously."

He turned away and pulled the sphere from his pocket again, holding it in one outstretched hand. The rest of us moved behind him, trying to prepare for whatever random result came.

"Reverse," he said.

The glow faded to a glimmer, barely a shade of blue at all, and that only toward the front.

"It worked," Graves whispered.

Peering over his shoulder at the globe showed us nothing, least of all a successful spell.

"How can you tell?" Amp asked.

Graves blew out a breath and dropped his hand to one side. "Because Spider is right there and it isn't glowing."

"Yeah, but—" Amp tried.

"And, I am feeling a distinct tug in that direction." Graves pointed off the road and across the fields, back toward the south where he and I had begun.

"The desert," Nila said.

I looked at her. "What?"

"You said the cultists had a hideout in the desert."

"That's what they said when they captured the caravan, or at least that it was nearby."

"Sounds like a place to keep kidnapped heirs," Nila suggested.

"It does, doesn't it?"

"We should go back to see the king," Amp said.

"Yes. Okay," I agreed. "Except, what did SilverStump tell us?"

"Not to come back without the prince," Amp replied.

"What would he do if we came back without Prince Rupert?"

"Hmm, well, after exposing his brother as being the weak link in his own security..." Amp faded, his version of growing pale. "Right, let's get moving. Desert of Nan, here we come."

"Is he talking?" Nila asked.

I shook my head. Given that Nila couldn't hear Amp, she would sometimes start talking while he was in the middle of his own dialogue. Not that we were always listening.

"If Graves's spell *is* working—" she said.

"Hey!" Graves interrupted. "If?"

We both stared at him.

He half-shrugged. "Yeah, okay."

"—then what?" Nila continued.

"What do you mean?"

"What do we do when we find a hideout full of cultists?"

"This was your idea, remember? Find them before they find us."

"We need a plan."

She was right.

"Okay..." I said. "Well, first we find out where they are. Then we rush to Timurpajan and get City Commander Norn since we can't get to the king."

Nila nodded. "Someone should go straight there."

That did make sense, but I was the most logical one to go. Norn had known my dad, and I could get to see him easier than the others, but I had no intention of leaving them on the cult's doorstep. We should have asked the king what they'd found out from the cultists in Timurpajan. Some of them must have been captured. Wouldn't Norn have discovered the location of the second hideout...unless the two groups didn't know about each other. What if the existence was only known by higher-ups in the cult?

"Let's find the hideout first," I said.

Nila agreed though she saw right through my thoughts.

Every time I think I understand leadership, I'm reminded that I do not.

You don't know what you don't know.

I jerked at the sound of my father's voice. How long had it been since I'd heard it, since I'd *needed* to hear it?

If only he had been a ghost like Amp, coming with us... I shook my head.

These are your adventures, son. Mine are done now.

And unlike Amp, Dad was at rest.

What did Amp need to do before he could move on?

\#

We camped outside of King's Corner that night, far enough from the road to avoid attention. Tomorrow we would start across the desert and hope to find the cultists hideout, while the heirs were still alive.

I *hoped* they were still alive.

"So, why *is* the cult hunting you, Spider?" Amp asked, floating between me and the fire.

"Well, it's a bit of a long story."

"I have time. All of eternity perhaps."

"You're working on sounding like a king's agent, aren't you?"

Amp shrugged.

THE WAYWARD SPIDER

I told my story of breaking into the tower and being sent to the warehouse, of stealing the goblet and rescuing Zadi only to hand him over to the high sorceress.

"It's a bit extreme," Amp commented, "the way they're pursuing you. All of that just to punish a thief."

"I guess they know how to hold a grudge." I turned to the ghost. "Did the cultists say anything while you were their captive?"

Amp shook his head. "Not really. They knew you were coming and got excited when the globe started glowing brighter. Made them forget about me. I thought I could escape while they were distracted, but we all know how that turned out."

"Ah, the life of a king's agent, right?" I said.

"Yeah. Sure." He turned away.

"No, seriously, Amp. You may have started that day as an accountant, but you ended it as an agent."

"King Vernion doesn't seem to think so."

"Well, give him time to think about it. He has a lot on his mind."

Amp's form gained a sharp edge and practically glowed.

That night no wailing kept us awake. Amp wandered off across the plain, muttering and getting into the occasional shouting discussion with himself. He was good enough to keep it far from us.

When the sun rose, he was nowhere to be seen.

We made breakfast and struck the campsite. The whole time I watched for the ghost and when he wasn't back in time to leave I started getting worried.

"Spider, he's dead," Graves said. "What more could happen to him?"

"Maybe he moved on," Nila suggested.

Without much left to do we slung our backpacks on and started across the plain toward the Desert of Nan. I kept an eye out for our errant spirit, even knowing if he'd been too far his transparent body wouldn't have been visible.

By lunch, I had convinced myself he had indeed moved on, and was happy for him. He deserved to—

"Spider," Amp whispered from next to my ear.

"Gah!" I said, spilling my tea into the dirt while trying to get away.

"I guess he's back," Nila said.

Graves chuckled.

"Where have you been?" I asked.

"Scouting ahead," Amp said. "I made it to the desert road. Do you know I never saw that road while alive? I had always intended on visiting Timurpajan, but there never seemed to be enough time. I—"

"Amp."

"Right. Focus."

"No, I just wanted to say welcome back."

Amp beamed.

"So what did you find?" I asked him.

"There's a slow caravan coming along the road."

"No sign of cultists?"

"None."

CHAPTER 27
A NEW CARAVAN, AN OLD ACQUAINTANCE

We plotted a course to intercept the wagons and see if we could get any news, hoping our friend Zachariah wouldn't be in charge.

Turns out there were worse people to come across than Zachariah.

"Well, well, well. Spider!"

Aw, crap.

"Hello, Farrobane," I said.

Graves and I stopped some paces away from where the caravan had set up their tents. We'd agreed Nila would stay behind the closest sand dune until we could show we meant no harm.

Thankfully most of the orange had faded from my tunic.

"What're you doing here?" Farrobane demanded. "Gonna steal another job from us?"

Farrobane's bully boys, ten smirking idiots in all, grouped behind their leader. They all snickered at this subtle bit of humour.

"I seem to remember you guys all being in jail."

"Yeah, and imagine our surprise when we got out and the caravan had left without us?" Farrobane said. "And in their desperation, all they had was a thief and skinny magician for protection."

More laughing, nothing good-natured in the tones.

I didn't rise to the bait. They could make their comments.

"Now, it would be bad for business if we just let this go by, you understand," Farrobane continued. "Wouldn't want others stealing from us."

The caravan drivers crouched around the fire, eyeing our

confrontation, ready to bolt if a sword was drawn. A couple of them had been on our trip to Grand Gesture.

"Uh-huh," I said. "And what are you planning to do?"

"Well, just kick your asses a little."

"A lot," one of his boys muttered from behind.

"Uh-huh," I repeated. "You heard that Graves changed all the bandit's horses into bears?"

"We heard. Sounds like fairy tales to me."

"It happened," a driver called from near the fire. "He—"

"Shut up, you," Farrobane said.

Two of Farrobane's boys had taken a step back, and a couple more had worried expressions on their faces.

"Way I figure it," Farrobane said, "he isn't quicker than a crossbow if he wants to fight that way."

"So, you're just going to fight us, eleven against three?"

Farrobane snorted laughter. "I only count two."

"Mmm, our third is behind you."

"Right, and when I turn to look, you what? Attack me? Run away?"

Two of the guys at the back did turn around, then turned white, and finally turned tail and fled.

Four more turned to see why they heard running feet.

"Um, Far," one said. "You might want to see this."

Farrobane heaved a breath of annoyance and turned to see Nila at the back of his group. She had her stone hammer resting against one shoulder, ready to swing.

"Looks like nine against three," she said

"Nine against...? Ha! Oh, no, no. We were just joking," Farrobane said.

"Sounded serious," Nila answered.

"Nah. Spider and me are old pals. We used to ride protection on his pop's caravans."

"Just that one time," I said, "when your guys got drunk on beer that was part of his shipment."

Farrobane scowled, opening his mouth to contest that then shook it off. "Ancient history."

"Uh-huh."

"Well," Farrobane said, stepping back from Nila, though several of his men remained between them. "We'd better be getting back to the caravan. Gotta take our protecting chores seriously."

One of his boys muttered as they retreated and Farrobane shushed him, looking back at Nila. She smiled, and the man shuddered. It was wonderful.

With an hour still left before sunset, we decided it best to get down the road a bit before setting up our camp, and better still to have a watch on tonight. Luckily we had a sentry no other people could see.

#

I had hopes that Nila's presence would be enough intimidation to keep Farrobane from doing a stupid nighttime attack, but that's optimism for you.

The moon was high when Amp shouted to wake Graves and me.

"Nila," I said.

She came immediately awake.

"They're coming," Amp said, "spread out across the desert with about ten feet between them."

The ghost sounded frightened, but also giddy. He was doing some actual spying.

"Okay, get back out there and keep an eye on them," I said. "Call back any information."

The ghost sped off into the night, almost saluting before he went.

Graves stood, twitching fingers at his sides.

"Can you hold off for a couple of minutes?"

He frowned and grunted, crossing his arms. "Of course."

I headed to the edge of our camp and spoke loud enough for my voice to carry. "Farrobane, it's not a good idea for you guys to be walking around in the dark. Anything could happen."

"They've stopped moving," Amp called.

"Now go back to your camp, Farrobane," I called.

Silence for two entire minutes.

"He says you're bluffing," Amp said, appearing at my side.

"Gah!" I replied.

"They're moving forward again," the ghost added.

"How could we be bluffing? We obviously know they're there. His boys are following him?"

Amp nodded. I cursed.

"Okay, we warned you," I yelled, then in a lower voice to Graves, "Have fun."

A gleam flickered in Graves's eye, like when that thief was turned into a pig. He raised his hands toward the blackness. "Sandstorm."

My jaw dropped. Sandstorms were vicious.

Wind whipped up, like a living, screaming beast. Farrobane's men screamed too as they were scoured by the sand.

"Don't kill them, Graves," Nila said.

"Spider said to have fun."

She squinted down at him, arms crossed.

"Spoilsport," Graves muttered, then waved a hand toward the desert. "Stop."

The wind increased, whipping and howling only feet from us. Graves stepped closer to the edge of our camp, a look of concentration on his face.

"I said, stop!"

With human-like reluctance, the storm slowed, increased, slowed again and then tapered to a stop. It had lasted less than a minute.

"I'll go check on them," Nila said.

"Wait," Graves told her, then pointed above her head. "Light."

"If I start to float..." she began, but a glowing sphere appeared overhead, following her movements. She disappeared into the night.

"Go with her Amp."

The ghost followed.

Nila returned in ten minutes, dragging Farrobane by one leg. She dropped him in front of us, and he jumped to his feet, ready to take flight.

"Still think he's not as fast as your crossbow?" I asked.

"Oh, hey, Spider. You gotta believe me. We were just coming to...um...to..."

I said, "Go dig your guys out of the sand and get back to the caravan."

"I pulled them out already," Nila said, then turned to the other man. "None of them are too happy with you right now."

Farrobane scowled. He would have to deal with that when he got back, and find some way to spin this in his favour.

"We're not going to see you again tonight, are we?" I asked.

Farrobane shook his head like a dog just come out of the water.

"Good, because next time Graves here will turn you into a pig."

He looked at the wizard, disbelief warring with fear. Farrobane had seen the sandstorm, but turning someone into a pig?

"It is hard to believe," I agreed and turned to Graves.

The wizard raised one hand.

"No," Farrobane said. "No, no, no. That's okay."

He stumbled backwards, tripped, got up and bolted for the safety of obscuring night.

Graves cocked his head to one side, pointing a finger at the fleeing man. "Piggy-tail."

Farrobane grabbed his backside and gave a squeal, then clapped both hands over his mouth and was gone.

"Piggy-tail?" I asked.

"It *should* stop at the tail anyway."

Amp followed them back to camp and kept watch through what was left of the night, though Farrobane wouldn't be able to convince any of his boys to follow him back a second time.

"Farrobane has a pig's snout," Amp said the next morning. "And hooves for hands, too."

"Huh!" Graves said. "Oh well, close enough."

"They were all pretty mad at him," Amp said.

"Well, that pig snout should get enough sympathy for his crew to not leave him behind," I said. "Did they say anything else?"

"No, but I wasn't really listening."

"Why not?" Graves demanded.

"My mind wanders at night when there's no one to hear me."

Looking at Graves got me a half-shrug, so the topic was dropped, for now. None of us had any experience with the dead. How did we know what was normal and what wasn't?

After breakfast the orb continued pulling us south, bringing us to the middle of the desert, more or less.

"We're still on the road," Nila said.

"So?" Graves said.

"We should be pulled off at an angle, assuming their other base is in the desert," she explained.

"The orb pulls us in a straight line," I added. "So, it must be at the edge of the desert, or on the plain?"

"Maybe," Nila said.

"There are caves," I suggested.

Nila nodded. "Could be better this way."

"What do you mean?"

"Closer we get to Timurpajan, the shorter the run for help."

"That's true," I said. "Another possibility... Hey Graves, are you sure the spell is still working?"

"Yes, I'm sure," he snapped.

He'd been angry since lunch when casting a spell had surrounded him with mocking, shrieking laughter for an hour. I couldn't blame him. It *was* annoying to listen to, and he'd walked alone until the spell wore off.

Graves stopped and came over to me, holding the blue sphere out.

"I trust you," I said.

"Fine. I'm just tired of being the one on the leash."

I took the sphere in my fist. The tug south was immediate and obvious. We were being pulled somewhere.

And that somewhere, as it turned out, was Timurpajan.

An hour from the city we couldn't pretend the globe had any other destination in mind.

"Why pull us here?" Graves said. "You did tell someone about the warehouse, didn't you?"

"Yes, of course I did."

Gar wasn't the forgetful type. He would have passed the information on to Norn, and that should have been the end.

"Unless there are still some cultists there," I said.

"Guess we'll find out soon," Nila said.

CHAPTER 28
FULL CIRCLE

We headed back into town from the same point Graves and I had left over two weeks ago.

"It all looks the same," Graves said, sounding disbelieving.

It's always the same after a trip. So much had happened that it felt like everyone else should have been affected, but the rest of Timurpajan had gone about their day to day routines.

Few would have even noticed we'd been gone. Just Gar and Lees...and Armentia too, I suppose. All of them would have expected us to be gone much longer too.

"Where to first?" Amp asked.

"Let's go see Gar," I said. "We can get a meal and find out what happened with the warehouse."

Nila looked at Graves and winked. The wizard nodded.

"What?" I asked.

"Potato fever," Nila said.

"You've been muttering about it for the last hour, once you knew for sure this was our destination," Graves added.

I turned to Amp who agreed.

Well, this was embarrassing.

"They are very tasty," Graves admitted.

"Looking forward to having some," Nila said.

Amp sighed.

The ghost wouldn't be the only disappointed one.

The Inn of the Sainted Ogre came into view, becoming more defined with each step we took. I tried not to rush.

As we neared the inn, it became obvious that the front door was missing from its frame.

"I guess that *was* the door I conjured near Grand Gesture."

Gar was going to have some words to say about that.

"Why hasn't he replaced it?" Amp asked. "That's not secure."

He was right. This had happened more than a week ago, and the door was still missing.

Something was wrong.

I rushed forward, the sounds of my friend's feet close behind.

Inside was a disaster, like a whirlwind had gone through the inn, destroying tables and chairs, gouging the walls, smashing bottles.

"This is from a sword," Nila said, her finger exploring the length of one wall gash.

Graves examined several scorch marks around the inn, nodding at each one. "Magic."

"What in the hells happened here?" I said. "Where are Gar and Lees?"

"Taken," a voice responded.

We all spun toward the door and the quick body that moved inside, into the shadows. Nila stepped forward, getting between us and this person.

"Thari?" I said.

"Hello, Spider."

The serving girl looked over one shoulder, out a window which was somehow the only intact item.

"I was off the day it happened," Thari said. "The town guard came and took Gar and Lees away."

"Why?" I asked.

"Story is they're traitors, members in some crazy cult."

"That's ridiculous."

"Of course it's ridiculous, Spider. You and I both know it."

"But Norn took them in?"

"Took them somewhere," Thari said, "but no idea where. Not the jail."

"We have to get out of here," Nila said.

I couldn't wrap my head around any of this.

"You told Gar about the warehouse," Nila explained, "and he told Norn. Then they got arrested. Coincidence?"

I rushed behind the bar and pulled up three floorboards which hid Gar's spot for less than legal merchandise. Inside was my satchel, and inside of that the goblet. Oh! And Zadi's padlock. I'd forgotten about that.

I clicked the lock into a leather loop on my tunic, like some odd thief jewellery, and slipped the thin key into my secret inside pocket. The satchel went over one shoulder.

"What do we do now, Spider?" Thari asked.

"We? Well, my friends and I are going to check out the warehouse, and you are going home where it's safe."

Thari shook her head.

"Yes. That warehouse is not a place for you."

She glared at me. "I watched for you to return. Making a show of being here to feed the pigs out back. I knew you would have a plan."

I drew in a breath and released it.

"A plan? Yeah, okay. So here's my plan," I said, handing her the satchel. "This was enough for them to chase me all over trying to get it back. Take it. Hide it."

She threw the bag over her shoulder.

"If I don't come back for it..."

Well, that was a great question. What does Thari do if we're all slaughtered inside the warehouse trying to rescue Gar, Lees, and the heirs?

"If we don't come back tonight, take it to Armentia, the high sorceress in the Tower of Wizardry."

Thari took two steps back, eyes wild.

"Knock on the door, and tell them Graves sent you," the wizard said.

She squeezed her eyes tight but nodded agreement. We could count on Thari. She was strong in both mind and body and wouldn't let the magic-users push her around.

"Spider," Nila said, "time to go. If Thari saw us, then others might have too."

"Okay," I agreed. "Everyone out."

"Good luck," Thari said as we exited the inn.

She gave me a quick kiss on the cheek, dragging a smile out of me. Then we headed in the opposite direction.

"So, on to certain death now?" Nila asked.

"It's not so bad," Amp said.

CHAPTER 29
WAREHOUSE, REVISITED

We made our way through Timurpajan and into the alley across from the cult's warehouse. The guards were still there, patrolling. It looked the same as it had that night. Was it really less than three weeks ago? It didn't seem possible.

"I can't ask any of you to come in with me," I said.

"Can't stop us either," Nila said.

I looked at Graves who threw up his hands in surrender. "Okay! So, you're right. Practical application of my spells is better than just sitting around and casting. Happy?"

"He means that we're coming too," Amp said.

"I don't need interpretation," Graves said but had no anger in his tone.

"Okay," I said. "We can't just sneak in the way I did last time, but I have an idea."

"Wonderful," Graves grumbled.

We dropped our packs against the alley wall. It was doubtful that a tent and bedrolls would be of any use inside the warehouse, and if we weren't successful, we wouldn't need them, or anything else, ever again.

I crossed the street and scaled the outside of the building, as I had on that first night. When the guard had passed, I pulled myself up and scooted across the roof in silence.

"Do you think this is wise?" Amp said.

I jumped but made no sound, focusing on the guard passing the entry door on the roof.

"Oh, right. You can't speak."

I shook my head once. The guard passed the entry, and I removed my picks, making short work of the lock and passing into the building.

"You're pretty quick with those," Amp said.

"Easy lock," I said, counting the guard's steps inside my head.

On the pegs were the same assortment of red sashes and other items to make guards appear like River Rats.

"Grab one and let's get out of here," Amp said. "I can't be hurt but I can still be nervous."

"There's no brown robes here."

"So?"

"We need a brown robe."

Amp groaned. "Okay, let me go see where they are."

That was the most sensible plan.

Amp was back in a little over a minute, or seventy-two footsteps.

"Bottom of these stairs," the ghost said. "On the back of a chair."

I grabbed a sash and made my way down into a room crowded with cultists. Mealtime. Cultists occupied the tables, eating and drinking.

"You could have mentioned the room was full," I said.

"Is that an important detail?"

"Just a little."

"Who do you speak with, brother?" one cultist asked me.

I bowed, making sure my hood continued obscuring my features. "Only myself, brother."

He turned to the woman next to him. "Why do cults always attract the crazy-heads?"

His friend puffed out a breath and rolled her eyes in answer. At least they decided I wasn't worth talking to.

The robe in question was on the back of an unoccupied chair and I took the few steps, grabbing it and turning back toward the stairs.

"And now he takes my robe," the same man said.

I bowed to him again, thinking quick. "Brother, this robe speaks to me.

It tells me it wants cleaning. Can you not hear it?"

Teeth gritted, the man turned away. "Keep it, crazy-head."

I hurried back up the stairs and got to the door.

"I've lost my count," I said.

Amp stuck his head through the door. He stayed like this for a minute before pulling back inside. "All clear."

"Clear like downstairs?"

"No, he just passed."

I cracked the door and looked outside. Sure enough, the guard was on his way to the other end. I hurried forward and over the edge, scaling down the side of the building.

"You've been gone a while," Nila said when we got back.

"Yeah, it was crowded, but we can use the number of people inside to make it easier for us to get through."

Graves and Nila glanced at each other then back at me.

"Okay, the plan," I said. "Graves, you wear this robe and bring me and Nila in as captives."

"Um..." he said.

"Yeah, I know it isn't perfect but—"

"No, it's just that my spare robe is this exact colour."

"Your...?"

"Yep."

I cursed under my breath with several ogre words Lees had taught me over the years.

"Should have asked," Nila said.

"Okay, fine. So here's the plan. Graves brings us in, then through to the lower levels, telling everyone we are heading for the cells. From there we rescue Gar, Lees, and the heirs and get back out.

"So simple," Graves said.

"Then we head back to King's Corner and let Vernion know what's going on here."

"*King* Vernion," Amp corrected.

"Yes, yes. Sorry. *King* Vernion," I said. "Any questions?"

The others stared back. Graves breathed one tiny, humourless laugh.

"If anyone has a better plan, I'm all ears."

"Oh, I get it," Amp said. "Because of the pointy elf ears."

Graves barked a laugh, short but heartfelt, and relayed Amp's interpretation to Nila who guffawed.

"Now can we go?" I asked.

Graves changed to his brown robe and dropped the cultist one against the wall.

"Mine is less scratchy," he explained.

"Right. Sure. Okay," I said. "Let's go."

"Wait," Graves said.

"What now?"

The wizard pulled out the orb and held it in his palm. "Reverse."

His eyes flared amber and the glass flared blue.

"Ready," he said, holding the globe toward me to confirm the blue glow would increase.

We crossed the street, Nila and I in front and Graves coming behind. We kept our hands in front, crossed over as if secured. She still carried the stone hammer on her belt, and we had to hope everyone would be distracted by Nila herself and not notice. She would need it if we had to fight our way back out.

"Here we go," Nila muttered.

Graves passed two surprised guards dressed as River Rats without challenge and pushed the front door open. We stepped into a narrow alcove which was only paces from the eating area. Two guards on duty blocked our way. After a heartbeat's pause, Graves grabbed my hood and pulled it off, exposing my ears. At the same moment, he took the globe from his pocket, not saying a word. The guards' eyes went wide.

"Well done," one of them said.

They parted, Nila and me stepping through the gap and into a room I had departed minutes ago. There were fewer cultists now, but not by much, and those present all stared at us.

Two more steps into the room and a wave of dizziness hit me. Next, a flash of light, like staring into the sun.

Then blackness.

CHAPTER 30
EVERYTHING GOES PEAR-SHAPED

Spider.
  Spider.
  Spider.
Spider.

A voice droned inside my dream, an endless, repeating monologue of one word.

"Let me sleep," I mumbled, it came out like *lem a slip*.

Spider.

Spider.

Spider.

"Wha?"

My eyes fluttered open and looked through the ghostly face of Amp, inches from mine.

"Gah!" I rasped, my voice a dry whisper.

Why do people always want to startle me awake?

Hold on.

Why was I asleep? The last I remembered...

I bolted upright.

Graves lay on a bed to my left, unmoving. Amp floated a foot away.

Stone walls and a steel door.

"A cell," I said. Obviously retaining my keen powers of observation.

"I've been trying to wake you for ten minutes. I would have given you a slap, but I can't do that sort of thing."

"Uh-huh." I gripped my pounding head.

"Nila is awake too. She's been calling, but I can't answer," the ghost said, then more to himself. "Can't do much."

Too many concerns were ahead of making Amp feel useful. I forced my feet under me and staggered toward the bed.

If Nila and I were awake, why wasn't Graves? He hadn't moved. Was he...?

No. He was breathing. Only unconscious.

He was also bound, wrists and ankles in X-shaped manacles. The cultists weren't taking any chances with a wizard. Wouldn't they be surprised to find he didn't need to wave his hands to cast a spell?

"Hold on, Graves," I said, patting my pockets and not at all surprised to find both my knives and lockpicks missing. I still had Zadi's lock attached to my tunic, and its key in my secret inside pocket. The cultists must have discounted both as useless, and they were right now. "Okay, plan B, then."

The two picks hidden in the bottom seam of my tunic were still there, and the stitching came free with some quick tugs. If Zadi had done something similar, he would have been able to free himself.

I got started on Graves's manacles. The trap was so obvious it insulted me, designed to take an unobservant thief's finger off.

"Crude," I said.

Graves was free in one minute, not that it helped to wake him.

"Spider?" Nila called.

"Yeah," I tried, making my way to the door where my voice would carry better. "Yeah, I'm here."

Looking through the undersized window confirmed where we were. Back in the hall of cells, upstairs from the ones Zadi had occupied. Across the hall were four doors, of which, the one directly opposite, had Nila's massive hands curled around the bars.

"You okay?" I half-whispered.

"Better than the...fragrant guy in here with me," Nila answered.

289

Ah yes, the rescued corpse. He hadn't escaped after all.

I groaned, remembering, and looked down.

My picks would be useless here. No lock opening existed on this side of the door, and the window was too high to reach it from the outside. Rattling the door confirmed it was about as solid as a cell door could be.

"Wonderful," I muttered.

"Spider?" another voice said, gruff but feminine.

"Lees?"

"Are you okay?"

"I'm fine, Lees...well, as fine as can be anyway. Is...is Gar...?"

"I'm here," Gar's voice came from farther away. "Just not easy to get my face up to the bars."

They were alive! I'd been dreading finding out what had happened to them, assuming the worst, but they were okay, for now anyway. They wouldn't be if we didn't get out of these cells though.

"Nila, can you break down the door?"

"Tried that. Too solid."

"She's been trying since waking up," Amp said.

"What happened anyway?" Nila asked.

I looked at Amp.

"The cultists all laughed while they brought you here," Amp said. "About us trying to sneak in through the front door even though none of them ever wear the brown robes outside."

"Ah. I see." I gritted my teeth. So much for my brilliant plan.

Nila pressed her face to the window. "What?"

I told her Amp's side of the story.

"Huh! Figured it was like that," she said. "So they hit us with a spell?"

Again I looked at Amp.

"There was a third guard. Some kind of magic-user."

And Graves had taken the brunt of the spell.

"Who's your friend?" Gar asked.

I introduced Nila to Gar and Lees.

"We saw your inn," Nila said.

Gar made an angry noise and called the city commander two physically improbable concepts, and one downright impossibility...without magic anyway.

"I sent word about the warehouse," Gar said, "but not right away. I forgot with all those pigs to deal with. Anyway, it was a couple of days later."

"What happened?" I asked.

"What happened was a squad of city guard laid siege to the inn."

"They weren't real city guard," Lees said.

"No. True," Gar agreed. "They were these villains made up like city guard."

"We saw them coming," Lees said, "and secured the inn."

"Then do you know what happened?" Gar exclaimed. "The bloody door disappears out of the frame!"

"Oh," I said. "That's...um..."

"Must have had a powerful magician with them," Gar said. "That door disintegrated without a trace. Solid oak!"

"We've been here ever since," Lees said.

I wanted to ask why they'd been kept alive but had the irrational certainty that would jinx it.

"A heartwarming reunion," an unfamiliar haughty voice said, coming from the cell to my right.

"Who are you?" Nila asked.

"Prince Rupert."

"Prince Rupert?" I said. "Your uncle is worried about you."

The prince let out a humourless laugh. "Good to know."

"Are the other heirs here?"

"Yeah, kid," said a gruff voice from somewhere further down. "Ransak Strong-Arm. First son of Fireaxe Strong-Arm, ogre chieftain."

"I too am here," came a pleasant feminine voice from between the cell holding Nila and the one with Gar and Lees. "Dorinda of the Caves, daughter of the dwarf king. My friends call me Pebble."

Two other voices came, speaking in a tongue which I couldn't understand. The ogre, Ransak, spoke back in an equally incomprehensible language.

"The last two cells," Ransak explained, "hold Bok, prince of goblins, and High Majestic Praetor Snuffy, of the orc kingdoms."

"High Majestic—" I started.

"Hey, I'm just translating here," Ransak said.

"So, no trolls or giants," I said. "No halflings—"

"Hey," Gar called out.

"Sorry, Gar. I mean no halfling royalty."

"No such thing. We elect our rulers through fair democratic process."

Rupert snorted his disdain for this.

"And the trolls and giants rule by whoever is strongest," Dorinda of the Caves added.

"Is that why the cult only wants these five heirs?" I mused.

"Six, actually," Rupert said. "They're hunting for some elf."

"Hmm, no. I'm the elf they were looking for, but that's another story."

"You're an elf?" Ransak said. "You don't sound stuck-up and prissy."

"I was raised by a human."

"Anyway!" Rupert cut in. "Ransom?"

"No," I said. "There's been no demands."

"Maybe to hold power over the races?" Amp said.

"Yeah, I'd thought of that too, Amp. But why do that when the heirs could be replaced with whoever's next in line."

"Is someone in there with you?" Dorinda asked.

"Well, yes. A wizard named Graves."

"Ah, that is who you talk to?" Dorinda asked.

"Well... No..." Great. Time to sound like a lunatic to a lovely princess. I hesitated.

"He's talking to a ghost named Amp," Nila explained. "The fourth member of our group."

"I am?" Amp said. "Part of the group, I mean? I thought you just let me stay because you felt guilty about killing me, and because you couldn't get rid of me. Me! Part of a group!"

The ghost started doing loops through the air, passing through the walls on each side.

"Woo-hoo!" he yelled as he spun.

"Okay, Amp. Calm down."

"Can he go get help?" Ransak asked.

"Yeah," Rupert agreed.

"Get help?" Amp said. "Yeah, of course. On my way."

"Wait," I said.

Too late. Amp was gone before I could point out the obvious problem of only Graves and I being able to see him and Amp not being able to affect items in the living world. How far would he go before he realized for himself?

"Okay, fine. Best we can hope is that Graves will wake up and get us out of here."

"Is he still unconscious?" Nila asked, sounding worried.

"Yeah."

I crossed the room and perched next to the wizard, also worried.

Worried for him if he didn't wake, and worried for all of us if we were counting on Amp to save us.

CHAPTER 31
THE MAD AS FROGS ORIGIN OF GRAVES

As I lowered myself next to Graves he started moaning, at first so only I could hear, but building to a prolonged groan.

"What is it?" Nila asked.

It stopped.

With no idea of what else to do, I reached out toward him.

His eyes shot open, glowing amber.

I was on my feet, backing away. Memories of forest-floods and horse-bears played through my mind.

Graves shot to his feet, back arching, arms out to either side, hands clenched into tight fists. He hovered, a foot of empty air between him and the floor while an amber aura built around him. It was difficult to look in his direction. Then, just as suddenly, Graves collapsed back onto the bed, leaving behind an after-image.

"Spider," Nila called. "What's happening?"

The after-image resolved into a glowing, amber version of the wizard. This second Graves turned toward the body on the bed, then back to me.

"Graves?" I said, taking another step back.

My back hit the opposite wall.

This glowing Graves started toward me, changing shape as it moved, morphing as it became...someone else.

A woman.

"Spider," Nila said. "What's—"

The woman touched me with one extended index finger and the world dissolved, except for me and her.

Be calm, Spider.

She spoke inside my head.

"What? Who? Graves?" I said, expressing myself to the best of my current ability.

Graves? Yes and no. I am a part of him that is magic.

"Oooookay..."

Confusing. I know. As for what and who, it's the same answer to both. I am Aneesa, goddess of luck and random chance.

"Um, I've never heard of you."

No. Few people know me these days, maybe a dozen in all, for I am of the old gods.

"Old gods?" I said. "Like Aniha-Morgo?"

My brother.

"Oh, fantastic."

Don't panic, I am not like him. He is the god of murder and fear, which is why he still has worshippers, still has power.

"But you have power. I've seen what Graves can do."

Well, of course, I still have power. I'm a goddess after all. But those spells are as much Graves as myself.

"I don't understand."

If you would but allow me to tell my tale, you would begin to comprehend.

"And you need to talk like that while you do it?"

That's for dramatic emphasis.

"Fair enough."

May I continue?

"Of course."

Very well. Graves was a sickly baby at birth and would not have survived.

With that, I saw the story of Graves's premature birth and the father who stalked from the room on seeing his disappointing runt.

A gardener on the estate worshipped me, and so I was present at Graves's birth.

The baby needed help, and I needed the same. Both of us would have ceased to exist in time. So I merged with the baby.

"Merged?"

Yes, but I became lost within, too weak to manifest myself. My godly powers merged with his innate magic to amplify the random chances around Graves.

"Oooooh, that explains a lot."

Now, after years of our power building, I can manifest outside him but only for a short period.

The story of Graves's life continued before me.

"Hold on."

The image froze in place, like actors on a stage.

"So all those spells were just random chance?"

Yes.

"You didn't influence their outcome?"

I...um...

"I thought so."

Well, I need to relieve the boredom. Heating up tea. Lighting candles. Boring!

"The bears."

Okay, that one got out of hand. I cancelled the spell though.

"Oh yes. He was surprised when the spell was negated. So that wasn't him?"

No.

I snapped two metaphysical fingers. "The dancing?"

Wasn't that hilarious?

The rules around Graves's magic took on some clarity. A sentience behind his spells would explain why we saw no pattern. It was all up to whim. This explained all those times when circumstances were just too convenient.

"Nila's portal. The rathagast."

You two needed some muscle travelling with you.

"And our trip to the other side of the mountains?"

The group needed to learn how to work together, and you needed time to become a leader.

"Hmm." I wasn't so sure that had been accomplished.

And you found that ring. That was fortunate.

"Ring?" I held my hand up and saw the trading outpost ring still there. "Big deal. Cheap tin."

No. That is a rare metal which neutralizes magic on contact.

"Really?"

Yes. So save it until the best moment.

"Maybe you should take it."

We can't. Graves and I are magic, and not strong enough to survive.

"Ah, right. Well, how will I know when it's the best moment?"

You'll know.

"That's a little vague."

Okay, if you don't figure it out, I will let you know.

"Oh. Yeah, okay."

Can I continue my story?

"Sorry. Please do."

Where was I?

"Um...manifesting yourself outside of Graves."

Oh, right. Thanks... So, together we have power, but apart we are still close to oblivion.

"So, you're stuck together. Does he know this?"

No.

"Don't you think he deserves an explanation?"

I...what would I say? What if he tells me to go away?

This goddess had experienced rejection on an unfathomable scale, but at its heart was the same fear we all have.

"Give him that chance."

She considered the idea then sighed. It was a weighty sound, stretching back through eternity.

I shall. Now, can I continue? It's kind of important.

"Right. Yes. Sorry."

Aniha-Morgo is poised to be reborn, and the world will suffer for it.

"Ah."

It's never the god of fluffy white kittens trying to come back, you notice that?

"Yeah, but who would stop that, right?"

I suppose. Spider, we need to stop him. I'm fond of this world, even if it has mostly forgotten me. The heirs cannot be sacrificed.

"Got it. Stop the sacrifice. Defeat the ancient god of murder. Easy-peasy."

Aneesa smiled, and I felt it all might be possible. How could we lose with a goddess at our side?

I must remerge with Graves now. I will help however I can, but our magic will be random again for the most.

Okay, back to being screwed.

"Wait!"

Yes?

"Can you unlock my door?"

She smiled again as the world popped back into focus with a *CLANK*.

"—happening?" Nila finished.

The entire conversation with Aneesa had happened between seconds.

Graves sat up on the bed, trying to get to his feet but lacking the coordination.

"Who said that?" Graves said, peering around.

The wizard cocked his head.

"Never heard of you," he said.

Our cell door swung outward at my touch.

"Yes! Thank you, Aneesa."

I removed my lockpicks and tried to decide between Nila's cell and the one holding Gar and Lees. Nila pushed her door open, followed a moment later by the others.

"Well, I could have gotten the rest myself," I muttered.

As it turns out I could not have. Sounds of approaching feet came from the stairs leading up.

We'd run out of time.

CHAPTER 32
RAISING AN ANCIENT GOD

"Well done, Spider," Norn said as he stepped into the hallway of our narrow prison.

To the city commander's right stood a priestess, and on his left a priest, each wearing the itchy brown robes I knew so well. They went through the complicated gestures and mutterings of casting a spell. Behind them were four cultists with crossbows aimed in our direction. These last stayed on the stairs for better line of sight.

I had to agree with Graves, I was getting tired of having crossbows pointed at me.

The goblin and orc were closest to the cultists and attacked first, Lees and Ransak a step behind.

Norn wore a calm expression, not flinching one step.

The priest shouted, "Bliksem!"

The four attacking prisoners struck a wall of electrical force and were thrown backwards, bowling down Rupert and Dorinda. They all rose to their feet, the goblin and orc mounting a second assault, only to be thrown back again.

Ransak spoke in their tongue and the two glared at the cultists but stopped the futile attack. A shimmering curtain of energy extended from wall to wall, floor to ceiling in front of Norn and the cultists.

"I don't know how you got out of those cells," Norn said to me, as if there'd been no interruption, "but that was impressive."

"You're a disgrace," I said, working my way forward.

"A disgrace?" he said. "Why? Because I've chosen the winning side?"

"No, because you've broken your vows of protecting people."

"Well, I was never much for that, even before the cult."

"My father believed in you."

"Your father died broke. What does that tell you?"

"Commander," the priestess said, "it is time. We must get the six down to the altar."

Six? So I *was* to be some elf proxy in all this.

"Bring them all," Norn said. "We can sort them out at the altar."

They bowed.

"Hold on. Why me?" I said to Norn, stalling for time. "Just because I stole that goblet? And set Zadi free?"

"*You* broke Zadi out?" Norn said, a grin on his lips. "We were wondering how the gnome escaped. Two cultists were flayed for allowing that to happen."

My guess would be those same two who had chased me around the altar.

"Thank you for solving that mystery," Norn said. "When Zadi and his lock disappeared, we had to change plans. We could no longer hope to contain—"

Norn blanched then waved the idea aside.

"Contain?" I asked.

He gave a quick shake of his head. "As for the goblet, I have no idea what you are talking about." He looked over at the priest. "Do you know about a missing goblet?"

The priest shook his head.

"Bolab's been moaning about his missing spittoon," the priestess suggested.

No, couldn't be... And, also, eww!

"But...then...why have you been chasing me?"

Norn laughed, a nasty sound I already hated. "Oh, Spider, it is a cliché but I have to say, you'll find out soon."

He made the motions of counting then turned to the priestess.

"One is missing."

She made several complicated gestures. "Trekken!"

Graves came hurtling from the cell, barely on his feet but being propelled forward. Nila stepped forward to catch him.

"Weak," he said. "Dizzy."

Nila held him up with one hand. "I've got you."

"Can't stand," he was silent, then. "Okay, yes... Look, I was going to... Just give me a second, all right?"

"Are you talking to me?" Nila asked.

Graves shook his head. "Thanks for your help, Nila."

"Sure. No problem."

"There," Graves said. "Are you happy now?"

Nila looked at me for explanation.

"Later."

"If there is a later," she said.

"Voorwaarts!" said the priest.

The shimmering wall of energy moved forward, striking the orc and goblin, sending them flying. How much more could those two take?

Ah, but they couldn't be killed, not here.

Lees caught the one while Ransak took the other. They turned their backs, ready to take the brunt of that spell as it reached them.

"Come on," I yelled. "Run."

And we did. Down the stairs to the next level, fully aware we were being herded but having no other option.

The wall next to Zadi's old cell was gone, pushed inward on two great hinges. I was impressed. Last time I'd seen no evidence of that being a door.

We continued on, Nila taking the lead while also carrying Graves.

Down, and down, and down we went. Norn and the priests keeping pace, the spell of energy always in front of them. We came off the stairs and into a massive cavern where the ends couldn't be seen on any side except for the one we occupied. All of Timurpajan could have been held inside here, only it *didn't* hold a city. What it held was a single, magnificent, obsidian altar which put the simple stone one upstairs to shame. That other was for sacrificing animals and nobodies, this one was for changing the world.

One man stood behind the altar, wearing robes of deepest blood red, watching our approach. A stone circle, perhaps a foot high and as big as a house, rested in front of the altar. Runes were etched into the rock around the edge, assaulting my head when I examined them too closely. Like the runes in the Tower of Wizardry, but malevolent, suggesting that drooling madness might not be such a bad choice.

Well, I did own a spittoon now.

"Come," the priest said.

No. If the others were priests, then this man was a corrupt apostle of pure evil. On the altar before him was an open book, emanating hate, murder and suffering in palpable waves.

From behind, the cultists who had chased us poured from the stairway, followed by dozens of others, all moving in the calm, unhurried manner of players in a game that was already won. Still more came from other parts of the cavern, from unseen stairs leading who knew where, coming together as a mob.

They seemed without end, a thousand and growing.

Norn and his two clerics pushed to the front, the nudge of their magic forcing us onto the stone circle. The evil apostle clapped his hands once, and every cultist started a low, moaning chant, filling the cavern with sound.

I scrambled to get off the circle.

"No," Graves said.

I turned, unsure that I'd heard right and he caught my eye, giving his head one quick shake. Nila set him down.

"Why are we here?" I demanded, spinning on the man behind the altar. "What do you want?"

There was no way of knowing if Graves-Aneesa had a plan, or if they were even lucid. If they *had* a plan, I had no way of knowing they could carry it off. What I did know was that me and my two lock picks were not going to defeat the cultists surrounding us. The answers to my questions were obvious, but it could buy some time.

"Aniha-Morgo shall rise," the apostle yelled.

"Aniha-Morgo," the cultists echoed. "Aniha-Morgo. Aniha-Morgo."

"Yeah, okay, but... how will this raise him?"

What villain didn't like to brag about their plans and how clever they were?

"According to ancient prophecy—"

"It's always ancient prophecy," Graves said, but the words sounded more like Aneesa's

"—the sacrifice of six heirs is powerful, malevolent magic," the apostle continued. "Powerful enough to rip the veil between worlds asunder."

"I'm not an heir."

"You are more than you think."

"Well, that's delightfully cryptic," I said, but he added nothing.

Was he some kind of lunatic? Of course he was. Who followed a god of hate and murder except for someone unhinged?

"Okay," I continued. "So, six lives to bring some old blind god back sounds pretty cheap. You sure you want him?"

"We have been weakening the veil for ten years with our sacrifices. Now, all is in proper alignment and the life energy of you six will finish the task. Aniha-Morgo shall stalk the earth again."

"Um...Graves or Aneesa," I whispered. "If you have a plan, this might be the perfect time."

"Aneesa?" Nila asked.

"An ancient goddess living inside Graves's head," I explained.

"Oh. Sorry I asked."

The wizard stood on his own, strength evident in his body again. Nila still held a hand at his back just in case.

"Protect," Graves said.

Magic coursed from his fingers, surrounding us in a sphere much like the power that had forced us here, except Graves's spell was visible, and crackled the air. The sphere enlarged to fit the raised circle, stopping at the edge.

The apostle chuckled. "That will stop people, crossbow bolts, and even most magic."

Yes! Graves had bought us some time.

"It won't, however, stop a spell of our ancient master."

With that, he read from the book before him, words which shouldn't be spoken, shouldn't ever be heard by mortal ears.

The pain was immediate and excruciating as if every part of my body and soul was set to burning.

I screamed and collapsed beside Rupert and Ransak, Bok and Snuffy. Dorinda followed a moment later. For her to remain upright after the rest was a testament to her strength.

The others, minus Graves who maintained the shield, tried to help. But what could they do?

While our souls burned, the apostle chanted a second spell from the book. A cold shriek of laughter filled the cavern as, above the altar, a rift in space opened. First the size of a coin, then a ball, ever growing until the size of a horse.

A breeze of hot, rancid beef pushed through the opening, caressing us in our agony.

"I smell my sister," a deep voice rumbled, like mountains being scraped together.

"Hello, Morg," Aneesa said in Graves's voice.

"I always hated when you called me that." The grating of his teeth sounded like entire civilizations dying.

Aneesa-Graves shrugged. "I know, Morgy."

"When I cross over," the voice said, "I shall eat your pitiful host and use his skull as my chamber pot."

The portal had opened to the size of a house, exposing the entire upper-body of this foul god. It was impossible to describe him in my agony, and even without the writhing, I suspect my mind would have wanted to focus elsewhere. All I knew for sure was that Aniha-Morgo was huge and had three eyes in a triangular shape, all of them blind.

"But you won't cross over," Aneesa-Graves said.

The voice laughed, and two rows of cultists collapsed. "It is inevitable."

"Is it? I don't think so."

"I have the six heirs, their souls flaying to open my portal."

I'm not an heir, I wanted to scream.

"Six? Nope, Morg. I count five."

You tell him Aneesa.

Aniha-Morgo glared sightless through the portal, counting.

The goddess-wizard smiled. "What do you say, Dorinda of the Caves?"

All was quiet, then Dorinda stopped writhing and got to her feet. "You knew, goddess?"

The apostle narrowed his eyes, scratching at one temple. Baffled.

I understood the feeling. How was this dwarf woman able to stand without effort when I could barely lie here not dying?

"Knew what?" the apostle said.

"This isn't Dorinda of the Caves," Aneesa-Graves said.

"I'm her double, her bodyguard," the dwarf said to the apostle and god then bowed toward our wizard. "And a humble follower of Aneesa, goddess of luck and random chance."

Random chance is right. I wish I could have laughed.

Aniha-Morgo screamed, and one line of cultists died. "You didn't confirm their identities? You unbelievable idiot!"

The apostle ceased his spell, relieving our agony. "Master, I thought—"

"Thought? No. You didn't. The veil between worlds cannot be destroyed with only five heirs. Read the prophecy!"

"I am sorry my lord. I will correct this."

"No," Aniha-Morgo said. "You are needed elsewhere."

A fist shot from the veil and grabbed the apostle. Aniha-Morgo's arm immediately started to flake, disintegrating in our world. The ancient god screamed his agony and pulled the apostle through to the other side.

"Do not expect to survive this," the old god said to the man in his fist, then, "Norn!"

The city commander stepped forward, sweating and shaking in terror. He bowed low. "Y...yes, my lord?"

"*You* shall correct the error."

"Of course, my lord."

"Find the real dwarf heir."

"You will find she is beyond your reach," Aneesa-Graves said.

"Then we shall just kill every dwarf in the land until this one is truly the heir," Aniha-Morgo said.

"Understood, my lord," Norn said.

"Meanwhile I shall use this man's magical life force to keep the veil open." Aniha-Morgo shook the apostle toward the opening between worlds. "It shall become permanent, but I cannot cross over without six heirs."

I tried to get back to my feet along with the others, stumbling. Dorinda grabbed an arm and helped.

"Thanks," I said, marvelling at this woman. Not a princess but willing to be in harm's way to protect the true Dorinda.

"Spider," Graves said in Aneesa's tone. "It's time."

"Huh?"

"The *best* moment." She rolled her eyes. "Remember?"

"The best... Oh! Right!"

I slid the ring off my hand and held it in my palm, wondering the proper way to do this. Aneesa had said she and Graves couldn't survive contact with this, but surely Aniha-Morgo *was* strong enough.

Okay. Here goes.

I cocked back my arm and let the ring fly. It sailed over the altar and through the veil, bouncing off of Aniha-Morgo's arm with a sizzle of god-flesh.

"Ow!" he yelled.

The ring rebounded, landing high on the apostle's robe.

"Where's that luck and random chance, Aneesa?"

The ring slid down the robe until it contacted the exposed flesh of the apostle's hand. It stuck to his flesh, bubbling and seething, like acid. In moments the man was gone, dissolved.

Then the veil slammed shut.

"What happened?" Nila asked.

"Without the apostle's soul, Aniha-Morgo couldn't keep the veil open," Aneesa-Graves said.

"Then, we did it!" I cried. "We won!"

309

"Spider," Nila said, gesturing out past Graves's protective spell.

"Ah, right."

We were still surrounded by a thousand cultists, minus those that had died from exposure to their god.

Norn leaned on the altar, his priest and priestess on either side, waiting for Graves's spell to expire. He reached down with reverence and closed the book, stroking the leather cover with one hand before picking it up.

"It shall be a decade before we can open the veil again," Norn said. "But you won't be here to see it."

Our group spread out within the sphere, around the runed circle. Nila and Lees stood shoulder to shoulder, shielding Gar and Graves. Opposite them were Ransak and Rupert, at the ready. Bok and Snuffy took one gap between those two groups, and I followed Dorinda, for lack of her true name, to the last.

Graves's spell remained steady, but it was only a matter of time.

We were going to die. But we'd saved the world.

Too bad no one would ever know.

"So, how is it," I asked the dwarf, "that you couldn't be a proxy for the true Dorinda, but I—"

"Spider!"

I spun around at the sound of Amp. He sped toward us and hovered over my head.

"It took forever to find you," he said. "I went back to the cells but—"

"Amp."

"Oh yeah. Right, right, right," he winked. "Prepare for transport."

CHAPTER 33
I WAS EXPECTING A RESCUE

"Transport?" I asked.

"Yes." Amp practically glowed. "I left here and didn't know who to go to for help. So I stopped and asked myself—"

"Amp."

"No, no. This is important to the story. I asked myself, who would be able to see me? So you know where I went?"

"The Tower of Wizardry," Graves said.

"The Tow...," Amp stopped. "Well, yes, exactly. I went to the top floor, and that really scary old lady could see me."

"Armentia," Graves said.

"Yes! That's the one."

"Is your ghost back?" Dorinda asked.

Graves's spell flickered, and we all looked up at the protective bubble, then at the surrounding cultists. *They* were ready. The shield flickered again.

"He have some kind of rescue for us?" Nila asked.

"Did you say something about transport?" I asked.

"Oh! Right! Almost forgot," Amp said, then shouted, "Now!"

A portal opened, centring on Amp and growing outward in a blinding flash.

"Ha! You lose, Norn," I yelled, relishing the shock on the city commander's face, hoping he could hear my parting words.

When the blinding flash disappeared, we were still on the raised circle of stone, but now in the desert under the hot sun. Being on the raised rock, we could see out over the heads of all the thousand or so cultists that had been transported with us. Every single one of them. Even the altar with

Norn. Oh, it took them time to get over the surprise of being teleported, but no more or less than us.

And we still had nowhere to go.

"You were saying, Spider?" Norn called.

"Graves," I said, "you're the only one that can do anything on a scale to affect all of them."

He half-smiled, nodded once, then passed out.

"A simple *no* would have been fine," I said, catching the wizard and easing him to the stone.

The force sphere over us flickered once, twice, then solidified again. I had no idea how long that spell could endure, but judging by the flickering, it was limited.

Certainly not the forever we needed.

A great shout sounded from the other side of the stone, and I turned to see hundreds of people rushing from caves in that direction.

I felt a surge of hope.

"More cultists," Nila said.

Well, of course. Why not? Help was coming, just not for us.

We had been transported to the other hideout, and now the number of cultists was doubling in size.

They really didn't need help against the ten of us...eleven with Amp.

"Amp, did Armentia mention if she was still mad at me?"

Amp shook his head. He was gazing around at the gathering cultists, his mouth hanging open.

"Amp?"

"Oh! Oh, oh, oh! Yes, of course."

I had no idea what the ghost was babbling about or who he was babbling to.

"They're in place," Amp said. "Now!"

The last time he said now, a great portal had opened and dumped us here. I didn't have faith in better things happening this time around.

A portal glowed into existence, about a hundred feet back from the cultists on their north side. This one was vertical, like a great, forty-foot-wide door. No cultist had noticed it yet, but Nila pointed.

Out of that glowing circle marched soldier after soldier, in full war armour. The gleaming silver stump of...well, SilverStump, flashed in the sunlight at the lead.

A battle was about to happen.

"Not enough of them," Nila said.

I shook my head. No, not enough to fight two thousand desperate cultists who had watched their god banished and their leader dragged to hell.

"Look," Ransak said, pointing.

Another portal opened, this one spewing an army of dwarves. The lead warrior was a twin of the Dorinda next to me. They could have been sisters.

"More portals," Lees said, who had put Gar on her shoulder to see better. "Two. Three. No, four!"

Out of these portals stepped armies of elves, ogres, orcs, and goblins. Some, ancient enemies for generations, saluted the others in the common cause of one enemy.

"Father," Ransak called, though doubtful any one voice could be heard over the din of that day.

The ogre chieftain led his people to battle, as did the orc king and the goblin...well, whatever their leader was called. On the other side were the elf king and his people, looking as Ransak had described, prissy and stuck-up. The prissy, stuck-up archers all drew back their bows and picked a target.

The other armies raised their weapons.

313

THE WAYWARD SPIDER

There would be no battle, only a slaughter. No cultist would escape from this, circled in as they were on all sides.

"Norn," I yelled. "Surrender."

Already cultists were dropping their weapons and throwing themselves to the ground. The cultist priests around Norn started to cast spells and were taken down by the excellent elvish archers and surprisingly not so bad goblin ones, leaving the city commander by himself.

Norn jumped onto the altar and shot his hands into the air in surrender, one hand still gripping the book. He spun to each side, ensuring the armies all saw his surrender.

Every cultist had thrown themselves to the ground now, from the farthest edge all the way to Norn.

Graves's sphere of protection flickered one last time, faltered, then disappeared.

"Crap," I whispered.

Norn was looking toward me, both arms raised, when our protection vanished. A wicked sneer crossed his face, and he leapt off of the altar, drawing a dagger as he headed straight for me.

The archers couldn't shoot him for fear of hitting us. Dorinda stepped between me and Norn, ready to take him on barehanded. Before she could defend me, two huge, meaty fists drilled into the city commander. Nila from the left and Lees from the right. Norn dropped the book at my feet and flew sixty feet, mowing down surrendering cultists as he went.

"I knew you two would get along," I said.

Dorinda stepped toward them. "I could have done that, you know."

"Don't be greedy," Lees said. "You got to help thwart the dark god."

"Leave something for the rest of us," Nila added.

Dorinda laughed, a sound like crystal wind-chimes.

CHAPTER 34
WELL, THAT'S THAT!

Armentia arrived through one final portal, no less impressive than the ones which had brought armies, though this one the size of one person. She crossed the open area to join the talks deciding what to do with these surrendered cultists.

The prisoners would be given the option: A one way portal to Aniha-Morgo's dimension, or be divided equally among the races for punishment, except for the elves who refused to take anybody. Most chose the first option rather than chance being given to the ogres, orcs or goblins who all had reputation for brutality. Lacking the dark apostle to punishment Norn was considered the next in charge. Prince Rupert considered the unconscious former city commander.

"Throw his through the portal," the prince said to SilverStump. "Let him be punished by his master."

Ransak, Bok and Snuffy approached together and bowed, giving their thanks to myself, Graves and Nila, swearing their friendship and taking ours in return. Then they departed with their people back through the portals which had brought them here.

SilverStump came forward and stopped in front of us, Prince Rupert by his side. The two had just finished disposing of Norn. "Well, I did say not to come back without the prince."

The man clapped Rupert on the shoulder. It was obvious he was as much a friend to the prince as a servant. Rupert stared back toward the portal.

"Is *he* here?" SilverStump asked.

I gestured to where Amp hovered.

SilverStump cleared his throat, drawing himself up to full height then gave a quick bow.

"Amper—" he stopped, gritted his teeth and tried again. "My apologies. Ample. Good King Vernion has bestowed upon you the title of King's Agent for however long you should remain in this world."

Amp stared at the man silently before breaking into sobs of joy. I wasn't sure he could cry, but he was doing a reasonable facsimile of it anyway.

"Um, he asks you to convey his thanks to the king," I said.

SilverStump bowed again, turned away and started for the portal, Prince Rupert following without so much as a glance at us. I hope he doesn't take the crown too soon.

The elf king approached next with Armentia by his side. He held out one hand, a glowing green globe in it. The light of this globe flared as he held it toward me.

"It is true. You are my son."

He said it without ceremony or fanfare, and without any thought of how such a proclamation would affect me. I wobbled, would have sat on the ground if Nila hadn't been there to keep me upright.

"There...must be some mistake," I managed.

"None," the elf king said.

This guy was a great conversationalist.

"Magistrate Salu's globe," Armentia said, gesturing toward the green glow, "is attuned to his son's lifeforce, much like the ones the cultists used. In some way, the apostle had determined you were still alive and sent his cultists after you."

I shook my head.

"You were stolen from me as a child," the elf leader said.

"It was assumed you had died," Armentia explained. "A kidnapping gone wrong."

Kidnapping? My father? No, that couldn't be.

Gar and Lees exchanged glances, unspoken thoughts passing between the couple. I would need to speak with them about this.

"You are my rightful heir," the elf said, "and one day you will lead our people."

I held up my hands, took a step back, shook my head. Everything I could do to convey how wrong that idea was. The elf king didn't react, and somehow that made it easier.

"I would like to visit and learn more about my heritage."

The elf king nodded once.

"But, I was raised by a human with help from a halfling and half-ogre," I said. "I'm about as elvish as Armentia there."

I glanced at the sorceress, suddenly sure I had overlooked elvish ears on her.

"No, Spider," she said. "I'm human."

Well, I wouldn't go that far.

I turned back to the king. "The elves should be led by a true elf."

The elf king cocked his head to one side, his gaze never wavering. "Well spoken."

With that he turned and strode away.

That's it? Hey, you're my son and see you later?

"How did Ransak describe them?" Nila asked.

"Prissy and stuck-up."

Nila grunted. "More like cold and emotionless."

I had to agree as I watched my birth father leave. Without a glance back, the elf king passed through the portal with the rest of his people.

I looked around at who was left and saw Dorinda of the Caves, standing beside Dorinda of the Caves. Both inclined their head in greeting.

"Your Majesty," I said, bowing toward one who smiled, turned and headed back through the portal with the rest of her people.

"You can tell us apart?" Dorinda asked.

"You aren't *that* similar."

Her mouth hung open, then snapped shut with a click. "Would you come and visit us as well, Spider? You and your friends, of course."

"I would like that," I agreed. "But, on one condition."

She cocked her head to the left.

"Could you tell me your real name?"

"Oh! Of course. My true name is Kimberlite, but I am called Kimb."

"When you aren't being Dorinda?"

"It does get confusing," she said.

"I will visit, and soon."

She smiled again and pushed one strand of hair behind her ear. "Thank you."

"Me? I didn't do anything."

"You brought this group together, held them together, led them," she shrugged. "Without you, nothing would have been in place."

My mouth opened to respond when the true Dorinda poked her head back through. "Kimb, time to go."

"See you soon," she said, then turned and followed her princess through the opening.

The portals had closed as the last of each army passed through, leaving we remaining few in the desert, near that horrific stone circle and altar.

Armentia gestured, and her personal portal shimmered, the Tower of Wizardry replaced by the Inn of the Sainted Ogre, door missing.

"You may return home," she said to Gar and Lees, not making it sound optional.

The two turned toward me.

"It's okay," I said. "I'll be home soon."

Lees turned toward Armentia, eyes narrowing, teeth gritting. The sorceress met her gaze and accepted the unspoken warning.

"I mean him no harm," she said.

"It's okay, Lees," I repeated.

Gar took her by the hand, and the two headed for the portal, stepping through side by side.

"Didn't I task you with keeping him safe?" Armentia said.

"You did," I agreed. "You also tasked me with making sure he got better with his magic."

"Hmm, he certainly has done that."

Graves stepped forward, hands wringing together.

"No, Graves. You are not yet ready to come back. There is still much to learn."

The wizard breathed out a deep sigh. "I agree."

"You do?" she asked.

"I've only been gone a couple of weeks, after all. Not the full year."

"I...see. Well then, that is settled."

"Great," I said, rolling *my* eyes for a change. "So I'm still saddled with babysitting you, am I?"

"Hmm," Graves said. "A bright yellow tunic this time, with cowbells."

I laughed, holding my hands up in surrender. Graves smiled too, briefly.

What happened to the loner thief?

Well Dad, at some point this group became a family of sorts. A strange, mismatched one, but family still. Besides, I still had almost a year to go on earning that ruby. Might as well enjoy it.

Armentia turned to Nila, hesitated before talking. "I am doubtful I can get you home, but I can try. There are certain spells I can look into."

"Thank you," Nila said, then turned to Graves and myself. "But take your time."

The sorceress turned toward Amp last. "The most I can offer you is a chance to move on."

"What do you think, Amp?" I asked. "Have you finished your final quest?"

"Not me. I'm a king's agent, and we never rest."

"Very well, now for the last item, Spider," she said, turning toward me. "That book."

She held one hand out, and I pulled the evil tome from behind me. I hadn't done an adequate job of keeping it hidden it seemed.

"We must keep it from the wrong hands," she said.

Well, we agreed on that. Question was, were *her* hands the right ones?

What else could be done? I handed Armentia the book.

"And what is this?" she asked.

Through two leather loops on the book, one on the front cover and one on the back, was Zadi's lock. The one I had taken from his cell a million years ago.

"Protection," I said. "To keep the book out of the wrong hands."

"Hmm," she said.

"It's a Zadi lock," I said. "One that the cultists had him making, to imbue with magic."

They couldn't have thought this one lock would control or contain a god like Aniha-Morgo, could they? Lunatics.

"That was never imbued with magic," Graves said, stepping forward. His eyes flared amber as he touched the lock. "Now it has."

I could hear Armentia's jaw muscles clenching. She could have crushed diamond between her molars. Without another word she turned and disappeared through the portal which changed from the inn to the tower, then back again.

"Now what?" Amp asked.

"Well, I thought I would help Gar and Lees get the inn back together."

Graves stopped and turned toward me. "You don't mean I'll actually have more than an hour to sit and practice?"

"Sleeping in a bed would be nice," Nila added. "And what about these spiced potatoes I keep hearing about?"

"You'll love them," I said.

"Maybe Lees and I can arm wrestle."

And all the bookies in Timurpajan would line up to take bets on that match-up.

CHAPTER 35
AN EPILOGUE...OR MAYBE MORE OF A PROLOGUE

A month later we occupied one of the tables at the Inn of the Sainted Ogre, eating lunch. Amp had the book from his room open in front of his place, asking for pages to be turned every couple of minutes.

The ghost was in his glory.

He'd helped Gar and Lees with their accounting and bookkeeping, using a go-between who could hear him, namely me. Nila had become great friends with the innkeepers, spending hours in conversation with Lees.

Graves had been practicing spells without any great backlash. Aneesa had gone dormant again, and it was only a matter of time before magical misfires started happening as the goddess fought the boredom of immortality.

With the reward King Vernion had given us for rescuing his nephew we'd been able to help Gar and Lees repair the inn, and taken a month of relaxation for ourselves in the meantime.

Nothing could have been more peaceful, calm and sedate.

"Uh-oh," I muttered.

Graves glanced up from a spell he was working on. "What?"

"I was thinking how nothing could be more peaceful, calm and sedate."

Nila jerked her head around, and even Amp paused in reading.

"Why not just curse the gods?" Nila asked.

"I'm sure it will be fine," I said.

Amp laughed and returned to his book.

Nila and I looked around the inn, half-expecting some danger to come through the inn's new front door.

Nothing.

She returned to the potatoes Thari had brought.

"What are you working on, Graves?" I asked.

"Just heating up my tea."

"Oh, I see... No, wait—"

Too late.

A portal opened in the space behind our table, two people wide and just as high. Nila grabbed her stone hammer, ready for trouble.

"Could be your way home," I said, getting to my feet.

"I'm already home," she answered.

Movement came from inside the portal.

"Aw, crap," I pulled my daggers free.

Graves waved his hands, trying to negate the spell before something leapt out. "Come on, Aneesa."

Too late again. The portal moved backward leaving an odd trio of confused people before our table. A warrior woman in armour, what must have been a wizard with his hood up, and the scrawniest barbarian I'd ever seen.

No one made a move.

The portal disappeared with a pop.

"Arthur, I don't think we're in Kansas anymore," said the possible wizard.

"Nay, Dead-Mike, we hath vacated the city of Morewood, not this Kansas."

Dead-Mike sighed. "It's an expression, Valeria."

The one called Valeria rolled her eyes.

"Who are you guys?" the skinny barbarian asked.

"Aye," Valeria added. "And doth thou know thou art haunted by a spirit?"

"You can see me?" Amp said, rushing over to her.

"Aye."

"Someone new to talk to!" Amp said.

Graves and I looked at each other and laughed.

"Might as well pull up some chairs," I said. "Hey, Gar, can we get more potatoes here?"

ACKNOWLEDGEMENTS

Behind every writer (every successful person really) is a long line of people who encouraged and motivated that person. Acknowledgments are a great place to show appreciation for those people, but it's a tricky job. The trick comes in not forgetting one of those important people. As I said in my previous book, this won't be my last, and if I forget anyone I apologize and will include you in the next. Promise.

To begin, a great big thank you to the people at Renaissance Press. Nathan, Marie-Claude, and Marjolaine not only publish books, but encourage their authors. They take the time to listen to concerns, and answer questions. It's a pleasure and an honor to be part of the Renaissance family.

As always, thanks to my web of personal readers: Allison Batoff, Kris Pichovich, Greg Neill, and my big sister Janet Haas. Thanks to Kevin Quirt, Jason Sharp, and Julie Lee for being first readers on this book and providing me with valuable feedback. Finally, thanks to fellow Renaissance writer Cait Gordon for suggesting the title. I struggled through fifty possibilities but think The Wayward Spider works best.

To my high school drama teacher, Mr. Gordon Day, who was the first person outside of my family to tell me I had talent, thank you.

Mom & Dad, as always, thanks for letting me be a dreamer.

To my two boys, Jack and Oliver, thanks for the motivation and encouragement, the laughs and crazy times.

Dreams do come true.

Renaissance.
Diverse Canadian Voices

Renaissance was founded in May 2013 by a group of friends who wanted to publish and market those stories which don't always fit neatly in a genre, or a niche, or a demographic.

This is still the type of story we are drawn to; however, we've also noticed another interesting trend in what we tend to publish. It turns out that we are naturally drawn to the voices of those who are members of a marginalized group (especially people with disabilities and LGBTQIAPP2+ people), and these are the voices we want to continue to uplift. Our team is the same; we seem to naturally surround ourselves with people who are, like us, people with marginalized identities.

To us, Renaissance isn't just a business; it's a found family. Being authors and artists ourselves, we care as much about our authors enjoying the publishing process as we do about our readers enjoying a great story and seeing a new perspective.

pressesrenaissancepress.ca
pressesrenaissancepress@gmail.com

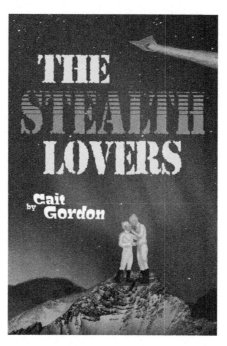

LGBT/Science-Fiction

MANY YEARS BEFORE THEY LANDED ON CINNEH, TWO YOUNG MEN STARTED BASIC TRAINING, ALSO KNOWN AS "VACAY IN HAY."

Xaxall Dwyer Knightly might only be a private, but his sergeant is fascinated by him. During a combat exercise, Private Knightly wins the distinction of being the first-ever trainee to throw an opponent through a supporting wall. The teen has the strength of five Draga put together.

Vivoxx Nathan Tirowen, son of General Tirowen, stands tall with a naturally commanding presence. A young man of a royal clan, the private has an uncanny talent with weaponry. The sarge is convinced that Private Tirowen could "trim the pits of a rodent without nicking the skin."

When the two recruits meet, Vivoxx smiles warmly and Xaxall speaks in backwards phonetics. Little do they know the bond they immediately feel for each other will morph into a military pairing no one in Dragal history has ever seen.

THIS IS THE STORY OF THE STEALTH— LEGENDARY, FORMIDABLE, AND FABULOUS.

Science fiction/fantasy

Will YOU be Everdome's next champion?

Everdome, a fantasy franchise derived from wildly popular novels by mysterious author S.M. Ardwur, is a world that was fractured by an immense magical disaster. Powerful mages rallied following the Cataclysm, forming magical bubbles over the fragmented pieces of the planet, creating twelve Domes, the twelve independent (?) kingdoms of Everdome.

When a man dressed as a knight offers thirteen people the opportunity to visit their favourite fantasy world and experience an immersive reality show based on the novels, there's only one answer they can give - a resounding yes.

But this experience is so realistic that some of the players start to wonder if fantasy has become reality.

Follow Abagail, Krista, James, Nicole, Richard and Megan as they navigate a high stakes tournament that might just actually be a matter of life and death.

pressesrenaissancepress.ca

MURDER AT THE WORLD'S FAIR

MJ LYONS

Steampunk

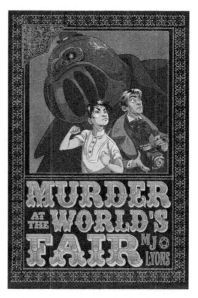

The year is 1893, and airships cloud the skies over the bustling metropolis of Toronto. The city is set to host the world's fair thanks in no small part to the work of two fantastical inventors. The New World Exhibition is to be a celebration of cultural and technological marvels; roving automatons, clockwork contraptions, the world's biggest steam-powered paddle boat, all to be fully lit by the wonder of electricity!

On the day of the grand opening, young Norwood Quigley, aspiring journalist, photographer and scion of a world-famous airship magnate, stumbles onto the scene of a murder; the victim: a Prussian Ambassador; the perpetrator: a Chinese assassin, or so the powers-that-be say. In truth, the suspect is Jing, a roguish but amiable youthful delinquent.

Concerned by Jing's claim of innocence and his assumed guilt by higher powers, including the British Empire's military, Norwood is thrown into a grand intrigue that hinges on Toronto's world fair. As chaos consumes the celebrations, he fears that his influential family is being manipulated in a plot to create an international incident that will lead to a war that spans the world.

pressesrenaissancepress.ca

Did you enjoy this book?

Independent authors and publishers rely mostly on word of mouth publicity.

Please consider helping others discover this title by posting a review of it online, on Amazon, Goodreads, a blog or social media.